Losing
Clementine

Losing Clementine

ASHLEY REAM

WM

WILLIAM MORROW

An Imprint of HarperCollins*Publishers*

LOSING CLEMENTINE. Copyright © 2012 by Ashley Ream. All rights reserved. Printed in the United States of America. No part of this book may be used or reproduced in any manner whatsoever without written permission except in the case of brief quotations embodied in critical articles and reviews. For information address Harper-Collins Publishers, 10 East 53rd Street, New York, NY 10022.

HarperCollins books may be purchased for educational, business, or sales promotional use. For information please write: Special Markets Department, HarperCollins Publishers, 10 East 53rd Street, New York, NY 10022.

FIRST EDITION

Designed by Diahann Sturge

Library of Congress Cataloging-in-Publication Data

Ream, Ashley.
  Losing Clementine : a novel / Ashley Ream. —1st ed.
    p. cm.
  Summary: "A new writer makes her fiction debut with a tale involving a renowned artist's impending suicide"—Provided by publisher.
  ISBN 978-0-06-209363-9
  1. Women artists—Fiction. 2. Suicide—Fiction. 3. Life change events—Fiction. 4. Self-actualization (Psychology)—Fiction. I. Title.
  PS3618.E2247L67 2012
  813'.6—dc22
                                                              2011027305

12 13 14 15 16 OV/RRD 10 9 8 7 6 5 4 3 2

Acknowledgments

Writing a book seems like a solitary pursuit, but behind me stood many people without whom it would not have been possible.

My husband, Austin Baker, and dearest friends, Janice Shiffler and Eric Stone, were my first readers and most trusted confidants.

My parents—Donna, Steve, Robin, and Joy—along with the entire "Gator in the Pool Gang" provided endless love and support.

My agent, Barbara Poelle, and editor, Katherine Nintzel, along with the entire team at William Morrow helped birth this book.

I am eternally grateful to all of you.

30 Days

I threw the teapot out the window.

It plummeted three floors and shattered into a hundred white porcelain pieces right behind Mrs. Epstein, whom I had never much liked anyway.

"Hey!" she yelled up at me.

"Sorry," I said, hanging half my upper body over the sill. Then I turned back inside, grabbed half a dozen teacups, and dumped those out, too.

I wasn't that sorry.

Crash. Crash-crash. Crash-crash-crash.

It was very satisfying.

"Have you lost your mind?" Mrs. Epstein screamed, dancing around in her sensible shoes to avoid flying debris.

"Yes," I said and used half my body weight to shove the sash back down.

It would've been more satisfying to slam it, but fifty years of paint made that impossible. Unfortunate. I was really into doing things that were satisfying at the moment. I had, just that afternoon, fired my shrink. When you've really and truly decided to kill yourself, what's the point of a shrink?

That was also satisfying. Both the firing and the deciding.

Then I positively on-purpose hit the car of the asshole who always parks six inches across my building's driveway. I took his bumper half off and did not leave a note, because he deserved it. I'll be dead in thirty days. Let him try to take me to small claims court.

Upstairs, I did not hang up my jacket and drank orange juice straight from the carton. I even spit in it a little because I could. All exceptionally satisfying. That's when I decided I didn't like tea very much.

Crash. Crash-crash. Crash-crash-crash.

I should've done this ages ago.

The edges of my studio are for living. That's where I keep my kitchen, my television, and, off in the corner behind some repurposed red velvet curtains, my bed. The center is where I work. That's not a metaphor. It's a spatial description. The commute rocks.

I flipped through a stack of stretched canvases leaning against the rough stucco wall.

No, no, no, no. Yes.

I picked a square one, four feet by four feet. That would do. I dropped it onto the easel. I'd fired Jenny, my assistant, the week before, just after she'd stretched half a dozen of these. Her last name is Pritchard, too, no relation. She's twenty-four and looks even younger. When I let her go, she looked at me as if I'd slapped her hard across the face. Even her cheeks turned red. Tears pooled in her bottom lashes, and she tore around the place snatching up papers and her bag and finally a coffee mug I'd given her when she first started. I should've had her prime the canvases, too, before she left, but I hadn't thought of it.

After she'd gone, I called the Essex Gallery in New York. The curator had a wife whose family made their money in upholstery fabric. He also had a young man tickling twenty-five whom he kept in an apartment in the West Fifties. I'd started out in that gallery back when I was just a little more than nothing. The curator and I liked each other in the way you have to like someone who knows more about you than they should. I told him he damn well better give Jenny a show of her own. She got a call the next day. Although I heard she turned him down. I can't imagine why. I mailed her last check with quite a bit extra thrown in, enough to keep her fed until she started selling on her own. That's what she should've been doing anyway instead of stretching my damn canvases.

I pulled a clean bowl out of the stack and shook the hell out of a bottle of gesso, a mixture of latex and calcium carbonate. Some form of the stuff has been in use since Cleopatra took goat's milk baths, except back then it was made of animal-based glue and PETA doesn't allow that anymore. I upended what was left into the bowl. I added a quarter as much of acrylic gloss, opened the bottle of water I'd drunk half of the night before, and added an equal part of it to the mix, too.

Chuckles jumped up on the worktable and switched his tail near the open bottle, making idle threats before winding his way around cans of solvent and glue. He walked over a stack of magazines and take-out menus and just plain trash I thought I might want to use in a piece someday. A *Vogue* slipped off the top and flopped to the floor. It stayed there because Jenny wasn't around to pick it up.

Finding nothing of interest, Chuckles jumped to the metal work shelves that line one wall. He sauntered past rows of magazines in archival holders alphabetized by title. *Car and Driver, Cosmopolitan, Food & Wine, Los Angeles, National Geographic, Popular*

Photography, Wine Spectator. He paid no mind to the plastic bins with printed labels: menus, travel brochures, maps (U.S.), maps (foreign), advertising (women), advertising (men), newspapers (U.S.), newspapers (foreign). Instead, he rubbed the corner of his mouth on the boxes that hold wallpaper scraps and fabric pieces organized by color, then turned his attention to the large rubber trash bins. They don't hold trash but keep bits of things I drag home off the street. I heard the *whomp* as he landed on one of the lids with all four paws. Jenny kept it all straight, so I didn't have to. She drew the line only at animal bones. Those I had to clean and boil myself. I was partial to birds' wings, but it was getting easier to order them online rather than collect what the coyotes left behind.

I worked the canvas from the top down in long, horizontal strokes with a wide brush, pushing the mix into the weave. It was grunt work, and I'd have to let it dry, sand it down, and do it again. This was why I'd hired an assistant in the first place. I dropped my brush into a can, remembered I had no one to clean up after me, and picked it up again along with the cat and carried them both to the sink. I washed the brush with soap and water. The cat got a reprieve. Gesso is ruinous for brushes. Might as well dip them in superglue. If Chuckles got into it, I suppose I'd have to shave him, which would make it even harder to find him a caretaker. Nobody wants a mange victim.

I tapped on the laptop keyboard a few times to wake it up and sat down with the carton of orange juice at the kitchen table. It was time.

"Got any requests?" I asked Chuckles.

He rubbed his face on my screen.

"Right," I agreed. "No kids."

I typed that.

"Anything else?"

He turned around on his short legs and showed me his brown butthole.

"No dogs."

I added that and typed out the rest of the notice.

> Male white Persian nonsmoker with strong opinions seeks adoptive home. Named Chuckles. Answers to nothing. Good grooming habits with a fondness for windowsills and feisty calicos. Current owner diagnosed with noncommunicable, fatal illness. Cat not responsible. House-trained. Healthy. No kids. No dogs. No Chinese restaurants.

I added a photo and showed it to him.

"What do you think?"

Chuckles didn't really give a shit, which was rather short-sighted of him.

I uploaded it anyway and considered dinner.

"You want me to bring you something?" I asked.

Chuckles didn't open his eyes, which were leaking discharge onto his squished face as usual.

I took off my gray denim work apron and picked my jacket up off the floor, no worse for wear. (Think of all the time I'd wasted over the years hanging it up.) I shoved my arms into it and left the door unlocked. The Volvo with the damaged bumper was gone, so I didn't have to hit any more cars on my way out.

My favorite restaurant is next to a tire shop off Sunset, which is either ten minutes from my studio or an hour, depending on just how fucked-up things have gotten. There is no such thing as rush hour in Los Angeles; sometimes the traffic is just somewhat more soul sucking than other times. I heard there was a guy driving around the freeways doing puppet shows out the back window of his truck while people were stuck behind him, staring out their windshields like gas-sucking zombies. Some journalist called it "emerging art." I thought it was another good reason to work from home.

After a medium soul-sucking thirty minutes, I ducked under a rainbow of faded and tattered Tibetan prayer flags, flapping in the draft from passing cars. A brass bell jingled over the door as I pushed it open, and the Pepto pink walls pulsed with goodwill and curry fumes.

"Clementine, come in. Come in."

Dolma has the most beautiful voice I have ever heard. It's the voice all good mothers should be born with. She is all controlled enthusiasm and warm light, and her accent tinkles like the bell above the door. I want her to come to my house and read me bedtime stories and smooth back my hair and tell me everything will be all right. She was wearing an orange caftan and jeans with Teva sandals, and her haircut looked expensive. Her children and nieces and nephews—who all work there, too—share the same deity-like beauty, although none are quite so beautiful as Dolma. Maybe it's because they are Buddhists. Maybe it's because they wear sunscreen and avoid free radicals. Maybe it's the great haircuts. I don't know, and it doesn't much matter.

Dolma sat me down under a square fabric lantern embroidered with one of those snakelike dragons. An air vent rippled the fabric and made the dragon look like he was dancing.

"Tea?" she asked.

I smiled and thought about my pot. Her tea was much better than mine. It really wasn't much like tea at all.

"Yes," I told her. "Lots. And beer."

"No Jenny today?"

"No. No Jenny today."

She left me one menu and went to fetch the drinks. Similar

to chai, the tea is heavy on the milk, cardamom, and ginger. She serves it unsweetened, which I fixed with one of those little blue packets. The beer was called Karma Beer. It said so on the label, which was the only reason to drink it other than its being cold and alcoholic. She also left a thin round cracker the size of a dinner plate that was pressed with spices I'd never been able to identify. I broke it up to dip in the small silver cup full of tamarind chutney.

"Samosa or momo?" she asked.

"Both."

Dolma laughed her bell-chime laugh. "You'll get fat."

"I don't have time to get fat."

She laughed again and disappeared into the kitchen.

The samosas were pyramids of fried pastry filled with vegetables just spicy enough to bring color to my cheeks. I broke them open and let the mouth-scalding steam escape before dipping them in a cool mint sauce as thin as milk. The momos were steamed, pale dumplings that looked like the flat round pillows on my aunt's couch. They were filled with chicken and much milder until dipped in the pickled tomato called *achaar*. Like a tangy, savory chutney, it was unlike anything else.

My taste buds were coming back. The medications I'd been taking for most of my adult life were slowly leaving my system. Things I thought I had liked were so much better than I suspected. Dolma brought a new cup of tea to replace the empty one. I considered drinking nothing else for the next month.

"I'm treating myself tonight," I told her. "All my favorites."

"All?" She tried to call my bluff.

"All." I made a big gesture with my arms.

The dining room had perhaps fifteen tables, half of them full. The bell over the door tinkled every few minutes as the dinner hour grew more respectable. Everyone came here, from broke clothing designers working out of their landlord's basements to marketing executives in statement eyeglasses. The food was cheap and delicious. Dolma had three nieces and a son taking orders and delivering water glasses and steaming dishes of curry.

Before my first main course arrived, my cell phone rang the *boom-chick-a-bow-bow* that signaled my ex-husband.

"Are you okay?" he asked when I picked up.

"Fantabulous," I said. "How are you?"

He had his serious face on. I could hear it in his voice. "Because last week you weren't so good."

"I'm better now." I dipped a bite of samosa into the mint sauce and put it in my mouth. Divine.

"Are you sure?"

"Come see for yourself. I'm at Dolma's. I've already ordered enough for both of us."

The food came long before Richard did.

Potatoes and cauliflower swimming in a thick orange curry sauce were first. One of the nieces set it down on the glass table topper that protected the postcards from Nepal underneath. The basmati rice and peas came next and covered a map of Everest.

I ordered green beans that were heavy on the anise, lamb vindaloo, and chicken korma. I had a noodle dish called chow-chow that tasted sweet and put off diners not expecting it. I ordered both naan and roti and then yak chili, which isn't much different from beef jerky except you can say you had yak for dinner. My table for two wasn't big enough, so Dolma's son scooted an extra chair close to my side and set the breads there.

When Richard showed up he was wearing a tie and crow's feet that didn't used to be there. He sat down and looked at the overburdened table. He didn't smile or laugh. He looked, if anything, resigned. Doubt, which lived behind my solar plexus, fluttered its wings, and I regretted asking him to come.

"You ordered all this?"

I was being scolded.

"Yes, have some." I pushed the plate of lamb toward him. A peace offering, a child trying to avoid punishment. He liked lamb.

Dolma glided up and deposited a cup of tea in front of him without a word and just as silently disappeared.

He took a sip and winced when it burned his tongue.

The week before—before I'd fired Jenny and my shrink—he'd come over. I'd refused to let anyone come in for three days and had stopped answering the phone. He used the spare key I'd given him for emergencies. An emergency is a gas leak near an open flame. What I was having was more like a situation. I was on the bathroom floor and determined to stay there until gravity stopped being so unbearably heavy or until I rotted away and died, whichever came first. I didn't have much of an opinion one way or the other, but Richard—being Richard—thought it might be best if I got up. Gravity had yet to relent, and so I stayed down. He cajoled, and I ignored. He threatened me with hospitals. Been there, not going back. I ignored harder. I ignored in the way Chuckles had taught me.

He would, he said, drag me all the way out of my studio and out onto the street and into the car and all the way to Cedars if that's what it took. He held me under my arms and yanked me off the floor. I fought. He pulled. One of us should have let the other call the bluff. I should've gotten up even if I didn't want to. He should've left me there. I shouldn't have given him a key. He shouldn't have come over. I shouldn't have had toast for breakfast. He should've chosen another shirt. Whatever the case, someone should've done something differently, because when he got me up under the arms and dragged me by force out of the bathroom and into the studio, he dragged me right past a bookcase, and on the bookcase was a small metal fan. I snatched up that fan, and before the idea could pass from my impulse center through something that controlled logic and humanity, I swung it behind me and hit him in the head with it.

He dropped me, and I landed hard on the floor, bruising my tailbone. The fan crashed to the floor, never to work again, and Richard pressed his hand to his cheek. There was blood seeping between his fingers and a look of shock and betrayal on his face. It was the sort of look you'd expect from a child whose mother had suddenly and inexplicably turned on him.

The cut had bled and bled as facial wounds do, and we had argued about whether it needed stitches. Sitting here at Dolma's now, I could see that the swelling had gone away, but it was still a little yellow and the cut had not yet healed. What I had done was unforgivable. Richard disagreed, but we all know when we have done something from which there is no going back, when we reveal to ourselves what we are capable of, even when we want to believe that we can and will do better. That was when I'd decided to fire my shrink. Those sessions had clearly been a waste of money. Having me around is like keeping a chimpanzee for a pet. It's only a matter of time before the maulings begin and someone has to shoot it.

Now Richard and I were pretending between us that it hadn't happened, because it was too humiliating for me and too embarrassing for him to watch my humiliation. Instead, I let the feeling of it make a home inside my intestines like a tapeworm. That, and I offered him my lamb.

"I can't stay," he said. "I'm meeting Sheila for dinner. I just wanted to check on you."

I held up the basket of naan and waved it under his nose. "Garlic. Your favorite."

He gave one of those fake smiles where the corners of his

mouth couldn't decide whether to turn up or down and instead twitched somewhere in the middle, which was always a sign he was going to pacify me. He tore off a piece of bread and put it in his mouth, washing it down with hot tea.

The tapeworm stayed where it was, but my doubt calmed itself a little. Plus bonus points that his breath would stink for his date with Sheila.

"Are you really okay now?" he asked.

"Perfect," I assured him and scooped a spoonful of korma onto my plate, using a bit of my own bread to sop up the sauce.

"Are you working?"

"Like a beaver."

"I'd ask if you were eating," he said, "but under the circumstances—"

"Don't worry. This is food for the week."

He looked at me, then at his watch, and stood up. "I have to go. I'm late." He leaned over the table, holding his tie against his stomach so it wouldn't drag through the *achaar*. "Moderation, okay?"

"In all things," I said.

After he left, I pushed my plate away, all the serving dishes still more than half full. Dolma came by, said nothing about his departure, and asked, "Dessert?"

"Yes, *kheer*," I said. "And some boxes."

I put the sack of leftovers in the fridge and took off my shirt and pants. There was some paint near the hem that would never come off. I stood in my underwear and pushed a finger into my bloated belly. Funny how overfull started to look like distended starvation.

I took an extra-large T-shirt out of a drawer and shuffled blindly to the bathroom as I pulled it over my head. I opened the

Losing Clementine 11

medicine cabinet, watching my reflection swing toward me and then away with the door. The bottom shelf was full of white-capped, brown-bodied prescription bottles. There were almost more than I could hold in both hands at once, but I managed, carrying them the three steps to the side of the tub. I sat down and set the bottles next to me, lined up like soldiers.

I opened the first bottle, performing the complicated adults-only press-down-and-turn maneuver that would prevent any clinically depressed toddlers from getting their mitts on my stash. I upended it into the toilet. The white and baby blue capsules plinked into the water and sent up a fine splash. A few drops landed on my knees.

"Good night, Depakote."

In went pink tablets. *Plink-plink-plinkplink.* Those had caused exhaustion.

"Adios, Seroquel."

I upended the bottle. Those were fun—dizziness, constipation, and weight gain.

"Ah, Thorazine." I poured the orange pills into my palm and spilled them into the crapper. They had made it impossible to fuck, plus I had been nervous all the time. "It was absolutely not a pleasure."

More tablets. More bottles. Finally in went the last of it: the pink capsules that had made everything taste like I was sucking on nails. I lost fifteen pounds on those, which was a change from some of the other meds.

For twenty years, my body had been one pharmaceutical experiment after the other. I walked around feeling as if the air around me were dense and thick. My movements and thoughts and sensations were slowed and dampened. I had taken things that drained my personality and, worse, my desire to work, to bathe, and to breathe. But when I stopped taking them, I was at the mercy of the fanged black monster that settled on my chest for days only to leap off and leave me thinking and moving in fast-forward. Two years before, I had locked myself in the bathroom for three days only to come out and repaint my kitchen cabinets in the middle of the night.

And that was nothing—nothing—compared to the horrors that could happen. I had seen them up close and personal and a repeat was unthinkable.

I couldn't live with the pills. That I knew for certain. And life without them was dangerous, not only for me but for those who got too close to me. That I knew for certain, too. So this was it. The only possible choice.

"Good-bye, Lithium," I said and flushed away the swirling pharmacy.

Somewhere in the bay, fish were overdosing on antipsychotics. Under no circumstances should they be operating heavy machinery.

29 Days

"State your business," I said into the receiver.

"Where are you?"

Carla ran the Taylor Gallery, which mostly made her in charge of corralling artists, who, as a general rule, are prone to things like getting arrested in Panama with a shipment of illegal parrots. She has a master's degree in art history from NYU and the self-flagellation tendencies of an Opus Dei follower. She deserves better. She wasn't getting it from me.

I dropped three strips of bacon into the hot cast-iron skillet and hopped back to avoid the spitting grease.

"I answered the phone. That's your first clue."

"You're supposed to be here. Your work is supposed to be here. We should be discussing placement this very minute."

"I've decided to devote myself to bacon."

In honor of that, I peeled another strip from the pack and tossed it into the skillet. The smell was a heady, intoxicating thing. There is nothing like the sweet, smoky smell of dead pig.

I heard Carla pull the receiver away from her mouth and mumble to someone else.

"I don't know what that means," she said when she came back to me.

"I'm not coming into the gallery."

I tucked the phone between my jaw and shoulder and opened the fridge. Carton of eggs. Pickled jalapeños. Shredded cheddar. Onion.

"You're not coming in today?"

"Ever. I'm having a transformative month."

"Is that some sort of artsy new age crap?"

"Probably not. There's booze involved."

"I'm going to have blank walls, Clementine. Big, blank white walls. I've printed a catalog. People are coming to the opening. Buyers are coming to the opening. Critics. They are going to expect the art in the catalog to actually be on the wall. That's how this works. That's how we make money. That's how you make money."

"Fifty percent of the selling price."

"You're negotiating now?"

"Nope." I pulled the bacon out of the skillet with a fork and cracked two eggs into the bubbling pork fat. "I'm not negotiating at all anymore. Not at all."

"I don't know what's going on with you, Clementine. Is Jenny there? Let me talk to Jenny."

"I fired her."

"You fired her?!"

I had to pull the receiver away from my ear.

"Last week," I said when the yelling stopped.

I dropped the cheese and jalapeños into the eggs and moved over to the kitchen table. I shook the computer mouse and waited for the screen to wake up.

"Clementine, the show is in a week."

"Gonna have to do it without me," I said and hung up.

Chuckles hopped up onto the table and sniffed my plate before giving me the pleasure of his puckered ass in my face again. Chuckles feels about jalapeños the way he feels about dogs.

"You keep that up," I warned him, gathering him up and setting him down on the floor, "and the best we're going to be able to do is a kitten hoarder with the petrified body of her dead sister in the backroom."

He meowed at me, which I took to be back-sass.

I'd started my Internet search before the urge for pig took over. This was the only meal I could make that turned out well reliably enough to be worth the effort. I picked up a strip of bacon and chewed on it. I couldn't believe how good it was. The fat was still soft enough to be harboring trichinosis, which was just how I liked it. A meal without the risk of parasitic worm larvae is no meal at all.

I'd already considered, researched, and discarded several plans, and it wasn't even 10 A.M. I was a marvel of efficiency. For example, hanging takes too long. Contrary to popular mythology, your neck does not break. You just dangle there twitching and gagging. And when it's all over, you are not going to look good. Firearms are much faster, but the cleanup is hell. The police don't do that, you know. They just take the body away. The brain matter lodged in the drywall is your family's problem. There was a suicide fad in L.A. several years back. People were parking their cars on train tracks, which hurt a lot of other people in the process.

As much as I hated those meds, I was starting to regret flushing them. Maybe I could've come up with some sort of antipsychotic cocktail spiked with a little gin and a twist.

I typed "intentional overdose" in the search engine and clicked on an archived newspaper story about elder suicide.

U.S. Customs officials have confiscated a record number of animal tranquilizers being brought north across the U.S.–Mexico border in recent months. Most confiscations are from elderly citizens and their families, who purchased the controlled substance over-the-counter in largely unregulated Mexican pharmacies. The tranquilizers, when used in high doses, are fatal to humans. Seizures have sparked new debate over the right-to-die issue.

Cases of terminally ill patients overdosing on these medications are on the rise, according to a review of records by *Times-Press* staff.

I read the rest of the article—all six pages of it.

Garden Grove sounds like a nicer place than it is. Thirty-five miles south of Los Angeles, it's tucked deep in the heart of Orange County, where the light and soil are just right for strip malls and Republicans. I would know. At fifteen, I moved there. I was the new girl in school, which is especially great if you happen to be six-foot-one and not inclined to look anyone in the eye. Bonus if you can also arrange for some really hurtful rumors about your family situation.

I exited the 5 and made two left turns and a right onto Spring Lake Drive. My aunt's house is the third from the corner on the left. It's important to count because the houses are all beige. They have driveways on the right, two windows, and porches with three stairs. They each have one tree in the front yard. Sometimes a tree gets sick and loses its leaves. This is a helpful, if somewhat unreliable, landmark. It's best to count. There was a rumor someone in the '70s tried to plant a rosebush and was never heard from again.

I parked in the driveway where my dinged right front fender would cause a motion to be passed at the next neighborhood association meeting. I climbed the three stairs to the beige porch and rang the doorbell, put my hands in my pockets, and sniffed. The place smelled the same, and I shrank inside my skin.

Aunt Trudy had been baking herself again. She was lubed from hairline to ankles with the same Banana Boat Dark Tanning Oil she'd favored for decades. I still couldn't smell a coconut cake without Vietnam War–style flashbacks.

"You coulda called first."

The skin on her legs drooped at her knees like a pair of stretched-out panty hose, and her arms, even though skinny, wobbled.

"What would be the fun in that?"

She looked me up and down. "Well, you might as well come in before the air-conditioning bill puts us in the poorhouse."

I stepped in after her. Her green and blue plaid one-piece was cut low around the legs and, when she turned around, bagged in the seat. She had the flat butt of an elderly man. She kept walking and I followed, past the living room and through the kitchen. She kept going right out the sliding glass door into the backyard.

Her usual chaise longue was set up by the pool I'd never seen her go into but which was maintained weekly. I knew. I paid the bill. She lay down and turned her nut-brown face to the midday sun. We can only assume skin cancer has some sort of preservative quality.

"Iced tea in the fridge if you want some."

She had her own glass at her elbow, the ice melted down to slivers floating at the top.

I sat in the opposite chaise, feet flat on the concrete patio.

"I want to know what happened to Dad."

She didn't look at me, but I saw the pattern of her rising and falling chest hiccup and change.

"Why?"

"Because I do."

She made a face like I'd asked her to hold my hair back while I vomited in her shoes.

"He run off," she said, eyes closed and face still turned to the sun, like either a blooming flower or a lizard regulating its body temperature, depending on how you looked at her.

"Do you know why?"

"Got himself another woman, I suspect. *How* is another matter altogether. Your father was not a looker."

My memory of my father was a child's memory; I didn't know if he was handsome or not. Even if he had been, I wouldn't have expected Trudy to acknowledge it. I didn't have any pictures of him, either. Not much had survived the dissolution of my nuclear family core, and what had had not made its way to me. No hand-me-down furniture filled my college dorm. No family photos sat on my mantel. Not that I had a mantel.

"Did Mom know?"

"Your mother did not like to talk about such things, and I didn't pry. Wasn't my business."

She turned her head just enough to shoot me an accusing look, reminding me it wasn't my business, either.

"Why are you asking me this now?" She used her disciplinarian tone of voice. Before marrying Bob she had been a schoolteacher and a feared one at that.

"I want to know."

The truth was I remembered almost nothing about my father. I remembered a lot about his leaving but almost nothing of before. He was a fuzzy, indistinct shadow hovering on the edge of memories, a grown-up on the edge of a birthday party or ad-

Losing Clementine 19

ministering chamomile baths the week my sister and I both got the chicken pox. I was pretty sure his hair had been brown, but that was really all I had.

"You picked a poor source of information," she said. "I never heard from him once he took off. Not a single word, and don't think that wasn't hard on your mother. Doesn't excuse her. I'm not saying it does."

"There was never a clue? A credit card charge or something?"

"Not that I ever knew about."

I looked down at my feet. They were big. Shoes never looked good in a size as large as mine, so I got around it by not caring what shoes I wore. That day they were heavy work boots, and my feet were baking inside them, sweat turning the insides into a foot swamp.

Aunt Trudy gave an exasperated sigh that sounded like it used a little spittle in the process.

"Leave it be, Clementine."

"Tell me what you remember, and I'll go home and you can get back to your sunbathing."

"I've already gotten back to my sunbathing."

I waited.

It worked.

"He was an accountant. He worked for a firm in Encino, an accounting firm. Parker and something, it was called. He had a mustache that he was always getting food stuck in, especially yellow mustard from the hot dogs. He had skinny legs and liked to wear his watch on the underside of his wrist, Lord knows why. He was tall like you. Your mother married him young and had you girls young. They met in the lobby of a movie house. Dated maybe six months before he popped the question. Jesus, Clementine, he could be dead now for all we know. What does it matter?"

I felt something sharp poke quickly into my stomach like a

pin into a party balloon. She was right. Mom was dead. There was no reason to imagine he couldn't be, too. Orphaned wasn't that different from abandoned. It just came without the possibility of parole.

"I have to pee," I said and went inside.

I opened the fridge, the same one she'd had since the '70s. The tea pitcher was heavy and glass with bright orange sunbursts around the middle that any midcentury collector would've creamed his pants over. I poured a slug into a matching glass from the cabinet and carried it with me down the hall. Posed portraits of Trudy and her second husband, Bob, lined the walls. They'd had them taken every few years since they'd married, and there were now a dozen of them hung in chronological order like a flip book of aging.

I passed the bathroom with the fuzzy pale blue toilet seat cover and went on to my bedroom, which wasn't my bedroom anymore. The walls were yellow and just far enough apart to hold a bed, dresser, and desk if you weren't too fussy about banging your shins all the time. Before my mother and sister died, it had been Aunt Trudy's quilting room, which saw very little quilting but a lot of soap operas on the black-and-white television set up in the corner. She moved the television out when I came in and put it back the day I left for art school. I walked across to the windowsill and ran my hand under the ledge. My initials, carved with a penknife, were still there, which I supposed was something.

I didn't remember much about the three years I'd slept in that room, and I didn't feel like trying. I really did, after all, have to pee.

By the time I made it back into the yard, Bob was back from the grocery store. The paper sacks were still sitting on the counter, but he'd stripped off his shirt and was sitting bare-chested

Losing Clementine   21

in a chair near Trudy. His entire body was completely hairless due to a genetic condition. He didn't even have eyelashes, which sounds like a small thing, but you miss it when you're looking at someone. He was nearly but not quite as brown as Trudy.

"Clementine!" he said.

I guessed Trudy hadn't mentioned I was there.

"Didn't know you were coming for a visit."

"Just going over some old family memories," I said.

He nodded. Bob had always liked me more than Trudy did. It was probably nice, looking back, having another freak in the house.

"Don't let me interrupt," he said, pushing off with his hands on his knees and standing to a full height of just under five-foot-six. "I've got ice cream melting away in there."

Trudy and I both watched him put his full weight into pulling open the sticky sliding glass door and then toddle inside.

"He's a good man," she said.

I didn't disagree.

"I was luckier than your mother."

She had always referred to her that way, as "my mother." Never by her name.

"Most people are."

I showed myself out, picking up a half-drunk bottle of Single Barrel Jack Daniel's from the open liquor cabinet on my way. I figured I'd earned it.

28 Days

"Would you say a chicken is like a person?"

Both the butcher's hands were flat on top of the meat case, his fingers sprouting black, wiry hairs between the second and third knuckle. Under the glass were rows of marbled red steaks stacked one over the other like shingles, waves of ground chuck, and prekabobed kabobs separated from one another with stiff, bright green leafy garnish that looked like it might be a petroleum by-product.

"You mean, like, spiritually?" he asked.

"I need to practice giving injections. Would you recommend a chicken for that?"

"I sure wouldn't recommend a frozen chicken." He pushed off the case and let his bulky shoulders settle down away from his ears. He put his hairy fingers in his lab coat pockets. "Fresh one might be all right."

"I'll take it," I said.

He disappeared through the swinging doors behind which,

I presumed, were the dismemberment tables where chickens, pigs, and wild-caught Alaskan salmon went to be disassembled into their most delicious parts. He came back with my chicken wrapped in white butcher's paper and plopped it down on the scale.

"One T-bone, also," I said.

"You going to give that shots, too?"

"No, that one I'm going to eat."

At home, I learned the hard way that Chuckles needed to be shut in the bathroom. He had no respect for scientific experimentation.

I had gone hunting in my metal supply lockers for the rubber doctor's gloves Jenny had used when mixing something she considered particularly toxic. Raw chicken juices seemed at least equivalent to cadmium. I wanted to kill myself, not get the runs.

Chuckles had taken advantage of my distraction and hopped from the floor to a stool to the kitchen counter, launching himself onto his prey as if it might sprout feathers and take flight. He'd gotten his fangs good and sunk into the ass end of the chicken when I looked up and yelled something at once profane and unintelligible. Ears flat to his overbred, smooshed-in head, Chuckles dragged the corpse, which was at least as big as he was, backward across the counter. Like Harrison Ford facing a leap from the top of a dam in *The Fugitive,* Chuckles threw himself and the bird over the side. It was a blur of cold, dead meat and fur, and it landed with a thud on the polished concrete floor.

"Chuckles!" I yelled.

I am almost certain I heard him let out an "oomph" as the air rushed from his lungs, and prey and predator rolled to a stop near the fridge. All four of Chuckles's legs were wrapped around the decapitated bird, holding it tight to his fuzzy chest like some horrific, interspecies 69 sexual position. His eyes were wild with meaty fervor as he unwrapped himself and tried to pull the five-pound bird under the kitchen table.

"Chuckles, you monkey's ass!"

I grabbed him by his scruff and separated him from his mate-slash-meal before carrying him at arm's length into the bathroom. I considered holding him down in the tub and squirting shampoo all over his germy body, but—if we're being honest here—it wasn't a battle I was sure I could win. And even if I did, there were revenge scenarios to consider.

"If you give me the flaming shits," I told him instead, "so help me God, I will feed you to the neighbor's golden retriever."

Then I dropped him on the bathmat and shut the door.

Chuckles yowled like a baby being fed into a meat grinder and stuck a white paw under the crack at the bottom of the door.

It took half a bottle of Lysol to make the kitchen right again. Afterward, I filled one of the repurposed glass jars I used for mixing glue solutions with tap water and dribbled in some India ink. I'd slept with a man for a couple of months who'd been diabetic. He'd left syringes in the bathroom, which I'd moved into the supply locker after moving him out of my bed. You never knew what would turn out to be useful. I filled one of the syringes with the diluted ink, like I'd seen people do on medical soap operas. Then, with the web's "most trusted medical site" open on my screen, I slid the needle slowly into the chicken's breast muscle before depressing the plunger with steady pressure. Ink emptied from the plastic cylinder and bloomed black under the translucent, creamy white skin, bringing up what looked like a very painful bruise.

I tried it a half-dozen more times until the carcass looked like it had been taken out into the alley and rolled for its wallet and watch. By then, it was also well into room temperature territory and starting to smell like, well, something dead. I put it in the fridge to arrest the stink or at least contain it.

If Jenny were here, she would've made a bologna sandwich with tomatoes, mayonnaise, and cheese by now. She'd have put it on a plate and left it along with a Diet Coke on the worktable behind the easels next to the tubes of acrylic paint. My stomach growled, and I thought about calling her and leaving a message on her voice mail or maybe just listening to her message and hanging up. Maybe she missed making my sandwiches, too.

Before I embarrassed myself, I held my breath, opened the refrigerator door, and pulled out some leftover Tibetan food. Inside the cardboard box, the curry had congealed into an orange mass. I put the whole thing, take-out container and all, into the microwave and hoped for the best.

To distract myself from Jenny, I found a Web page for Parker, Combs, and Jimenez, an accounting firm "serving its clients since 1965." Aunt Trudy had faults, but her memory wasn't one of them. The page was just as gray and conservative as you would expect the Web site of an accounting firm to be. There were school-photo–style head shots of the partners along with short biographies that made you hope you would never be seated next to one of them at a dinner party. There was no mention of my father or any other employees. No photos of company picnics or even the office lobby. Though I did find a brief company history and quotes from satisfied clients extolling the firm's core values of "transparency, accuracy, and accountability." You'd have thought they were running for public office.

I tried to imagine my father in a beige cubicle somewhere in Encino, these men in the head shots behind him like a Greek chorus. I tried to picture him toiling for decades to be as transparent and accurate as possible, his hair going gray and his posture getting more and more stooped over time. He was vague in my memory, a compilation of physical traits like the description of a fugitive on the evening news. Caucasian. Above average height. Brown hair. Last seen wearing a mustache. It wasn't a very clear picture.

I plugged the address into my phone and looked down. I was wearing the same work boots as the day before, the same jeans worn to strings around the ankle hems, a different ribbed tank top. At least I'd changed my shirt. Blue paint had settled into my fingerprints and the creases in the palms of my hand. It had gotten under my short fingernails and made a home around my cuticles.

After letting Chuckles out of the bathroom and taking a shower, my hands were no less blue, but my black hair was damp, combed straight, and smelled like juniper shampoo. I put a drop of Moroccan oil in my hands and worked it through to the ends that just touched my shoulders. I made a part on the left and tucked the bobbed ends behind my right ear. Makeup is more mysterious to me than alchemy, but I took out a pressed compact made of swirled beiges and browns, golds and bronzers. I touched a big, fluffy brush to the center and put it to my cheeks, then coated the pad of my finger and rubbed more across my eyelids. They were crepier than they used to be. The skin wasn't as taut, and the lines around my eyes had settled in for keeps. I pulled the glass stopper from a bottle of floral perfume and touched it to the soft indentions under my jaw.

My study of the womanly arts had been interrupted. My mother and younger sister died when I was fifteen. If my father had just waited around seven more years, he could've saved himself the trouble of having to leave them.

He'd disappeared after we went to bed. I don't know what time. Mom never said, and he didn't wake me up. My sister and

I got up the next morning and ate pancakes off paper plates and watched *Scooby-Doo* reruns on television. All three of us thought he'd come back. For a while, two of us didn't really understand he was gone. All he took was a suitcase and his hot rod car, which had a small tear in the passenger-side seat I had made with scissors. When we went to school on Monday, he wasn't back, and my sister had to go to the school nurse because she was too upset and it was disturbing the class. My mother came to get her. I didn't know that until I went to ride the school bus home, and my sister wasn't on it. I flipped out pretty good, because third-graders get that way when family members start disappearing en masse. He didn't send a postcard or call, and he never did come back. Sometime after Christmas, we stopped expecting him to. By summer break, Mom had thrown out his underwear and pants but not his shoes, because shoes aren't cheap like underwear.

Encino is a small community in the San Fernando Valley smashed up against and completely indistinguishable from all other Valley communities. You can drive from one to the other, passing the same dry cleaners, dubious sushi restaurants, and gas stations, without so much as a sign to mark your transition. It does not, frankly, matter much where you are. If anything at all marks Encino from its clone neighbors, it's that it isn't aging quite as well. Sherman Oaks and Woodland Hills have kept their figures and shown up on time for regular collagen injections while Encino is really starting to let itself go.

I took the 101 either north or west, depending on which sign you happened to read. That's one of the joys of the L.A. freeway system. I exited onto a main commercial street and waited at a light every four blocks until the chandelier and rug stores next to the nail salons and curry take-out shops faded into tall and then taller business towers. Afternoon Valley sun, hotter and brighter than suns across the rest of the country, reflected in the dark windows that focused the light like giant magnifying glasses, threatening to burn us all up like ants.

I parked on a side street at a broken meter, prayed for no ticket, and walked through the front door. It was heavy and *whooshed* open with the suck of air-conditioning and atmospheric pressure. No guard kept watch over the large black desk or the white plastic orchid that looked liked overdeveloped labia. The building smelled like printer toner and recycled air, and the sudden change in temperature turned the sweat on my back to slushy ice. The directory by the elevators listed Parker, Combs, and Jimenez on the seventh floor. Lucky.

The elevator was lined with mirrors, which I tried not to look into because if I looked I'd start fussing, and seven floors wasn't enough to fix what was wrong. I watched the floor readout tick up in glowing numbers, and at seven a bell dinged and the doors slid open. The wall in front of my face, the one on the other side of the lobby that should've held some sort of sign, maybe brass, telling me what lair I had entered, was blank and scratched. Hanging hooks still protruded from the drywall, and someone had spackled over but not yet painted a small hole near the baseboard.

I stepped off anyway. To my right, the clear glass entry doors were shut, and beyond them the reception area was empty. A built-in desk to the left stood as lonely as the one downstairs. Lonelier even. No plastic flower. There was no other furniture. No signs. No fluorescent-light–loving office plants. A bit of brown packing paper was wadded up and lying on the gray industrial carpet.

I tried the door. Locked. I would've been surprised if it hadn't been. I turned my back, pressed the button to call the elevator again, and didn't look back.

Downstairs in the lobby, I walked to the desk and waited. A woman in a black skirted suit came in from the street and *click-clack-clacked* her way across the marble to the elevator, which opened as soon as she pressed the button. Still, no one came to the desk. It was quiet except for faint voices too high and fast and excited to have anything to do with corporate accounting. I followed them around behind the desk and put my ear to a plain black door painted to match the surrounding walls. Now I could make out a Spanish-language soap opera, the one the cleaning service people who came once a week to my studio liked to watch. The star wore a lot of silver bangles and favored off-the-shoulder blouses that showed off improbably round, full breasts. She looked as if she should be advertising Tecate. She probably did.

I opened the door. A security guard in gray sat with his back to me. The air smelled a little sweet and a little like rotten skunk. The front legs of the guard's chair smashed down as he tipped it back flat and spun around to face me, smoke curling out of his nostrils. I was willing to bet the television in front of him, one of three, was meant for security tapes. On it, a man and woman were embracing passionately while music swelled and the credits started to play.

I smiled. He didn't.

"Off-limits, ma'am. I need you to wait outside."

I didn't care about the pot, but I didn't much like being called "ma'am."

"*¿Quiere compartir?*"

He had the joint down by his side, a little behind his back.

I stood there quietly while he weighed the risk. His eyebrows pinched together over his nose, and I thought I'd be sent away. Then he relaxed.

He passed me the joint, and I took a hit, turning my head to the side as I exhaled and handed it back.

"What happened to Parker, Combs, and Jimenez on the seventh floor? They move?"

My Spanish was too slow, clunky, and unreliable for a whole conversation.

"They closed," he said. "Packed up everything and had a big auction for the furniture." He shrugged. "I bought a couch. It was a good price."

"Forwarding address?"

He shook his head and took another drag off the joint, which had burned almost to his fingers. He stubbed it out in a bright green plastic ashtray and blew out the last of the smoke.

"I don't know anything. They owe you money or something?"

"I'm looking for one of the employees. It's a family matter."

"Yeah?"

"Yeah."

I heard the elevator ding in the lobby and so did he.

"A lot of the people who worked there went to another place in Studio City, a big place with its own building and parking lot. Gave them free gym memberships and everything."

"You know the name?"

"Something Mayer, like Oscar Mayer, you know?"

A *whoosh* from the front door and more *clackity-clacking*.

"Thanks, man," I said. "For the puff, too."

He nodded and turned back to his T.V.

"All dressed up for nothing," I told Chuckles when I got home over an hour later. While I'd been chasing geese, the 101 had been filling up and overflowing, backing up cars onto the entrance ramps. There were stoplights that let only one or two cars merge at a time. It was supposed to alleviate gridlock. It did not.

Chuckles was standing on the worktable and raised his smooshed nose toward my neck when I bent to pet him. He sniffed and turned his face. He disapproved of the perfume.

The answering machine blinked the number 4 at me. That was four more messages than were usually there when I got home. I poured what was left of the Jack Daniel's bottle into a juice glass and pressed the PLAY button.

Carla's voice came out of the speaker all four times, each time angrier and more desperate than the last. She threatened to call Jenny. She threatened to sue me. She did call Jenny. I hit DELETE after all of them then stripped naked and dumped the clothes in the overflowing hamper after first pulling the ones from that morning out.

I put my gray denim work apron on over my tank top and jeans and went to mixing acrylics. I made up a dove gray with a little blue, the same color as the guard's uniform. I mixed a lot of it and chose a good-size brush and started at the bottom of the canvas. I laid it on heavily and blended upward. Darker at the bottom and feathering until it disappeared into the gesso white. It wasn't enough. I added a little black and blended it into the mix on the palette. Blend, blend, blend. I loaded my brush and went at the base again, brushing up toward the center. I added some dark, dark green and blended. I brought the color up higher and higher until only a strip toward the top stayed white. Then I started a new mix, blending more blues this time. I started at the top and painted down, down, down. The bristles of the brush scratched at the canvas surface as the paint deposited and left the bristles dry and unlubricated.

I took a step back and then forward and mixed again, yellow this time, using my brush to pull some of the blue and gray mixes from before into it, making it murky and dirty. I started in the middle where the two colors already on the canvas met and became one. Beginning on the left, I made long strokes up and down, blending in both directions at once. One-third of the way across the canvas, I stopped and left it.

27 Days

Chuckles was yowling inside his carrier as if all the vets in California were after his testicles. I put him in the backseat and went to toss my bag into the trunk.

Mrs. Epstein, who was nearing Aunt Trudy's age, was standing in front of her own trunk unloading cases of soda and oversized bottles of dishwashing detergent and toilet paper. She stared at me out of the corner of her eye. I had not been forgiven for the teapot incident, nor should I have been. I did, after all, lack remorse. I was a hardened criminal.

"You going on a trip?" she asked, looking at my bag as if it might be full of venomous snakes.

"Yep." I avoided eye contact, closed the trunk, and opened the driver's door, which unmuffled the sounds of brutal torture coming from inside the carrier. It was possible Chuckles was throwing his body against the metal door. Soon he'd start expelling fluids from every orifice. I hoped to be at Richard's house when that happened.

"Where are you going?"

"Tijuana."

"You can't just drive to Tijuana." She dropped her detergent to the concrete floor with a thud, barely missing her off-brand tennis shoe. "You could be kidnapped and turned into a drug runner." She pointed at me. Her finger was weighed down with a large silver and turquoise ring. "I saw a program on CNBC where women were forced to be prostitutes and carry cocaine in their lady parts."

I hadn't considered exactly how I was going to smuggle the tranquilizers back across the border. That was an interesting possibility.

"Thanks for the warning," I said, dropping into the driver's seat and pulling the belt across me. "Have a nice week."

"There is something wrong with that cat," she spat, just as I slammed the door closed and pushed the button to raise the gate.

Richard still lives in our house. He got it in the divorce. I still consider it part mine in a cosmic sense. This is preferable to the literal sense because the house is in Sherman Oaks, which is less suited to painters than to Amway salesladies and people who purchase potpourri in bulk. Also, Sheila has taken up semipermanent residence on my side of the bed, which would be awkward if I were still sleeping in it.

The last time I was over, which was two breakdowns ago or about a month, Richard claimed Sheila just came over a few days a week to visit, but when I riffled through the bathroom cabinets, I found two of her prescriptions, both for urinary tract infections. One I knew from experience turns your pee orange. Part of me hoped her doctor didn't warn her about that ahead of time.

Richard objects to my referring to it as "our" house, but when you know where all the Tupperware lids are, even the ones that always go missing, I don't know how it can be otherwise.

I parked in the oil-stained driveway and heaved Chuckles,

Losing Clementine 35

who had given up yowling for a throaty growl, out of the car. I pushed through the wrought-iron gate in the hip-level hedge that surrounded our front yard and took the cracked walkway up to the front door. Then I laid on the doorbell because I was in that sort of mood, and there were no teapots around.

"Jesus Christ, Clementine, what do you want? And what happened to the front end of your car?"

The cut on Richard's cheek was almost healed. He was wearing a wrinkled T-shirt that he'd probably slept in and a pair of bright green soccer shorts that went *shish-shish-shish* between his thighs when he walked. Richard had played intramural soccer in college and still liked the uniform.

"Here." I shoved the carrier at him. Chuckles gave his best yowl.

"I am not adopting your cat." He threw up his hands as if I were handing him a leaking bag of poop, which, depending on how quickly he took the carrier and let the cat out, I might be.

"It's just for a couple of days. I'm going on a trip."

"Rich," a high-pitched voice called from the kitchen, "who is it?"

"I didn't see Sheila's car," I said.

I looked back over my shoulder and scanned the street for her lime-green new Beetle, which, in my opinion, was a car better suited to cheerleaders than tax attorneys. Maybe it was her way of rebelling.

"It's in the garage," he said and then called over his shoulder, "It's Clementine. She's trying to drop off her cat."

Sheila did not respond. We didn't like each other, Sheila and I. That had always been true, and I didn't know if she knew about the incident with the fan or not. The injury was unmistakable, but Richard could have made up a story: I fell down the stairs. I ran into the doorjamb. They were shameful abuse-victim stories, and I still hoped he'd told one, because I didn't want her to know how much better she was than me.

"Why can't Jenny take care of him?" he asked.

"I fired her. I don't think she'd do it pro bono."

"You can't fire Jenny. You'll die."

I decided to appreciate that joke on the inside.

"Take him," I said, "or he'll make himself vomit."

Richard took the carrier.

"Where are you going?"

"Tijuana."

"You can't go to Tijuana. There's a drug war. You'll be killed and abducted into slavery by gangs."

"That appears to be a very popular opinion," I said, remembering it was Richard's habit of telling me what I couldn't do that had played a large part in our divorce.

He scowled at me the way he did when he thought I was being unreasonable and I thought I was being clever.

"Why are you going?"

"That's where they keep the medicine."

He set the carrier down with the door pointed toward the kitchen and pinched the release mechanism. Chuckles went shooting out like flames were coming out of his butt and disappeared behind the couch.

"Why do you need medicine? Are you sick?"

"Yes."

"With what?"

He was looking toward the couch, and I answered the back of his head.

"Cancer."

The lie just popped right into my mouth, and I paused to taste it. I liked it even if it was false. It was sort of like how strawberry candy doesn't taste anything like strawberries, but we all collectively agree that red dye number five and corn syrup will be called "strawberry" anyway. My disease would be called "cancer." And it was, in its way, like cancer. My brain had certainly turned on itself.

Richard looked me right in the eye. "That's not funny."

"I didn't think it was particularly hilarious myself."

We stood there facing each other on opposite sides of our threshold. His hair was standing up on top like he'd been running his hands through it a lot and maybe hadn't showered since yesterday morning. He didn't look so good now that I was looking. The wrinkles that sprouted from the corners of his eyes were deeper, and something was pulling down on the corners of his mouth. I tried not to look at the faint pink line across his cheekbone.

He watched me, and I watched him until eventually it started to feel like a staring contest. As much as I wanted to win, I couldn't help but let one eye wander to the white scar down the middle of his chin that looked like a Cary Grant cleft and was the result of a skateboarding accident when he was thirteen.

He acknowledged his win by speaking.

"Are you serious?"

"I am."

His face broke right down the middle. "Oh, God." We stood there looking at each other for a beat. "Jesus. Where is it?"

"In my brain." *Strawberry, strawberry, strawberry.*

His eyes were a mixture of disbelief and pity. "When did you find out?"

"Something's been wrong for a while." Truth.

"How are you treating it?"

"Palliatively."

"Clementine, fucking hell, can't they do anything?"

I shook my head. I was starting to feel a little guilty and didn't know why. This was more humane than being honest. It did, after all, explain a lot.

He chewed on the inside of his cheek then spun around on his heel and headed back toward the hallway that branched off into our bedroom. His shorts *shish-shish-shished* until he had almost disappeared.

"Wait for me in the car," he called over his shoulder. "I'm coming with you."

He took longer to come out than it would take to pack a duffel bag for a couple of days. He took just the exact amount of time I estimated it would take to pack a duffel bag for a couple of days and have a big argument with your maybe-live-in girlfriend about taking a road trip with your ex-wife to purchase illegal prescription drugs. It was an argument I knew he'd win, because even a lawyer can't find a loophole big enough to jump through in "she's dying."

When he came out, a small dark cloud was hanging over his head, and it followed him all the way to the car. He opened the passenger door and shoved his bag between the two headrests, knocking the sunglasses perched on my head. He'd changed into jeans and a gray T-shirt with fewer wrinkles.

"You never said what happened to the front of your car."

"I hit somebody."

"An actual somebody or a car?"

"A car."

"On purpose?"

"Pretty much."

He shook his head but smiled a little, which is easier to do when you're no longer on my insurance policy.

"Sheila's allergic to cats, you know."

I started the car and tilted my head to the side like this was new information. "Is she?"

Losing Clementine 39

"You can't possibly have to pee again."

"You're right," I said. "I just have a burning desire to see what kind of paper towels the Jack in the Box uses."

"You don't have to get pissy."

"You don't have to complain every time I have a bodily function."

He pushed back into the passenger seat and leaned against the headrest. I left him there while I went inside. By the end of our marriage, we had stopped traveling together. He would fly to San Francisco while I drove. That turned out to be only the most temporary of solutions.

Tijuana is a straight shot on the 5 south from L.A. I took the last U.S. exit, which spit me out in front of a series of giant parking lots, one after the other all the way to Mexico. The monotony of row after row of cars was broken only by bright neon signs over small offices advertising Mexican auto insurance. I pulled into a lot and took my ticket, promising to pay my eight dollars a day and agreeing that should I fail to return after more than two weeks, they could tow and auction off my car.

I chose a spot at the back of the lot and pulled forward until the nose of my car was three feet from the border fence, an ugly metal wall that snaked off over the hills and disappeared with the horizon. I'd heard it didn't even stop at the beach but kept right on going into the water just in case you had any ideas about wading out and around.

It was faster to walk across the border than to drive. I put my bag on my back, and we headed for the series of revolving metal gates that were heavy enough and spun fast enough to make you worry about losing a finger. A guard waved us through. No passport check. No baggage search. On the other side, a troop of brown-skinned children juggled for tourist change, and beyond them cabdrivers in dark sunglasses and pressed yellow dress shirts offered overpriced rides.

"You need taxi?" each asked as we passed, despite having watched us say no, no, no, no to the other four guys in front of him. Hope springs eternal.

We shook them all off and headed toward our hotel. A huge McDonald's was off to our right along with a billboard advertising human growth hormone at "lowest price!" Cars snaked back toward the U.S. border, inching forward like rush hour on the 405. Vendors walked between the lanes pedaling snacks and drinks. Rolling carts like out of a county fair offered warm pork rinds crumbled into bite-size pieces off whole back sections of skinned pig. Last chance for a bouquet of flowers, a bag of tamarind candy, an out-of-season Day of the Dead skull.

Those cars not in line to cross the border were zipping around traffic circles marked in the center with gargantuan statues. One was abstract and looked like Chinese chopsticks, another clearly portrayed an Indian chief, and a third was of Abraham Lincoln holding a broken chain and looking as if he, too, didn't know how or why he had come to be there. People were everywhere, enough to fill the city of Houston.

It was less than a five-minute walk to our hotel. With practiced efficiency, we were ushered into the air-conditioned lobby, and the receptionist with perfect English took my credit card. Beyond the front desk was a coffee shop and bar pushed up against the wall to make room in the center courtyard for an acre of slot machines, all of which flashed and jingled whether anyone was playing them or not. Encircling them were twelve floors of rooms. The doors faced out onto interior balconies that looked down on the gamblers. Unlike Vegas, which blocked out all time-of-day indicators as if it were conducting a scientific experiment, the whole hotel interior was topped by a glass sky-light. It felt more honest that way.

A bellman took us up to the fifth floor. He opened my room with the key card, flipped on the lights, and accepted the two-dollar tip. Everyone took dollars here just the same as pesos and would give you change in either currency. That, at least, hadn't changed since my last trip across the border some dozen years before.

Richard looked at me with the creases around his mouth forming deep gullies. "I don't know about this."

I wondered if I should've paid the bellman more to stay.

"About what?"

"Maybe you shouldn't take anything you buy here." He gestured around the room like I was considering fishing around under the bed and swallowing whatever I happened to find there. "It might not be safe."

Richard and I had always had different opinions on what constituted safe.

"I'm hungry," I said to change the subject.

"Already?"

"I'm anticipating it. I'm going to take a shower and a nap first."

"What am I supposed to do?" he asked.

"Find a room."

"Why can't I sleep here? We slept together platonically all the time while we were married."

Good, I thought. I'd been hoping to use this trip to rehash old marital arguments.

I opened the door and let in the jangle of the slot machines below. "Out."

"Why?"

"For being an asshole. Get your own room."

He picked up his duffel bag with all the wounded huffing he

could manage, and I let the door slam on its heavy, autoclosing hinges behind him. Even with it shut, the hyper ringing of the slots penetrated the room. That was going to bug me.

I was good to my word and turned on the hot water. The room looked like any hotel room in Cleveland, Ohio, or Oklahoma City, Oklahoma, except stocked with free bottled water for those with delicate constitutions and a fear of microbes. I stepped under the spray, yelped, and put my hands over my nipples. The hotel had fallen under the sway of high-pressure, low-water shower heads that threatened to pierce your skin with needle spray.

I turned my back and unwrapped a bar of soap. I liked this. Being away had always felt good to me. A fast car or an airplane could almost always outrun whatever black cloud was chasing me. Most times it would take a day or more for the cloud to catch up.

After having the sweat and dust knocked off me by the water cannon, I needed tequila, so I pulled on a pair of my nicest jeans.

Across from the hotel was what looked like a strip mall but was, the bellman assured me, an enormous discotheque several hours from being open for business. Next to it was a bar that at capacity couldn't have held more than fifty. At the moment, it held nothing but a bartender and several neon Tecate signs. The sun was still up and only thinking about starting to retire.

I sat at the bar and in two awkward sentences established that my Spanish was slow, error prone, and confined to the present tense. I pointed at the drink menu. Margarita on the rocks. The barman, who had been flipping through a magazine, looked pleased to have something to do, and the drink came strong and without salt.

Rock *en español* was turned up loud, and a flat screen TV behind the bar played videos to go along with it. I watched a cartoon where a man's limbs were being cut off one by one like a Monty Python sketch until he fell into the ocean as nothing but a torso and head and was rescued by topless mermaids. The bartender set down a bowl of snacks. They looked like small, matte brown marbles and tasted like honey-roasted peanuts. They were light and crunchy in your mouth and addictive in a way only Cheetos and cigarettes had been before. The bartender and I ate them and watched the cartoon morph into amputee porn, which was funny in both our languages.

Too soon the video was over, replaced by the Mexican version of The Cure, and Richard had taken the stool next to me.

"I asked the bellman where you went," he said.

I pushed the bowl of snacks toward him.

He took a handful. "These are delicious."

The bartender came over, and Richard pointed at my drink. I went back to watching the excessive male eye makeup on-screen.

"Would it help," he asked, "if I owned up to being a jerk right now?"

"Which time?"

"What do you mean which time?"

I took a healthy sip of my margarita, reached over, and pulled the bowl of nutty goodness back toward me and out of his reach.

He conceded defeat. "In the hotel room. I shouldn't have brought up sex."

To point out just what he was missing, I brought one of the nut snacks to my mouth in a slow, sexy motion like one of those ridiculous burger commercials with the lady in the bikini.

"And I should not have commented on the frequency of your urination."

"That was wrong of you."

"Yes, it was."

I let him have a nut snack.

"What *are* these?" he asked, putting a palmful in his mouth.

"The vehicle of my redemption."

He ignored that. "We should eat all of these and then go to dinner. I have a place."

I took my eyes away from the television. Richard had never once in the history of our rather rocky and complicated relationship made a dinner reservation.

He shrugged at me. "I asked the bellman for that, too." He ate a nut snack. "It's possible we're supposed to order rotten corn." He looked sad. "It won't be this good," he said and ate another snack.

Huitlacoche translates roughly into "raven's excrement," which is another way of saying bird poop. What it actually is is corn that has been infected by a fungus and morphed into black tumors. The chef mixed it with Oaxacan string cheese and served it in a purse-shaped crepe with poblano chili sauce. It's better than even the nut snacks.

The cab ride to the edge of town had taken less then fifteen minutes. The driver had dropped us at the foot of a steep, circular drive. Above us one of the priciest restaurants in Tijuana was perched on a knoll, surrounded by transplanted palm trees and aloe plants all dramatically lit with uplights buried in the ground cover.

We had been ushered inside and seated promptly. The host had held out my chair and even placed my napkin in my lap, which I admit was a little overly familiar.

I scooped another bite of the *huitlacoche* onto my fork. "Tasty, tasty tumors," I said and laughed because sometimes you just crack yourself up.

"Don't joke about that," Richard said.

"Why?"

"You know why."

There were only four other occupied tables, and the dining room had the judgmental hush of a library. We were close to attracting attention.

I took a sip of light red wine. The waiter had assured us in perfect English that it came from a local vineyard.

"Tumors," I whispered.

"It's not funny."

That was interesting because I was pressing my lips together to hold in the giggles, which was forcing them down into my diaphragm and making my ribs pulse with unexpellable energy. Richard cut a ladylike bite from his edible purse of bird poo.

"Tuuuumors."

"I am serious."

I couldn't help it. I started laughing. I laughed until I disturbed the chickadees hanging in cages around the restaurant. Their chirps echoed off the tiled floor of the indoor courtyard, where a small child had escaped his mother's table and was slapping the water in the central fountain. I wiped tears from my eyes. Richard concentrated on his food, but his dimples were showing.

"Mmmm . . . uncontrolled cell division."

That was enough to make him put his knife and fork down, which brought one of our four waiters scurrying over to take away the plate.

"You are insane," Richard hissed, but he lost the battle with his cheeks, which split open in a wide grin.

"I win," I said.

"You do not win." He took a sip of wine and laid his hand on mine, slipping two fingers into my palm. I squeezed them.

"I want to go with you to the doctor," he said.

"What?"

"When we get home, I want to go with you to your doctor visits."

"Richard."

"Have you made arrangements? For your care, I mean, not for—. Do you have a place to go?"

"I'm working on it."

After duck *carnitas* with blue corn tortillas, tamarind sauce, and cilantro, we stumbled out of the restaurant and into a cab. The four waiters waved us off, bidding us a quick return. Tourism was really down.

The sun had set while we worked our way through the courses, and Tijuana, like Los Angeles, was at her best at night. The soft-focus light of restaurants and bars took the edge off.

Traditionally, someone sits up front with the cabdriver, and Richard's Spanish was even worse than mine.

"Dónde música?" I asked the driver as we headed back toward town.

"Discotheque?"

"No," I said. *"Personas."* I mimed a fiddle.

He nodded, and we were off, with neither of us being absolutely certain we had understood the other.

The cab had seen better days. Part of the door's plastic lining was missing, and the dashboard had been loosely upholstered with a Muppet-like faux fur. Unlike the sharply dressed drivers standing vigil at the border, our chauffeur that evening was fraying at the edges. He looked to be near retirement and relying on the faded picture of Jesus taped to the center of the steering wheel to get him through. I guessed that meant I was relying on Jesus, too, and under the circumstances, that was worrying.

We drove through town and by the Zona Norte, the city's famous red light district, where tourists were warned not to go.

Losing Clementine 47

Another turn took us past a few small bars and then deeper into a neighborhood full of seemingly nothing but apartments already gone dark for the night. The streets got smaller, one after the other. The radio was not on, and I could hear Richard shifting in the backseat. Just before he could get nervous enough to reach over and tap me on the shoulder, the cab stopped, and the driver said in his best English, "This good place for music and for drinking."

I was all for a good drinking place.

"*Gracias.*"

Cabs in Tijuana don't have meters. Everything is negotiable. I offered him a five-dollar bill, and he nodded and accepted it.

A small wooden sandwich board sat on the sidewalk, painted in a curlicue font I couldn't read in the dim light. The sound of guitars floated out of a window, and every inch of curb space was taken up by cars sporting some amount of scrapes and body damage. Driving here was a full-contact sport.

I opened the metal storm door and stepped inside with Richard behind me. His hand was pressed against my lower back. The temperature outside had dropped, and he felt warm against me. Wine and tequila were sloshing around in my veins and making that seem like a very nice thing.

The whole place was filled with tiny round café tables with no room at all for standing. Men and women sat close together. Sometimes women and women, too, whether friends or something more it wasn't clear. Three guitar players sat on a small stage finishing a folk song, and a host who looked like a high school student in a black apron approached us.

"*Dos,*" I said.

He nodded, and we followed him to one of the only three empty tables, which were all down the steps and in the front row. The crowd applauded the last song as we sat and were presented with menus. The young men on stage were lit gently and glowed varying shades of brown. All three had oiled black hair and eyes too dark to discern where the pupil stopped and the iris started. They were dressed in khakis, and the one in the center had long hair pulled into a ponytail and a plaid, hipster porkpie hat pulled low over his eyes. He could have slid past the velvet ropes at a Hollywood club and had his choice of women.

They nodded their thanks to the audience, and the one closest to Richard and me took a swig from a bottle of cough syrup. A woman from the audience called out to him. I didn't follow her words, but he held up the bottle and blushed. Everyone but us laughed.

I ordered a carafe of the house red wine and waved off the offer of more food by patting my stomach to indicate "too full."

Paintings hung on the walls with little papers next to them listing titles and artists. It was a gallery along with everything else, and it felt as if the universe were having a joke with me. The paintings were almost all of naked women, most turned and bent so at least some of their sex was exposed. The artist wasn't trained—or at least not trained well—but he was passionate about his subject.

The wine came quickly and was not as smooth as the cabernet at the restaurant, but that hardly mattered. I filled Richard's glass and then mine.

The player on the far end leaned into the microphone and began his words the way a slam poet begins his, something between a rant and a song. The middle guitar started softly and picked up speed and volume to keep up. Richard reached over and slid his arm around the back of my chair. The song stretched on. It was Mexican folk, and it was improvised jazz. The notes swirled around each other, found their center, and came back to the original runaway beat. It grabbed you by the shirt and

Losing Clementine 49

pulled you forward with it until your feet were barely skimming the floor. All three men leaned forward and belted out the final words a capella, and the tables erupted.

I stopped our boy waiter, all but grabbing his pant leg as he passed.

"What was that song?" I asked without bothering to try to translate.

"*Narcocorrido,*" he said before the music began again.

Mexican gangster rap, glory to the drug runners and the killers. I didn't care. I loved it anyway. I was full of booze and food. The people around me smiled when I looked at them. I wanted to stay, rent an apartment, and learn the language by immersion. I wanted to eat blue corn tortillas every day. Let them tow and auction off my car.

Richard refilled our glasses.

I leaned into him so he could hear me. "Let's stay," I said. "Let's not go home."

He smiled. He didn't think I meant it. Maybe I didn't. There are some things you can't outrun.

The music was slow then, all three guitarists working together, no break after the marathon they'd just run. A saxophonist stepped out of a small door in the back that most certainly led to the kitchen. A black-aproned waiter carrying a flan dodged him. A smattering of polite applause welcomed the new musician to the party. He brought the instrument to his lips and joined the ballad.

Richard touched my arm. I turned to him, and he kissed me. I kissed him back once and then twice. He tried to slide his tongue into my mouth, but I hadn't anticipated it and didn't open for it. I reached over and squeezed his thigh to make it okay. He rubbed a finger along the back of my neck.

He never would've done that back home, and I never would have let him, but there is something about crossing borders that makes other boundaries easier to cross, too.

We watched for two more hours. The waiters brought more drinks as the musicians waved for them, but not once did they take a break. All three plus the saxophonist were still there singing to full tables when we stepped back out onto the sidewalk. The alcohol sloshed around in my brain, and the pavement seemed to shift under me with each step.

We wandered down the narrow residential street toward the slightly larger one ahead. Outside of the club, the air was quiet. It was midnight or somewhere close. Some small, weak-voiced part of my brain wondered if it was safe for us like that, leaning into each other and walking alone, not quite lost but not knowing where we were, either. The night's wine reached up and patted my back. There, there, little one, it said, and I forgot to worry anymore.

"Do you think we'll find a cab?" Richard asked.

"Probably on the next street," I said.

We came to the intersection and turned toward the heart of the city and our hotel, but the road was quiet. A few cars passed, perhaps three a minute, but none of them were taxis. We passed businesses shuttered for the night. Metal gates were drawn down over their entrances. Graffiti hung like lace on all but one, which had been painted with a blue face so sharp it seemed the bone structure underneath had been honed. Abstract green and yellow shapes swirled around it with the words *"amor y respeto por las culturas indigenas."* Even I could read that.

We were alone on the sidewalk, which turned to dirt and broken concrete at intervals as if a jackhammer had been taken to it but no follow-up work done. No caution tape or safety cones blocked off these uneven, ankle-twisting sections. We were, it seemed, expected to use our own common sense, and it was our problem if we didn't.

We walked for what seemed like a long time, and still there had not been any cabs. I knew only in the most general direction where our hotel was, and knew it was much farther than I cared to walk, even on whole sidewalks. I wondered if we'd have to sleep in a doorway. The wine was patting me on the back again when we both saw it.

Up ahead at the next cross street, many blocks from where we'd left the club, a cab passed. Richard gave a whoop and held up his hand.

Hopeless, I thought. Too far away, going too fast. I patted his arm. Nice try.

We continued on a few steps before we saw it. The cab had shifted into reverse and come back into view, zipping backward to our street and turning down to meet us.

When he stopped, I opened the passenger door. *"Buen ojo,"* I said. Good eye.

For another five-dollar bill, we were delivered back to the air-conditioned comfort of our hotel. The bellman opened the door and greeted us in English. We fought with the buttons in the elevator but had no trouble with the key card to my door. I don't know if Richard's key worked in his door. We didn't try it.

I saw the kiss coming this time. I opened my mouth to him and tasted the last of the wine on his tongue.

Richard is taller than I am. Taller and stronger with a chest and arms that can swallow me, and when they do, I feel small and feminine, which is not nothing at my size.

We stood just inside the room by the bathroom door and mirrored closet, our mouths open and locked onto each other. He pressed his pelvis into me, and I felt his swollen cock, shoved uncomfortably down the leg of his jeans. Blood was rushing to my cheeks and my chest, and my underwear was damp.

I worked a hand in between us and rubbed my palm against him. He groaned into my mouth and pushed harder. His belt was new and stiff, and I had to yank to get the buckle loose. I fumbled with the button and pulled down the zipper, and the jeans drooped off his narrow hips. I gave them a tug, and they let go, falling to his feet. He was still wearing his shoes and had to hold onto the wall over my shoulder while he kicked them off. I pulled on his boxers, and he took those off, too, so when he stood up straight he was wearing nothing but a T-shirt down to his hips and ankle socks.

His cock was sticking straight out from his body, and I grasped it, but without a tub of Vaseline, I couldn't do much more than massage him without a friction burn. He had one of my breasts in each hand, cupping and squeezing them, and trying to pinch my nipples through my shirt. I let go of his cock and undressed myself (top, bra, jeans, underwear) in the utilitarian way of couples who have done this many times before. I wondered if I'd gained weight since he last saw me naked, figured I had, and wished the room had kinder lighting.

I got down on my knees. The industrial-grade carpet bit into them, but sex is always intermittently uncomfortable. I kissed the length of his cock and took it into my mouth. It was familiar in a way I had forgotten.

Richard rested his right hand on the back of my head, trained by years of girlfriends not to press down. His breathing quickened into a pant, and I pulled back, letting him slide out past my lips for fear that it would end before I'd begun.

He lifted me up off the floor by my armpits, and I struggled to find my footing in time. He slipped his hand between my legs, and we worked together to rock his fingers into place. I buried my face in the crook of his neck while he found his rhythm and blood swelled me around him.

Too much and not enough, he took his hand away and steered me backward across the room to the bed. He pushed me back onto the comforter, and just for a moment I imagined all the unwashed bodies doing just this on top of it. Then he pushed his face between my knees, and I cared less about the biohazards.

Richard had always been good at this—enthusiastic and near worshipful—and when I had clutched and groaned and clawed and bucked without half of the restraint he had shown earlier, he stood with his knees crosshatched and red and guided his cock inside me to take his turn.

I had forgotten how good it could be when I wasn't half dead on medication. This was better. This was much better.

26 Days

When I woke, I had a low-grade headache to remind me of why it's never a good idea to order wine by the vat. Richard was still there. The comforter with all its biological contaminants had been kicked off onto the floor, and nearly all of the white sheet was wrapped around his narrow hips, leaving me with cover up to my thighs and no more.

I wondered whether I should wake him or if I should get up and shower, letting him slip out the door in yesterday's clothes. We could agree to pretend the night before never happened. We might, if we were deft, be able to agree without ever mentioning the agreement. We would just start talking about breakfast and then never stray into other territory. I wanted to know what he wanted to do, but by asking him what he wanted to do I would by default mention the sex and thereby eliminate not mentioning it as an option, leaving only the possibility of dealing with it.

It was a goddamn logic puzzle, and I was dehydrated and headachy.

I got up and went to the bathroom, because peeing wasn't really taking a position on anything.

When I came back, having spent some time trying to read the back of the bottle of complimentary shampoo in Spanish, he was awake and wearing pants.

"There's an espresso bar in the lobby," he said. "You want me to bring you something?"

"Yes," I said.

Was this the deft agreement or just a desire for caffeine?

"You still like it the same way?"

"Milky, weak, and sweet," I said.

He pulled his shirt over his head and didn't bother looking in a mirror to see what state his hair might be in, which is the sort of thing that had sparked in me from an early age the sneaking suspicion that I had gotten the short end of the gender lollipop.

By the time Richard came back, I had showered, carefully protecting my nipples from the power wash, dressed, and was fighting with the hotel-provided blow dryer, which was about as effective as someone repeatedly sneezing on your head.

He had done more than fetch coffee. He was shaved, washed, and wearing new clothes, which made me wonder if he had been stalling. The fact that I wondered that made me angry at myself. I was sure he wasn't psychoanalyzing my personal hygiene, so why was I being so needy about it?

He set my *café con leche* on the bathroom counter along with two packets of sweetener, gave my shoulder a quick peck, and then disappeared into the bedroom. I heard the television switch on and the unmistakable cadence of a soccer announcer's voice.

Great. What did that mean?

I sneeze-dried my hair just until it was no longer dripping down my back, then parted it to the side and pulled it into a stub ponytail at the nape of my neck. People who are trying not to appear needy don't spend too much time with their hair.

The bellman directed us to a local breakfast place that looked much like an off-brand Denny's and was located in a strip mall next to a nail salon.

The waiter brought us a basket of room-temperature pastry with our menus. There were a couple of minibaguettes, what looked like a single-serving pumpkin pie but surely wasn't, and a bit of folded dough that strongly resembled a British pasty. I bit into that one and was disappointed. The goo inside was from a fruit I couldn't discern but was not unlike the gel that surrounds chunks of apple in a pie. I left most of it uneaten.

We each ordered combo plates and orange juice. The juice came right away in old-fashioned fountain glasses with straws. Richard wasn't talking much, and when he did, I felt like a visiting relative he hadn't seen in several years. ("Hey, look at that. A lady cabdriver. Don't see that too often, do you?") We had officially entered the postsex twilight zone, where everything was off and potentially dangerous. It was a relief when silence settled in to stay.

I watched a middle-aged married couple divide their food. She gave him her beans. He passed her extra tortillas.

"We never got there."

"What?" I looked over at Richard, who was looking at the same couple I was. "We never got where?"

"Never mind."

Our food came. My breakfast was ham, tortilla, eggs, salsa, and bacon piled one on top of the other with a side of beans and tripe. The tripe had the texture of a fibrous vegetable combined with the undeniable flavor of meat. I left it on the plate.

"What are we doing today?" Richard asked.

I picked up a crumbled piece of bacon with my fingers and ate it.

"I have some medicine to buy."

"Where are we going to get it?"

The orange juice had bits of pulp bigger than normal. It gave me the odd feeling of needing to chew what I sucked up through the straw.

"I'd rather go alone."

He put his hand on my knee under the table. I'd put on shorts that morning, and his hand was hot on my bare skin. I wondered for a moment if he had a fever.

"Would you stop trying to do everything by yourself?"

My heartbeat started to pick up, and my skin felt cold and damp. What would I say? Yes, Richard, just step around that dog food while I ask about some large animal tranquilizers?

"Just this part," I said. And the part where I jam a needle into my vein while lying in the bathtub, you know, in case of fluids.

"I want to come with you."

"You are here with me."

"You know what I mean."

"Let's have *carnitas* for lunch."

"We're eating breakfast right now."

"It's never too early to plan."

After we paid the bill, we made our way out to the street to flag down a cab, which was turning out to be easier to do here than in New York, and offered another five-dollar bill to be taken across town to Avenida Revolucion.

The heart of Tijuana sits in a bowl surrounded by hillside neighborhoods packed so tight there is not one bit of ground to be spotted between the houses. At sea level, we zipped around the traffic circles, which replaced every major intersection, and past billboard after billboard mostly advertising mobile phones.

The air felt twenty degrees hotter than when we left the hotel. Even the sky looked bleached and faded from too much UV exposure. I scooted away from the window, a futile exercise trapped in the front seat. There was no air-conditioning, and I felt my spleen start to melt. There wasn't enough sunscreen in all of Mexico. I put a thumb against my delicate forearm skin and pulled away, inspecting how quickly the white spot turned back to pink. Was I burning or just getting heat stroke?

We passed a sushi restaurant, a disco shaped like a cave, and a BMW dealership. When we stopped at a light, street vendors walked between the cars with armloads of candy, flowers, newspapers, bottled water, and sunshades. School-aged kids braved the intersection to break-dance for coins. I was considering purchasing a sunshade when the light turned green again. We turned, and the neighborhood got less affluent. An auto repair shop made out of corrugated metal had a mural of a bikini-clad woman painted on the side. It was surrounded by a fence topped with razor wire and, every so many yards, a cross. Lust, self-protection, and, when all else failed, prayer. I could appreciate that.

The taxi pulled over on the south end of Revolucion. "This okay?" our driver asked in English.

It was. We climbed out and started down.

The veterinary shop I'd read about was two blocks off the avenue on the northern end. Somewhere between where we were and where I needed to go, I had to find someplace to stash Richard.

The avenue was nothing like what we'd enjoyed the night before. Quickly the stores on either side of the street became nothing but trinket shops, strip clubs, and tequila pushers. On every block stood a donkey painted in black-and-white zebra stripes. Its owner stood ready to hoist a tourist onto the beast's back and plop a sombrero adorned with the word *Tijuana!* and pom-pom fringe on his or her head. Now and again, the keeper would toss a corncob onto the ground for the animal to chew and would try to wave us over.

Store clerks ran out to us as we passed. "Come inside," they demanded in English, "just for the hell of it."

We shook our heads and kept going.

Old men with nut-brown skin approached us with silver necklaces that would turn your neck green. They pushed them toward our chests.

No, no, no.

A few feet later another man holding the same necklaces.

No again.

The strip club bouncers took their turn. The barmaids. Hostesses at restaurants. "Mexican food!" one of the women in a waitress uniform shouted at us, trying to shove menus into our hands.

I stopped looking at faces or scanning the storefronts for fear of attracting more attention. I heard myself saying no, no, no, no, thank you, no, on a loop. I was developing tunnel vision.

At the end of the avenue, mariachi bands in full dress stood on the corner, perhaps half a dozen of them, waiting to be picked up by a passing car to play a party. On the opposite street corner, women in high heels and skirts not made for the hour waited for passing cars and parties, too. To the left and down a couple of blocks was the Cathedral of Our Lady of Guadalupe. Its spires stood tall over the city, watching. The hookers paid it no mind. To the right, somewhere down there, was the store I needed.

I nudged Richard and pointed at the church. "I'll meet you in there."

"Where are you going?"

"I'm not doing this again."

"Clementine."

I had been pushed passed sympathy already.

"You can wait for me at the church or you can go back to the hotel, but you're not coming with me."

"That is ridiculous."

"If you try," I said, "I will scream bloody fucking murder, and everyone will look, and it will be a scene, because we're white."

"Are you actually trying to use racism to your advantage?"

"If I have to."

The muscles in his neck and face were tight, but he shook his head and turned his back on me, headed to the left. I turned, too, and went right. I had gotten the directions from a newspaper article, which had been none too discreet about describing just how scofflaws were obtaining and smuggling deadly poisons across our precious border.

I crossed the avenue without looking back at the hawkers and pushers and strippers and zebra-painted donkeys. Within a block, I was out of the tourist zone, back in the rest of the city. I passed a gas station, a two-story shop selling terra-cotta, and a street that seemed to house nothing but dental offices, most with signs in English offering oral surgeries for a fraction of the northern price. There were cheap clothing stores and botanicas, just like in L.A., selling their mixture of Catholicism and voodoo.

The farther away from the avenue I got, the more normal and poorer the neighborhood got. I went one block, two blocks, three blocks farther than I'd expected. I stopped and swiveled my neck. Something close by smelled like a sewer. This couldn't be right. Maybe I had passed it. Maybe it had closed. Maybe the newspaper had obfuscated more than I thought. I kept going like a gambler throwing dollars on the table to win back those already beyond his reach.

No, no, no, no, no, no, no.

Yes.

To my right, just one shop up, was a sign across a small store-front. Most of it was beyond my meager Spanish, but I recognized *veterinaria,* and in case I didn't, above it were painted two large fighting cocks in a face-off. My relief at seeing those two birds—an abomination to PETA supporters everywhere—was like three martinis on an empty stomach.

I stepped under the fighting cocks and into the store. Sunlight penetrated only the first six feet, and beyond that no artificial light illuminated the merchandise, what little of it there was. Advertisements for pet food were pasted in the window and had been for some time. The red inks had faded, leaving nothing but the blues and yellows, which made the human and golden retriever look a washed-out green.

A woman sat in the back of the shop on a plastic chair with a young boy. I smiled at them, and they stared at me. I had planned to subtly browse the wares undetected before getting up my nerve and approaching the register to inquire about things kept "in back." So much for subtle, but still I went through the motions.

As in all the shops I'd passed, goods on the shelves were slim. No twenty-seven kinds of toothpaste to choose from. No six varieties of food to suit the aging small dog, the aging large dog, the aging large dog with a weight control problem. There was one doghouse of questionable quality and a wall displaying a sprinkling of leashes and collars, a few sizes, a few colors. If those were too fancy for you, there were three spools of metal chain—small, medium, and attack-dog size—that you could buy by the meter. Above that was a lone, empty birdcage. Either it was for sale or its occupant had died. It wasn't clear. The rest of the small space was taken up by an L-shaped counter with a glass front. Behind it were old-fashioned wooden shelves that reminded me of a small-town candy shop or perhaps an apothecary.

I feigned interest in a small blue collar. It was a difficult ruse to keep up. Everything was dusty, and I didn't see anything to bring home to Chuckles. I gave up and walked toward the register. Inside the glass display case were two bright orange castles for decorating a tropical fish tank. No fish or fish flakes or aquariums or plastic plants or turquoise tank gravel to go with them. They looked sad in their forced frivolity.

The woman left the young boy to play with his toy car and joined me on the other side of the counter. "Can I help you?" she asked in English.

I had written down what I needed and pulled the piece of paper out of my pocket. I unfolded and smoothed it out. The paper felt thinner from the heat and sweat of my body. I was lucky the ink had not smudged.

"Do you have this?" I asked and pushed it toward her.

She turned it around, squinted at it, and nodded.

The shelves behind her had the same barren, postholiday-rush look. She walked the length, reading labels, and when she got to the end, I began to worry she had run out.

She had not. She bent down and picked a clear glass bottle off the bottom shelf, double-checked it against the paper, and brought it to me for my inspection. I, too, double-checked the name and the dosage against the paper. The label matched. I nodded, and she moved over to the register to ring it up.

Forty-five dollars.

I paid in cash, and she put my purchase in a purple plastic shopping sack.

When I stepped out of the shop, I was blinded by the sunlight and a case of nerves. No problem to buy it here. Contraband back home. I clutched the bag in my hand and hurried back the way I had come.

Richard was standing outside the church with his arms

Losing Clementine 63

crossed over his chest. His nose had turned pink from the sun, and his mouth was drawn tight across his face. Behind him the doors of the church were open, but yellow tape blocked them off. I looked over his shoulder to the inside. Construction men were knelt down over the terrazzo floor working. At the end of the nave watching over them was Our Lady of Guadalupe herself, aglow in her rainbow aura. I liked seeing her there. Women were so rarely in charge in these sorts of places.

"So you didn't get to go in, huh?"

It wasn't so much a question as a statement of the obvious, and Richard ignored it.

"Did you get what you came for?" he asked.

"Yes."

"Fine."

Half an hour of silence later, we found a restaurant with a sign that featured a cartoony pig eating a less cartoony pig. Inside they served us *carnitas* by the pound with freshly made tortillas and salsa. We ate and ordered tequila. The food and the booze thawed Richard. He looked at the purple plastic bag I carried but didn't ask about it.

When we left the restaurant, he took my hand, and we walked that way until we found a market. It was permanent but not much more than a series of lean-tos. There were *moles* and red and green chili powders mounded up in clay bowls, bins of every dried and fresh pepper known to Mexico, pinole, tamarind pods, tomatillos, plantains, brown cane sugar dried into cones, tubs of rock salt, and all kinds of nuts, both plain and covered with chili powder. Cheese was displayed in boxes with mesh sides for air circulation, and dried fruits of all colors filled glass bins like candy at a five-and-dime. Men stood in the aisles cleaning the spines off cactus pads, and above them hung piñatas in the shape of Mickey Mouse and SpongeBob SquarePants.

I bought chili powder and coffee, pretending I wanted them to eat and to drink. What I really wanted was to slide my glass bottle down inside them when we crossed the border. There could be sniffer dogs. You never knew.

That night Richard and I had sex again, just once, and then fell asleep.

25 Days

"Do I look okay?" Richard flipped down the visor and opened the mirror. The two lights on either side illuminated two inches worth of darkness. He smoothed his hair and checked his teeth, perhaps for pubic hair.

I could've said something, but I didn't. He looked vulnerable with his nose up against six square inches of low-grade reflecting glass, trying to see if *adulterer* was written across his forehead in invisible ink.

Our trip north had been uneventful. There had been no dogs. We simply walked through the processing building and stood in line with our blameless white skin and showed our passports to the agent. It was air-conditioned, which dried my nervous sweat. I tried to think boring thoughts. The agent asked no questions. Our bags were x-rayed and set off no alarms. My stomach relaxed. That was that. It was easy, really. Uneventful. I suppose smuggling always was until it wasn't, and it was my lucky day.

Now we were home. I had a pound of coffee and red chili powder for no reason, and Richard would go inside, and his girlfriend would be there. He would be unusually cheerful one minute and disparaging of me the next. He'd say I was miserable company, as all sick people are, except, in my case, much worse. He'd lay out a list of my annoyances and end it with "She's not like you." He might even suggest that I smell funny, like bologna gone off. Then, when he was secure in her gullibility, he would excuse himself to shower. He would take an extra long time and be thorough, and I didn't begrudge him any of this. It was what he needed to do, and he'd earned a pass or two over the years.

"You look completely normal," I said.

"Yeah?"

He looked up his nostrils.

"Yep."

"Okay then." He flipped up the visor. "Right." He climbed out and opened the back door to fish around for his duffel bag. "I'll bring Chuckles out."

I watched him walk toward our house. Dusk was hanging on by its toenails, nothing but a sliver of salmon-colored light on the edge of the world. His white T-shirt glowed in the near dark, and there were a dozen little lamps shoved into the ground along the pathway to the door, illuminating Richard's sneakers. The lights were new. That was something I never would've done.

When he unlocked the door with his key, I could see it was dark inside. I wondered what that meant. Maybe Sheila had gone to her own house. Maybe she was out back in the small shed that had been my studio for a year. That was as long as I could take the tiny space. It wasn't big enough to organize my supplies and store my work before sale. It was either too hot or too cold. It had terrible ventilation, and it made me feel claustrophobic.

On my birthday at the end of that first year, I'd gone out and rented myself a work space, different from the one I have now. There was no kitchen, and it was smaller and zoned commercial. I didn't have Jenny then. My shelves were a mess, and no one made me sandwiches. There had been a fast-food restaurant around the corner. I walked there covered in paint and ate a lot of french fries and gained five pounds.

I found Chuckles on my way back one afternoon. I'd had a paper sack forming a whole Rorschach test worth of grease spots and saw him dart under an old blue pickup truck that had been parked seemingly unmoved next to the building for as long as I had been renting there. He was emaciated and not more than a couple of months old. Persian kittens look like dandelions gone to seed, and I was lonely in my studio all by myself all day. I got down on my hands and knees in my stained jeans and T-shirt and tore a piece off my chicken sandwich to lure him out. Half an hour later, I had him, and it wasn't until I gave him a bath and cut the mats out that I realized his fur wasn't supposed to be gray. I kept him and never bothered looking for an owner, even though Persians aren't known for their street cred.

Ten minutes later, Richard came out with Chuckles in his carrier. Chuckles was not going easy into the good night. Richard opened the back door and put the carrier on the seat, and I rolled down my window. He put one hand on the roof of the car and the other in his back pocket and stared off toward the neighbor's house and then down at his shoes, which was never a posture that foretold good things.

"I'm sorry, you know, about us. I just didn't know how to handle it. You were sad all the time, and I couldn't make it better."

At first I thought he was talking about Mexico, and then I realized he wasn't.

"I know," I told him. "It wasn't your fault."

"You seem better now. I mean, you know, mentally." He blew out a puff of air. "I guess it's not really fair, the timing, with the cancer and everything."

I smiled through the windshield.

"Give Sheila my best."

When I got home, Jenny was sitting on the floor in front of my door. Her hair was falling out of her ponytail, and there was a hole in the knee of her jeans. Chuckles yowled with joy and started to cough something up.

"How long have you been sitting here?"

I set the carrier down, and Jenny leaned over to open it and scoop Chuckles into her arms, which is not something other humans are allowed to do to him.

"Too long. Where have you been? Have you been to the Taylor?"

"Mexico. And no, why?"

I leaned over her to unlock the front door, and she followed me inside carrying the cat and my bag. She put both next to the unmade bed and started straightening the covers. What I really wanted was for her to make me dinner. I pulled one of the blue painted stools up to the counter that floats in the middle of the floor, marking the kitchen's boundary, and tried to look hungry. If she didn't mention her firing, neither would I.

"Elaine's stuff is up. She got the show before yours."

"I'm not having a show. You want pancakes?"

"You don't know how to make pancakes."

"That was sort of my point."

"And what do you mean you're not having a show? Did they cancel? Is it because of Elaine, because I swear to God, she is a thief."

"We can talk about it while you make pancakes."

"You're not listening to me." She stopped straightening and faced me.

"Yes, I am," I said. "I'm listening now. Tell me."

Chuckles hopped up on the half-made bed and lay down.

"Elaine stole your stuff, and it's hanging at the Taylor right now."

I stopped caring about pancakes. "What are you talking about?"

"It's just like what you've been working on. The layers, the scale, the colors, the Americana themes. Everything."

Elaine Sacks had been the Lex Luther to my Superman for years. We'd come up in the business at the same time, except I had talent and she had less but supplemented it with a few well-placed blow jobs, or so I'd heard. She was also a copycat. She showed at the same galleries I had after I'd established myself there. She'd moved to L.A. a year after I did. She took up mixed media after I'd switched from oils. It was like having a pesky younger sister who always wanted to borrow your clothes and get a ride to the mall with your friends. Except in this case she was also dipping into my client base. Because I'm above that sort of thing, I hadn't yet set her car on fire, but we had an understanding. She stayed away from me, and I wouldn't spit on her. That was generous on my part, I thought.

But this was too much. The twelve pieces I'd assembled for the show that wasn't going to happen were still there in my studio. I'd gone off on a subversive Grandma Moses track. All rolling farm landscapes and small towns with little houses and people and lots of red, white, and blue until you looked close and the cow has two heads and the guy working the hay barn is in slavery shackles and the milkmaids are getting it on. It was some of my best stuff. When I kicked it, it would be worth a fortune. Jenny would get a lot of that money, though she didn't know it yet.

"Show me," I said.

It was black dark by then, and downtown was deserted except for clusters around the valet stands of bars and restaurants. The well-funded ones were still pushing through and hoping the promised gentrification, which had come to a fiery end in the real estate crash of '08, would find its feet again. The jury was still out on that. The homeless still owned huge tracts of the sidewalks, and the pull of the suburbs had not ceased. But the hipsters and galleries and nearby USC students were dug in. So maybe. Just maybe.

The Taylor Gallery was located on one of the quieter blocks. There were no bars and restaurants to keep people nearby after the offices closed at six o'clock. The gallery, too, was closed. It was open in the afternoons and by appointment, and most of my work sold on opening night anyway and sometimes before then to a few clients that John Taylor cultivated and called my patrons.

Jenny parked in a yellow loading zone. I climbed out first and walked up. The huge plate glass windows were dark, and the white lettering at chest level done in Times New Roman all caps glowed. ELAINE SACKS—HOMESTEAD. A large piece hung on a freestanding display wall a few feet behind the window. Grandma Moses redone.

It was like standing in a sensory deprivation tank. I couldn't hear the whoosh of traffic on Figueroa. I couldn't smell the old salami wafting out of the closed deli across the street.

The piece in front of me was larger than what I did. Sacks still operated like she was an unknown. A new artist's work is priced according to size. No one says that aloud, but it is. You don't know where the market will take the artist yet, so you buy the painting like any other commodity, like corn or chickens or industrial carpet. You paid by the square foot. The scale of her work felt a little desperate to me.

When Jenny touched my arm, I jumped. I hadn't heard the car door open and shut or her footsteps crunch on the dirty sidewalk. I'd have made for a fine mugging victim in that state.

"You didn't tell anyone about my work, did you?"

"No." Her voice was level and firm. "I wouldn't do that."

I took a rattled breath. "I know."

"Can you sue?"

Maybe someone could sue on my behalf. I wasn't going to be around long enough for that. What I was around long enough for was for her to show before me, to establish this style as her own, to devalue my work, and to throw doubt on my integrity. I'd be dead and people would say crap things about my work, and it shouldn't matter but it did. It made me angry. It made me raging-bull, rip-your-guts-out, beat-you-to-death-with-a-metal baseball-bat angry.

The rage went in two directions. Elaine took half. Probably more than half. The other went to the gallery assistant. I didn't remember her name anymore. I hadn't remembered it the minute after she'd told me. She'd come by with a check. I was on her way home, she'd said, could she stop by? Jenny had already left for the night. The assistant had worn all black. I remembered because it was the required uniform of assistants, and it had told me what to think of her, which was nothing. Black leggings, black shoes, black top, black scarf, black bag. She'd had the check from my most recent sale, and I'd stuck it to the fridge with a magnet. Jenny would take it to the bank. The assistant had asked if she could look at what I was working on. I didn't see why not. It was right there out in the open. The piece in progress was on the easel. Others leaned up against the walls. She didn't even have to ask, but I said yes. She'd walked up to each. She'd made comments. I don't remember what. She was the only other person to see them. Elaine had already signed with the gallery. I knew that. She'd had a show there already that I hadn't attended.

"You should go home," I said to Jenny.

"What are you going to do? How are you going to get back?"

"Don't worry about it."

"I can help."

Jenny looked like a half-grown Gerber Baby. She loved Jesus and knew in her heart that Jesus loved her. She knew how to make peach cobbler, and she said please and thank-you.

"No, you can't."

"Are you going to break in?"

"Go home, Jenny."

"I have paint in the car. House paint. My friend had it left over from her condo. I was going to do my bathroom."

I looked at her, turning my head just slightly from the bloody accident in front of me. "What color?"

"Robin's egg blue."

I crinkled my nose.

"I know," she admitted. "I would've brought red if I'd known we were going to deface property."

"Leave the paint."

"Take the cannoli?"

I really loved that girl.

"I'm staying," she said. "What's the plan?"

I looked through the window. I couldn't get close enough to see if the milkmaids were doing it, but her buildings weren't as detailed as mine. The colors weren't as well chosen. The piece lacked balance and flow. Your eye had no obvious place to land, no path to follow. A good artist took you on a tour, led you by the hand where she wanted you to go. I wasn't just being knocked off. I was being knocked off badly. The back of my neck was hot.

To the right of the piece, there was a red dot stuck to the wall. Below the dot, a card announced in perfect script:

> *Homestead #3*
> *Elaine Sacks*
> *36 x 40*
> *Acrylic and Mixed Media*

Buyers could be so stupid.

"Jenny?"

"I'm getting the paint."

She went to the trunk, pulled out a gallon bucket by its thin wire handle, and set it on the curb. With a small Swiss Army knife that dangled from her key chain, she popped off the lid then brought it to me.

"You don't do anything," I said. "You're the lookout. It's all me. No arguments."

She scowled. I didn't care.

"You have a lug wrench?" I asked.

Her eyes got big. "Okay, I'm lookout."

"And the wrench?"

"In the trunk."

I followed her to the car, looking in both directions. The buildings stood fifteen stories high on either side of the street, making an urban canyon that swept sandwich wrappers and plastic bags through on focused air currents. Other than trash, it was empty and silent. Not even a bum. Maybe Jesus did love Jenny. I pulled up the stiff, thin flooring and took the wrench from next to the doughnut spare.

"Start the car," I said. "Keep it running."

I waited for the engine to turn over. Jenny turned the key in the ignition, then climbed out of the driver's seat and looked at me. I pointed down the road in both directions, and she slowly dragged her eyes away and checked for witnesses. A car passed two blocks away. I waited and looked up at the dark windows above the gallery. It was office space, an architect. No one seemed to be working late. Nothing indicated a cleaning crew was in residence.

"All clear?" I asked, keeping my voice at its normal register. There was no use whispering. Things were going to get loud.

Jenny looked both ways. "All clear."

The metal was heavy and shaped like an *L*. I choked up a little on the long end and took one last look at that piece-of-shit painting and the smug, precise lettering on the window. Then I swung like I was shooting for the cheap seats, aiming the lug wrench right for the middle of her name.

The glass shattered with a crash so loud it startled even me. Less than a breath later, the alarm went off, and the *EEE-EEE-EEE* made the breaking window sound like a whisper.

There wouldn't be much time.

I stepped over the broken shards and snatched the painting off the wall. I dropped one end onto the ground and shoved my work boot right through the center of it. I couldn't hear, but I imagined a satisfying rip of the canvas. I dropped the frame to the ground, turned around and snatched up the half-full bucket of robin's egg blue paint, and dumped it onto the ruined canvas.

There were more paintings inside, each more horrible and offensive than the last. Each just as deserving of stomping and tearing and splattering, but the one would have to do. I was out of time. I dropped the bucket and ran for the passenger-side door. Jenny saw me and threw herself behind the wheel. I didn't have the door shut yet when she jerked the car out of park and mashed her tennis shoe down on the accelerator. I grabbed on to the seat with my left hand and grunted as the door pulled hard on my right shoulder. I yanked it shut, and the sound of the alarm faded quickly behind us. I listened for police sirens but didn't hear any. Not yet.

Jenny was laughing so hard tears ran down her face.

I smiled so wide my cheeks hurt from it. "That was very satisfying," I said.

24 Days

I sat on the hood of my red '68 Corvette, the first of the Shark Generation. It still needed front-end repair. I was leaving it to Trudy's Bald Bob. Let him take it to the body shop.

The parking lot was full, and it was a few minutes to five. I was holding a piece of cardboard, which I belatedly realized made me look homeless. On it, I'd written my father's name, Jerry Pritchard, in white paint. My sign was starting to droop in the heat. Studio City is in the hottest part of the Valley, which is always twenty degrees hotter than the coast, which meant 103 degrees in the shade. If I had to sit out there much longer, the sun bouncing off the hood would slow-roast my buns.

I was tired. Jenny had been too wired to sleep and didn't want to go home. I'd climbed into the shower to wash off the splashes of blue paint, and she'd made pancakes. She didn't leave until after two in the morning. Chuckles wandered off the bed and into the kitchen to yowl his complaint like a crotchety downstairs neighbor. We didn't talk about me firing her, and I didn't know if she'd be back. Some things you just don't have a right to ask about.

So I sat there and waited for five o'clock.

The second hand had just ticked past due north when the front doors opened and the employees of The Mayers Group spilled out like candy from a ripped bag. The building was only six stories and located right next to the freeway, which was loud and carcinogenic, but it was a big enough company to have its logo on the facade, even if the directory said they only occupied three of the floors.

I held my sign over my head, and women in skirts and high heels parted around me. The men stared and poked the sides of other men, their blue and gray ties blowing in the wind like flags. They made their way to Accords and Camrys and a Lexus or two. They set their to-go coffee mugs on the roofs and unlocked doors, deposited briefcases, and tossed in purses. No one spoke to me, and I'd even bothered to find clothes without paint or food on them.

I kept scanning the crowd for gray hair, all of which turned out to be at the bottom of the spilled bag of employees. The older women, who had seen it all and sent it to college already, didn't bother to glance at me, which was fine enough. I spotted three men with varying degrees of hair loss bringing up the rear and slid down the sloped nose of the car, making for them.

One of the men wore suspenders, and all of them slowed when I approached. I let my sign drop to my side and tried to look polite. Engines were starting all around us, and cars were flowing toward the exit in a practiced ballet.

"Excuse me," I said. "My name is Clementine Pritchard. My father was Jerry Pritchard."

The man in the suspenders whistled. "That's a blast from the past."

The man to his left, who had a close-clipped full beard and mustache several shades darker than the hair on his head, said, "Doesn't sound familiar."

"You wouldn't know him. He was in my department at Parker, Combs, and Jimenez. God, was it thirty years ago now?"

"I knew him to speak to," said the third gentleman, whose most notable feature was not having any notable features.

"What brings you here?" asked the man in the suspenders.

"I'm looking for him."

The parking lot was almost empty but for a handful of cars, all of them black and dark gray and a pay grade nicer than the ones merging onto Ventura Boulevard.

Suspenders looked apologetic. "Well, none of us have seen him since we were young and handsome."

Everyone smiled.

"I was hoping he'd kept in touch with someone."

Suspenders looked at Nothing Notable, who shrugged. Beard had figured out this conversation did not concern him and was waiting for the earliest possible moment to extricate himself.

"You could try Martin Mathis," Suspenders offered. "He came from PC & J after the layoffs, too. He's never mentioned anything to me, but you never know."

"Where can I find him?" I asked.

"He's been out sick all week."

"There's something going around," Nothing Notable said.

"Maintenance needs to clean the air ducts," Beard agreed, having found something to contribute.

"He'll probably be back by next week. You could call then and ask for him."

"Thank you all," I said in my most polite, responsible adult voice. "I appreciate your time."

We all shook hands as though we had concluded a successful business negotiation, and the three headed for their black sedans. Beard threw a glance over his shoulder as I made toward the Corvette.

"Yours?" he called.

"Mine," I confirmed.

"Nice."

I nodded. He couldn't see the fender from his angle.

I had no intention of waiting until next week to call. While the other three pulled out of the parking lot, I dialed information.

There are a surprising number of men named Martin Mathis in the greater L.A. area, which has a population slightly larger than that of the Netherlands. This explains the traffic. But you had to figure in the commute and assume that none of the Mathises wanted to live too far from their cubicle. I chose the closest one, which was only three miles or twenty minutes away in traffic.

This Mathis family lived on a wide street lined with parked cars and jacaranda trees that dropped their showy purple flowers onto windshields, driveways, sidewalks, and lawn furniture the way a stripper sheds day-old glitter. They had remodeled sometime in the past fifteen years. The facade didn't match the houses on either side, which were growing old gracefully.

I parked as far away from the jacarandas as I could, because no one wants lawn debris in her convertible, and walked to the door painted the same red as the Corvette.

Martin Mathis opened the door in his bathrobe. He didn't say anything. He just stood there with his pale shins sticking out the bottom of the grayish-blue terry cloth. He was wearing a white T-shirt underneath, and he hadn't shaved in several days. Whatever was growing in the air ducts had felled him good. I didn't offer to shake hands. When you only have twenty-three days left to live, you really don't want to catch the accounting flu.

"My name is Clementine Pritchard," I said.

"The artist?" he asked.

"Yes." That was unusual. I normally wouldn't get recognized if I went around with my résumé stapled to my T-shirt.

"I knew your dad."

Now we were getting somewhere.

"That's why I'm here," I said. "Can I come in?"

He cast a worried look over his shoulder. It looked like the front door opened into a large living room that was scattered with papers and toys.

"I don't want to be rude, but do you mind if we talk on the porch? The baby is napping, and you wouldn't believe what I went through to get her down. Six months old and going through a sleep regression." He shook his head.

I raised an eyebrow. Mr. Mathis was old enough to be my father, and I medicated my own sleep regressions with vodka and Lunesta.

"Second family," he said.

Maybe it wasn't the air ducts that were getting the better of him after all.

"Sure," I said. "I'll try not to take up too much of your time."

He stepped out onto the porch and closed the screen door behind him.

"I saw an article in the *Times* about you a few years ago. I said to my wife, my first wife, I mean, 'That must be Jerry's girl.' And it was. I only remember on account of your first name being so unusual."

He didn't mention that infernal song, which was good. I would have had to stomp on his bare foot.

"Have you spoken with my father since he left the accounting firm?"

Martin scratched his beard growth. "Not that I remember, but

Losing Clementine 81

that was a long time ago. You were knee-high to a grasshopper when he left Parker and Combs. It wasn't even Parker, Combs, and Jimenez yet when he left."

"I'm trying to find him."

"I gathered." Martin put his hands in his robe pockets and looked down at his welcome mat. "We were all real surprised when he left like that. I don't think he even gave notice. Rumors went around that he'd packed up and left you and your mom, too."

"And my sister," I said. "I had a sister."

Martin didn't comment, and I couldn't tell if he hadn't known or maybe just didn't remember because she hadn't lived long enough to be a famous anything.

"Maybe he kept in touch with someone or you heard something about where he might have gone?"

"I sure wish I had something to tell you. I'm surprised he stayed gone. I would've thought he'd send word or come to his senses."

"I'm not sure he had senses to come to," I said.

"I understand how you must feel that way, but I really can't help you. Jerry and I just worked in the same department, you know? We didn't have beers after work or anything. Our wives didn't know each other. Kept to himself mostly." A baby fussed, and Martin looked in through the screen door. "All I can really tell you is that he was good at his job, if that means anything."

I didn't know if it did or not.

"If you think of anything—," I said.

The fussing got louder.

He nodded, murmured a good-bye, and went inside.

I missed the ceremony on purpose, showing up late in a bright yellow dress that went down to my toes and gathered under my boobs. When the wind blew, I looked six months pregnant, which was something I hadn't realized when I bought it.

The botanical gardens took up more acreage than all of LAX with the runways and international terminal thrown in. There were more than a dozen subgardens, including a Japanese garden, a rose garden, and a jungle with a waterfall inside its own glass house. A sign near the entrance told me there were more than fourteen thousand varieties of plants on the premises. I'd have to take its word for it.

Discreet signs pointed me through the main building, where they showed introductory films to visiting schoolchildren during the day. I followed the arrows out the other side and down a winding but still wheelchair-compliant path, where I didn't see another person until I followed another sign around a dense grove of live oaks. Through the twisting branches, I made out fairy lights twinkling in the distance.

In a grassy clearing, near a path that broke off toward the lily pond, round tables with white cloths were set up. Guests held small plates and wineglasses and talked in small groups. The seated dinner hadn't started. I was still fashionably late, just this side of rude.

I stood and watched for a moment. I knew nearly everyone by reputation and some well enough to speak to. I pulled my wrap around my arms—deserts are cold at night—and watched, looking for my landing spot. The people organized themselves by category. Old college friends moved together. Faculty joined and split and rejoined. Artists who were not the groom's former students formed a subset, as did gallery owners and a group that stayed to the sides, wearing flat shoes and conservative garden party dresses. Family, I decided, and gave them a wide berth, pointing myself instead toward old college friends.

A reflecting pool, wide and rectangular, was full of floating candles. I took the path that wrapped around it. The closer I got, the more the hum of the party dissolved into high-pitched laughter and snippets of words. A uniformed waiter intercepted me with a silver tray half-empty but still also half-full of little toasts topped with shaved salmon and something white and creamy. I took one, and he handed me a napkin. I ate the toast in one bite. Dinner couldn't come soon enough.

There were two more waiters. One carried tall flutes of gold champagne, a thin layer of bubbles still clinging to the surface. I took one of those and a bacon-wrapped shrimp from the other guy. The shrimp was still in my mouth when Jeremy spotted me through the throng of guests. He hurried over and threw his arms around me. I hadn't yet wiped my fingers, but I hugged him anyway. Bacon grease wouldn't show on the back of his black tux.

"S-s-s-s-so glad you came, Clem-m-m-mentine."

"I wouldn't have missed it for all the world and the one after that," I said, which was true.

I hadn't seen him in two years, which is one of those things you let happen and doesn't feel like anyone's fault but is.

"Have you m-m-met Mark?" He put a hand on the bicep of the identically dressed man to his left, who put out a cool, smooth hand to shake.

I took it. "It hasn't yet been my pleasure," I said. "Clementine Pritchard."

"Of course, I know who you are. You're Jeremy's most prized former student."

I smiled, and Jeremy blushed. "I n-n-never played favorites."

Jeremy had short, spiked silver hair and wore small round glasses with black plastic frames. He had been my professor in the painting department at the Art Institute. We both liked to work late and eat meatball *banh mi* sandwiches from the Vietnamese fast-food place down the street, which wasn't a restaurant so much as a building with a hole cut into the side that dispensed food. Everything came wrapped in wax paper and without enough napkins. We would spread out our dinners on the worktables in the studio and drink sodas from the machine chained to a pipe outside the side entrance. No one was waiting for me to come home, and I guessed no one was waiting for him, either. It was nice not to have to eat alone, and he was a good teacher. He was a better teacher than he was a painter. I sensed he knew that and didn't mind it much.

"I did," I said. "Jeremy was my favorite professor."

The tips of the grass tickled the sides of my feet in my open sandals, and another waiter approached with more salmon. I took one and so did Mark. Jeremy waved him off.

"I haven't said hello to everyone y-y-yet, and we're about to have dinner."

"Go on then," said Mark, leaning over to kiss him. "I'll talk to Clementine."

Jeremy waved as he went and then threw his arms open to new arrivals. Mark watched him go. He looked young enough to be Jeremy's son and handsome enough to get paid for it.

"What do you do?" I asked.

"Nothing to do with art."

"Then keep talking to me," I said.

"You don't want to talk about art?" he asked. "You don't want to pontificate on how the viewer's experience completes your work? I could tell you how your latest piece was positively ovulating."

He smiled. His teeth were as white as the tablecloths and glowed in the dim light of the candles and strings of fairy bulbs. It was distracting, and it felt like he was flirting with me. It might have been the sort of flirting that all very attractive people do as their way of moving through life. He could have been flirting to garner praise the way waiters work for tips. Or he could be a smarmy little shit.

"So what do you do really?" I asked.

"I'm a lawyer."

Two strikes.

"Will you hold that against me?" he asked.

"Yes, but I will pretend I don't because it's your wedding night."

I looked over his shoulder like I'd spotted someone, which I hadn't.

"Please excuse me for a moment. It was wonderful to meet you and congratulations."

"Jeremy is a wonderful man," he said, slipping both hands into his pants pockets and crinkling the hem of his jacket in the process.

"Yes, he is." Somehow my words came out sounding more like a threat, which I suppose they were.

I stepped away, picked up another glass of champagne from a tray and deposited the empty, and began wandering the tables, looking for my name card. People swirled around me in flowing dresses and gray and khaki slacks. Above the tree line, the spiral that topped the glass conservatory stood watch.

I found my card in the back third of tables. In the center was a small urn of white and cream flowers with long, spiky bits of greenery like uncut grass coming out the top.

"Oh, God, Clementine, did you hear? Oh, this is me." Susan Kimball, a ceramic artist, held up her name card, which placed her two chairs over. "I think we're having dinner soon," she said. "All the nibbles have disappeared."

Susan showed at the Contemporary, several blocks over

from the Taylor. She made extremely large-scale pots with very narrow openings that looked to be melting the way chocolate does in bright sunlight. For a while, she'd been favoring greens and blues but had recently entered a warm period.

"Did I hear what?" I asked.

I looked around. The uniformed waiters had indeed evaporated, probably into the white tent tucked a discreet distance from the guests. I hoped there was more food in there—and champagne. I downed my second glass and set it next to my name.

"What happened at the Taylor. Surely they called you."

Susan sank into her chair. I'd been seated not with the Art Institute group I had hoped for, many of whom had gone on to practical jobs involving cubicles and office baby showers, but at what looked to be the artists' table, with a collector or two thrown in for our potential economic benefit. I recognized the name card to my left. He had bought something from me but not recently. I had the vague notion he worked in real estate. I would no doubt hear all about it tonight.

"No one called," I said.

Some sort of staff member walked to the heat lamp behind us and relit it. Instantly the air was twenty degrees warmer, and the goose bumps on my arms relaxed. I let my wrap droop off my shoulders.

"Oh my God, it's all anyone is talking about," Susan said.

She leaned in toward me as though we weren't entirely alone at the table. She'd pulled her brown hair into a messy knot at the nape of her neck, and there were small, shiny barrettes holding her bangs out of her eyes.

"They were vandalized. It was horrible." Her eyes sparkled as if it were anything but. "They were showing Elaine's work. You know Elaine. The vandals broke the front window late last night, threw paint on one of her pieces, and smashed it to bits. Can you believe it?"

I opened my mouth, but she went right on.

"I mean, is that art criticism or what—secretly we all just love it because, well, it's a spectacle, and isn't that what we're all about, but also Elaine is such a you-know-what, and the work she was showing, I mean really, it's so obvious, just hit the viewer over the head, why don't you, it's too bad for the Taylor, but on the other hand, you know what they say about all publicity being good publicity." The whole spiel came out in one long sentence. "I even heard the guy who bought the piece was ecstatic. Thinks it's worth more now."

"Really?"

She nodded and took a simultaneous breath and a sip of her champagne.

Some sort of silent signal must have been given, because everyone was taking the seats around us.

"Personally," Susan went on as people pulled out chairs and bumped into us and jostled the table, making the candles wobble and flicker, "I'm experimenting with luster right now. How about you?"

"I'm thinking about death."

"Aren't we all?" she said and laughed.

The arm of a waiter reached around and set a chilled white plate in front of me with a small pile of greens and one curl of Parmesan cheese.

23 Days

When I woke up, all my limbs felt a hundred times heavier than they did on other days, which was how I knew. Chuckles jumped up on the edge of the bed and picked his way on light paws up to my head. He bent down and sniffed my eyelashes. If I killed myself, I thought, before finding him a home, he'd probably start eating my body within a couple of days. That would be pretty gross.

My mind floated, or maybe it was sinking. I didn't want to get up. Not then and possibly not ever. I did have to pee. I considered this from a distance, like it was someone else who had to pee and not me. How important was it to try to make it to the toilet when your limbs weighed five hundred pounds each? Wouldn't it be better just to stay where you were?

Then someone knocked on my door.

I screwed up my eyebrows because that often made thinking easier, except today was one of those days, and nothing would be easy no matter what I did to my eyebrows. I really did need to make some sort of plan for my remains. That wasn't something you wanted to trust Aunt Trudy with. Lord knew what could happen.

The knock came again, which meant it wasn't some delivery person leaving a box. It also meant the main door downstairs had been left open for every tweaker and Jehovah's Witness from here to Oxnard.

I opened my eyes, which took a supreme effort, and wished I'd remembered to train Chuckles to open the front door. He really wasn't pulling his weight. I thought about that for a minute, while the addict-intruder-religious nut banged some more, and I decided not to pee on the mattress.

I went to the bathroom and avoided looking in the mirror the way a Hasid avoids *Hustler* before pouring out some cat chow for Chuckles. When I'd finished all that, the knocking was still there. I looked through the peephole and opened the door, wearing underpants and a tank top through which you could almost certainly see my nipples.

"So you're alive."

Carla's hair was as short as hair could be and still be said to exist. It was nothing but a shadow over her chocolate-colored scalp. If you had a head as perfectly shaped and perched on as long a neck as she did, you might shave your head, too.

I didn't respond.

"So are you having one of your artist's moods or are you just rude?"

I wanted to go back to bed, and so I did. I just walked away from the door and left Carla standing there. I heard her come in a few moments after I collapsed in a heap. I heard the soft *tap-tap-tap* of her ballet-slippered feet across the floor. Even her footsteps were elegant.

She stopped before she got anywhere near the bed.

Chuckles meowed.

In the garage, someone activated the gate.

The air conditioner kicked on.

My arms and legs got heavier.

I started to forget Carla was there until I heard the shuffle of canvases. The pieces, my pieces, which were so much better than Elaine's, were still lined up against the wall. I ignored her.

A while went by. Quite a while maybe. On days like today it was impossible to judge the passage of time. Minutes got stuck in tar and stopped moving. Eventually, I felt the mattress sink with Carla's weight.

"I'm not going to press charges," she said.

"Pin a rose on you."

"How did it happen?"

I didn't open my eyes. "With a lug wrench."

"How did the art happen?"

I opened my eyes some but not all the way, so her form was a fuzzy black and brown shape in the near distance.

"Are you asking if I copied her or if she copied me?"

"Yes."

"Fuck you."

"Okay."

"You knew and you didn't tell me." The programs for my show had been printed more than a week before.

She let a breath out. "It could have been a coincidence."

"Bullshit."

"It wasn't our place."

"How many crimes happen with that as the excuse?"

"Don't blow this out of proportion."

I considered punching her. Six months' worth of work and my reputation were on the line. I was exactly in proportion. In fact, I wasn't sure I'd done quite enough.

"Fuck you again, and you need to vet your assistants better."

Losing Clementine 91

"I don't know what that means."

"It means you don't send anyone from the gallery to my studio again."

"I never have."

"You did."

"I didn't."

"She brought my check."

"I send your checks certified mail. I keep the receipts."

"Not this one."

"When?"

"Six months ago."

"I'll look into it."

"You do that."

I heard the clatter of Chuckles's tag as he scratched his neck with a back paw. The weight on the edge of the bed lifted, and Carla *tap-tap-tapped* to the other side of the room. I didn't hear the door open. I wished it would. I wanted to be alone.

I heard the suction release as the refrigerator opened. That wasn't the door I'd been thinking of.

"Do you know you have a blue chicken in here?"

"Yes."

"I don't think you should eat it."

There were food noises. Cabinets were opened. Cutlery clattered on plates. There was the *whish* and *purr* of a gas burner sparking. Chuckles meowed. The air conditioner turned off. *Whish purr clatter tap-tap-tap whish tap-tap-tap clatter.* A car siren went off in the distance, and I started to fall asleep.

"Clementine."

I woke up. Carla was still there, leaning over me and shaking my shoulder. I didn't know what time it was.

"Clementine, you have to eat."

Eating involved sitting up, and I didn't want to sit up. Sitting up sounded like a lot of work.

Carla set a plate down on the nightstand, hooked a hand under each of my underarms, and hoisted. My butt dragged along the bed as she pulled me into a seated position. My underwear scooted down under my cheeks. She was frighteningly strong, and this seemed too personal. I didn't have enough energy to struggle, so I scowled.

"Are you taking your medication?"

"No."

"I figured. Eat this."

My nose started to work. I smelled breakfast smells like in a diner. Pork fat. The unmistakable smell of pork fat. She set the plate on my lap. On it was a sandwich on toast with fried egg and strips of bacon and cheese melted on both slices like glue holding the whole thing together. I wasn't hungry.

"Can I call Dr. Gothenburg?"

"I fired him."

"Are you seeing another therapist?"

"Nope."

A small blob of cheese had leaked out the edge and started to solidify. I picked it off and ate it. American. It was the flavor of childhoods and picnics and then it was dust on my tongue. I wanted to spit it out. I heard Carla gathering her patience, or maybe I felt it. I don't think I saw it, but maybe I did.

"What time is Jenny going to come?"

"I fired her, too."

"Clementine."

I closed my eyes and leaned against my headboard. It felt cool and hard against my back. All of me felt cool. Goose bumps came up on my arms and legs.

"I don't feel right leaving you alone," Carla said.

"I wish you would. Why did you come?"

"To talk about your show. To discuss how we were going to handle it after the incident." Her voice got tight on that last bit.

"I'm not having a show. I told you."

"I don't think you should at the Taylor."

"Elaine showed first. Even though she stole from me, it won't look that way. It'll look like I'm copying."

"It could hurt sales," she admitted.

"And the gallery isn't going to defend me."

Carla didn't respond to that. "Eat the sandwich. You've lost weight since I saw you last. No one earns points with me looking like an African famine victim."

She got up from the bed and walked back to the kitchen. She picked up the phone and started pushing buttons, flipping through my caller ID history. She pushed another button and put it to her ear. I made a note to be offended tomorrow or the next day. That was an invasion of privacy. I looked down at the sandwich on my lap and realized my underpants were still pulled down under my butt. That was an invasion of privacy, too. I pulled them up.

Carla talked to someone on my phone. Told them I was sick. Asked them to come over. I set the plate on the nightstand and slid back down onto my back. I found the corner of a sheet and pulled it up to my chin. I thought about the drugs I'd flushed. Goodnight, Thorazine. Goodnight, lithium.

That's the last thing I remembered.

22 Days

When I woke up, the light in the apartment was pink and orange. I blinked and wondered if it was sunrise or sunset. Jenny was on the blue stool pulled up to the worktable. She was sorting the stack of magazines and papers. The ones Chuckles had kicked off were no longer on the floor. I rolled onto my side and pushed up to sitting.

Jenny looked up.

"Are you going to work?"

"I'm thinking about underpants," I said.

"Okay. Do you need to put some on?"

"I need to get rid of some."

I got up and shuffled to my dresser. I had to pee again. I made a note to deal with that later. I opened the top drawer and started digging through my lingerie. I was wearing cotton briefs. They'd been black, but too many hot washes had turned them dark gray. I liked them. They were comfortable. I pulled out the underwear I didn't like. I pulled out the ones that were binding and made of silky, non-natural fabrics that didn't breathe and gave you yeast infections. The underwear I'd bought for the men I'd dated. The sexy underwear I hated to wear. I pulled out the thongs. All the thongs. The thongs were the worst offenders. I dropped them all in a pile on the floor, and when there was nothing left in the drawer but cotton briefs that had gone through too many hot washes, I scooped up the pile and carried it over to the loveseat.

"Bring me some scissors, please," I said.

"What do you want with them?"

"Just do it."

The corners of her mouth turned down, but she did what I asked. "I put the sandwich Carla made in the fridge," she said. "Do you want me to heat it up for you?"

"No."

"You didn't touch it."

I picked out a hot pink thong and started cutting.

"Clementine."

I made long strips and put them in another pile on the other side of my lap.

"Clementine, why are you doing that? I can go buy you underwear to cut up if you want. You don't have to use your own."

I picked up a black satin pair next.

She came at me another way. "Carla said she would move your show to the Contemporary. She called while you were asleep. It's all set. It'll matter less about Elaine's show if you have yours there."

"It'll matter exactly the same amount."

"Maybe not quite as much."

I put the strips into a pile.

"I wrote the dates down," Jenny said. "They're expecting your call."

I kept cutting, and Jenny went into the kitchen. People were always going into my kitchen. A few minutes later, she set a bottle of sparkling water by my feet. "Are you going to cut up the rest of your clothes?" she asked.

I really hadn't thought about it. One project at a time.

By ten o'clock that night, the television was on, and the sandwich crusts were on a plate by the sink. Jenny had gone off to meet her new boyfriend, and I was weaving my strips into four-inch squares.

The phone had rung three times before Jenny left. I'd told her not to answer it. I could see the red light blinking on the machine. I didn't need to listen to the messages. I knew what they said. I'd heard them when he left them. Dr. Gothenburg wanted to come over. Carla had called him when she got back to the gallery. That seemed like an invasion of privacy, too. I was going to have to do something about that.

I put a loop in the corner of the square I'd just finished and held it up—one perfectly functional potholder. It was far more functional than the underpants. If I hung them on a gallery wall, critics would talk about the sexual symbolism, the conversion to a homemaker's tool, the whore-to-mother business. Bullshit. I hated those underpants, and everyone needed potholders. Even Carla.

I stood up from the loveseat and almost fell down. I'd been sitting cross-legged for so long I couldn't feel my feet. I was numb from the knees down. I waited for the pricking and stinging and tingling to start as the blood opened the veins up and the flesh came back to life.

Yep, there it went. I curled my toes. That never stopped hurting no matter how old you got. It hurt when you were a kid and hurt when you were an old lady in her underpants. That reminded me I should probably change my clothes. I might smell.

I gathered up the potholders I'd made and found a large manila

Losing Clementine 97

envelope in Jenny's desk. I picked up a Sharpie marker from the cup of pens and wrote the Taylor Gallery's address on the front, shoved the potholders inside, sealed it, and set it by the door to go out, right next to the overnight bag I had never unpacked.

I unzipped the bag and pushed around dirty laundry until I found the small bag of coffee and carried it to the kitchen sink. I slipped a paring knife out of the block and used it to slice through the tape holding the coffee closed. It split, and the smell of mornings and cafés and an ex-boyfriend with a serious espresso addiction came rolling out. I upended the grounds into the sink until I heard the *ka-chink* of glass on metal. I stopped pouring, picked up the small bottle, and dusted it off.

Dropping the half-empty bag in the trash, I carried the vial of liquid to the bathroom, rolling it between my palms, heating up the glass, appreciating how open to transference the material was. I flipped on the light, knocked a few stray grains of coffee off my palms and the bottle, and moved my toothbrush holder to the left. There was a small shelf above the pedestal sink and below the mirrored medicine cabinet. I slid two bottles of perfume over a few inches and placed the tranquilizer right in the middle, spinning the vial around so the label was facing forward. Then I looked at it. The display was calming. I could feel my blood pressure dropping and my shoulders relaxing just standing there. This, I thought, is how some people feel about fish tanks.

I gave it a few more minutes, and when I was as relaxed as I was going to be, I flipped off the light and went to bed.

21 Days

"Well, that could've gone better."

Chuckles was in his carrier licking the pouf of fur on his chest. He was refueling. All the reserve hair in his stomach had been yacked up on the carpet of the only people who had responded to our ad. They were going to "think it over" and "call me," which I was pretty sure was code for "leave the state" and "never speak of this again."

The yowling hadn't helped either.

"Is he always this vocal?" the young couple had asked.

They were newly married, newly moved in together, both with jobs that involved cubicles and their own extensions. The husband had given me his business card when I arrived. I assumed that was new, too. The condo looked like they'd robbed the showroom of a Pottery Barn. I suspected Chuckles was to have been their practice baby. They'd given me a tour of the place when I arrived, and there was a suspiciously underdecorated spare room that seemed to be waiting for something to happen. "Why buy decorative throw pillows," it seemed to say, "when you're just going to have to pick out a crib?" And I was okay with that. They were nice enough, unlikely to use Chuckles for dogfighting bait, and had brought out the good cookies for guests.

We were seated on the sofa, which was upholstered in pale green chenille. Chuckles was newly freed from his portable jail cell and sniffing all the furniture for signs of poodle. I had finished chewing my dark chocolate Milano and was eyeing another. I hadn't eaten breakfast.

"He's very quiet most of the time," I said. "He just doesn't like the carrier."

That's when he'd heaved and convulsed and yacked all over the floor.

"Oh," the woman had said, putting a hand to her chest and fiddling with her diamond solitaire pendant. "Oh."

Once the ball of fur was out, Chuckles shook himself off and rubbed his face on the man's bare ankle. He'd stopped yowling, but it was too late.

"We're sorry about your illness," the man had said as he ushered me toward the door, past a Taiwanese-made urn full of tall fake grass. "Maybe you'll get better."

"It's terminal," I assured him.

"Well, you never know," he chirped and shut the door.

Shit.

I started the car and pulled away from the curb.

"I have another appointment," I told Chuckles. "Behave yourself."

Forty minutes later, I parked at a meter on Lincoln Boulevard. Palm trees lined the east/west streets that veered toward the beach a mile away, but the doctor's office was crammed between a liquor emporium and a gas station advertising two-for-one candy bars and a sale on cigarettes.

I took Chuckles inside with me because *20/20* had warned me about leaving pets in the car. His fur could catch on fire even if the temperature was a good ten degrees cooler this close to the ocean. A bell tinkled over the door, and the receptionist looked up. A small fan was pointed at her and another whirred and oscillated in the waiting room.

"I have an appointment," I said.

She pointed to a sign-in sheet on the other side of the bulletproof glass. She didn't mention the cat, and I didn't, either. The rest of the room was lined with green plastic lawn chairs. Maybe they'd been two-for-one next door along with the candy bars. I signed my name.

"A consultation is a hundred dollars. That's not refundable whether the doctor makes a recommendation or not."

I slid a credit card through the slot in the glass, signed the receipt, and took the new patient sheet she shoved through. It was short, and once it was filled in, there wasn't much to do. There were no magazines and no television, but someone had left the classified section of the *Times*. I checked the date. It was a week old. An elderly woman with a footed metal cane sat four chairs down and didn't look at me. I figured that was proper etiquette and didn't look at her, either.

A middle-aged man in a button-down shirt tucked into his jeans stepped out of a door at the end of the room. "Mrs. Shipley?"

The woman rose up, leaning heavily on her cane, and shuffled toward the open door. I spent my time using the toe of my work boot to clean scuff marks off the floor. No one else came in. The receptionist read a magazine she didn't offer to share. I leaned down to look in Chuckles's carrier. He was lying flat with his squished-up face on his front paws. His eyes were closed and his breathing was shallow. He was either asleep or moving toward the light.

Losing Clementine 101

Five minutes later, Mrs. Shipley came shuffling out of the room and headed for the door. She left a trail of skid marks on the floor with her footed cane. Old people. You can't take them anywhere.

The same middle-aged head came out. "Ms. Pritchard?"

I picked up Chuckles, who woke up and started pacing around, throwing off the balance of the carrier and making it rock like ocean waves. It was hard to hold and made me walk funny. I was trying to look sober and responsible, and this wasn't helping. The doctor didn't mention the cat, and I didn't, either. I gave him my new patient sheet, and he scanned it.

"Have a seat."

He was made of various shades of beige. His skin was oatmeal and his hair khaki. His eyes were a light brown, and he used them to avoid looking at mine. He had a metal desk shoved all the way to one side and a guest chair next to that. There wasn't room for anything else. Someone had sent him flowers, and they sat next to his laptop, which was open and playing a fractal screensaver.

"What brings you here today?" he asked my collarbone.

"I'm anxious," I said. "I have anxiety."

"I see."

I waited a beat and nothing happened.

"I'd like to be able to control that without prescription pharmaceuticals."

He nodded and used his toes to push himself forward and back a little in his rolling chair. "Do you have any allergies?"

"No."

"Are you taking any other medications?"

"No."

He was reading the questions off the form I'd filled out and handed to him.

"Any other medical conditions?"

"Healthy as a horse," I said. "Except for the anxiety."

"Right."

He sniffed. I imagined this was not how he'd pictured himself in medical school. He probably hadn't been very good at it, just good enough to get by but not enough for a good specialty. It was the worst kind of smart, just barely smart enough. No oncology or surgery or even gynecology for him.

"Okay, I'm going to write your recommendation. You can present it to any dispensary. It is not a prescription, and they may choose not to fill it at any time."

"Got it," I said.

He pulled out a piece of cream-colored paper the size of a paperback book and embellished with more scrollwork than my high school diploma. He filled in the blanks, slipped it into a black envelope made of equally nice stock, and handed it over. I didn't know whether to use it or frame it.

"Thank you."

"Use it responsibly."

Chuckles and I walked out into the offensively bright sunshine and down half a block. I could smell french fries bubbling in grease somewhere nearby. A Hispanic woman my age and wearing a Bebe T-shirt pushed a shopping cart loaded with recyclable bottles past me, and Chuckles let out a hiss.

"Can it," I told him and opened the door.

The dispensary was air-conditioned and quiet with a mild herbal smell. A long wooden counter stained a dark walnut stretched from one end of the small space to the other. On the other side of the shop, tables and shelves displayed natural soaps and shampoos alongside bottles of vitamins and supplements for which you did not need a doctor's recommendation.

A young woman with blond hair pulled into a loose knot stood behind the counter reading a book. She had a hoop inserted into her earlobe that stretched the skin around it. She looked up.

"Is that a cat?"

"Yep."

"Cool."

"I have a recommendation from my doctor," I said.

By "my doctor," of course, I meant "a guy I looked up in the Yellow Pages whom I'd never see again." She didn't care. I wondered if anyone ever tried shooting spitballs through her stretched earlobe hole.

"Cool. What do you want?"

She looked behind her, and I followed her gaze. Large glass apothecary jars were displayed on the shelves behind her. Dozens and dozens of jars, each with a carefully hand-lettered label on the front. Some were more full than others. Inside, each batch was a slightly different shade of green. Together the jars formed a subtle, mossy rainbow of forest colors. All pharmacies should be that beautiful.

"What do you recommend?"

She slid off her stool and pulled down three jars, lining them up on the polished counter in front of me. She opened each in turn, announced its name, and held up some for me to smell and inspect. It was like a tasting at a good wine bar. I started to really like this girl, even if the book she'd flipped over and laid spread out to hold her place was by Ayn Rand.

I chose weed number two, and she filled a small glass jar with a screw-on lid for me, the way department stores package custom-blended cosmetics. I showed her my recommendation, and she rang up the purchase. The whole thing was very civilized, much better than anything I did to score in high school. For one thing, I didn't have to drive to the Valley and end up in some kid's basement bedroom with a fistful of small bills and a cold sweat.

"Do you take your cat everywhere now?"

"Yes. Didn't I fire you?"

"Disturbingly, that's so, but I felt a duty to my fellow man to make sure you didn't starve to death."

Miles, who was sitting in front of my door with his unnaturally long legs stretched out in front of him, held up a paper grocery sack by the top loop handles. Something green and leafy was sticking out the top. I couldn't remember the last time I'd eaten something with leaves, and Miles was the sort of cook who knew what a béarnaise sauce was.

"Bribery, Dr. Gothenburg?"

"You didn't return my call. I raised the stakes."

I set Chuckles down and rubbed the ball of my shoulder. It was going to be diet kibble for him.

"You know, this is the second time this week I've found someone I've fired leaning against my door. The pattern is starting to concern me. I think it's a sign I'm not being forceful enough."

"Would you like to talk about that?"

He'd come from his office. You could tell because he was wearing his work uniform. Dark slacks, pastel shirt, and tie. He had a weekend uniform, too. Gray T-shirt and dark jeans in the summer, fine-gauge sweater in the winter, or what passed for winter in Los Angeles.

"If I wanted to talk about it, I wouldn't have fired you."

"Okay. Who else did you fire?"

"Jenny."

"I liked Jenny."

"A little too much."

"That's not fair. Why did you fire her?"

I ignored the question. Chuckles reached a fuzzy white paw through the carrier's gate and batted at Miles's shoe. Traitor, I thought.

"I'm going inside now."

Miles was bent forward playing swat-the-paw with my cat. When I put my key in the lock, he folded up his twelve miles of arms and legs and got to his feet.

"Am I coming in?"

"Depends."

"State your terms."

"You can come in as friend and chef. You may bring the green leafy things. Leave the psychology crap out here."

He pretended to consider my offer. It was a bad bluff.

"Deal."

"Carry the cat. The bastard weighs a ton."

Inside, I pulled off my boots and rolled up the frayed edges of my jeans to my calves. Miles freed Chuckles, who ran under the bed to collect his dignity, while I slipped my dark gray work apron over my head. When it settled around my neck, Miles's lips were on mine. They were dry but soft, and he tasted like peppermint. He ran his tongue between my lips, and I let him in. He slid his hands under the back of my T-shirt and then down into the low-slung waistband of my jeans. I didn't wear them tight, and he got his hands in up to his wrists, his fingers cupping the bottom of my ass.

I backed out of the kiss. I wasn't sure if I'd also broken up with him when I'd fired him.

"Are you helping with dinner?" he asked, opening his eyes slowly like a sun-drunk lizard.

"No, I'm smoking."

I took a step back and pulled the small jar of green buds from my jeans pocket along with a sheaf of rolling papers the girl behind the counter had thrown in for free. Once I'd owned a very pretty blue glass pipe, but that was a couple of cities, many domiciles, and a marriage ago. I might still have it. I might have donated it to the Goodwill. It was impossible to know.

"That's new," Miles said.

"No, it's old. The habit, I mean, not the pot. The pot is fresh." I held it up for his inspection. The sappy crystals sparkled under the kitchen light. "I can't remember why I stopped."

He took the sack of groceries into the kitchen. "Because it makes you paranoid?"

"Nope."

I laid a paper out on the counter and crumbled the stinkweed into it. It smelled sweet and herbal like the shop. Miles watched.

"I haven't rolled a joint since high school," he said.

I twisted the ends closed.

"Hand me a lighter out of that drawer there." I pointed, and he obeyed.

I flicked the flame to life and brought it to the joint, inhaling. The smoke was smoother than I remembered it being. No burning, no coughing. I held it for a count of three and then blew it out through my mouth, using my lips and tongue to make rings that floated up and disappeared in the late afternoon light streaming through the window.

"Show-off."

Miles had pulled a brown onion from the bag and sliced off its hairy end. I held the joint out to him, and he took it. A large pot of water had materialized on the stove, and a fire was on high underneath it.

"Don't tell my patients."

"No patients here," I assured him.

We smoked and he chopped and I watched. I turned on my

computer to play some R&B. The Temptations sang over the sizzle of onions in butter on the stove. Miles unbuttoned one of his shirt's middle buttons and tucked the end of his tie inside. My head was warm and not quite attached to my neck. He laid two pink, fleshy chicken breasts onto a blue plastic cutting board and sliced them both across their middles, pressing them open like a book. He opened a frosty bottle of white wine and poured some into the pan.

"Your glasses still up here?" he asked, opening a cabinet.

"Mmm-hmm."

He took two down and filled them. I took a sip from mine, then carried it with me as I floated on bare feet across to the canvas sitting on the easel. I gathered my hair into one hand and pulled the elastic that was always on my wrist around the ponytail. I picked up my pencil from the worktable, took up my glass again, and began to sketch and drink.

I laid lines over the long-dry background paint. Starting at the bottom where it was grayest, I drew a head bent over forelegs. Back hooves up in the air, arching through the yellows, and a tail curled wild like a comma, pointing at the bluest of the blues.

Ben E. King was begging his woman to stand by him.

The back line of the animal from the nose to the paintbrush tuft of fur at the end of the tail was a serpentine *S*. I went over it again, smoothing it out. Underneath that curve were the bent legs and blowing nostrils, all angles and violence and sharp edges.

I stepped back and emptied the last of the wine into my mouth. I liked my drawing. It could've been the booze and the weed, but I still liked it.

"That's what we call flow, Elaine Sacks. So fuck you."

"What?" Miles asked. I had forgotten he was there.

"Nothing."

I took my empty glass and set it next to the chopping board for a refill. Miles had garlic cloves minced fine and was sprinkling coarse salt onto the board. He lifted the bottle of wine, now half-empty, and poured one-handed into both our glasses. The chicken had disappeared into a skillet, and I could see the surface of the water pot bubbling away. I drank more wine and unscrewed the top from the bottle of weed before deciding I didn't want any more before dinner and put it away.

Miles squinted at the canvas. The lines were hard to see from there.

"That looks different from your usual stuff."

"I'm entering a new period."

"That's exciting."

I made noncommittal noises. Miles didn't know much about art, which was fine. That was my work. Of course, we couldn't talk about his work, either. Miles mostly wanted to talk about movies and baseball, neither of which I watched much.

He opened a box of angel hair pasta and dumped a sheaf into his left hand, then broke it in half before dropping it into the water. He picked up his own glass of wine and reached for my wrist. I let him have it. He pulled me close and pressed me to his hip. I was still wearing my apron, and it kept his leg from slipping between mine. He bent down and kissed behind my ear where the hairs that were too short to go into the ponytail lay in wisps. I didn't lean into him and didn't pull away, choosing a neutral ground.

The chicken breasts were dredged and simmering up to their waists in a creamy sauce. Capers bobbed around the edges. Miles dipped a soupspoon into the pan, blew on the tasting of sauce, and held it out for me. It was lighter than it looked and a little acidic. Not just wine. Lemon, too, I thought. I was hungry. Those cookies were a long time ago.

Miles patted my butt, dismissing me from his side, and reached for a pasta serving spoon. He fished out a thin strand, tried it between his two front teeth, and then lifted the roiling pot and carried it to the sink. He leaned back out of the steam as he poured.

When the phone rang, I didn't pick it up. It rang until we were both hostage to listening to it, just waiting for the machine to pick up.

"Ms. Pritchard, my name is Michael Ma from the *Times*. Your assistant, Jenny Pritchard, contacted me. I'd like to talk to you about some of the work being shown at the Taylor Gallery right now. If you could return my call at your earliest possible convenience." He left two numbers.

"What's that about?" Miles asked.

"No idea," I said, even happier than usual he didn't know about my work. "Let's eat."

I cleared my laptop off the small dining table, and he replaced it with two plates of pasta and chicken. I brought up the rear with the wine and salads. We hadn't turned on any light, and evening was falling like a cosmic dimmer switch.

"I have a constant need for approval, so you have to tell me you love it," he said.

"I love it."

"You haven't tasted it yet."

"You're right. It could be crap."

"My ego feels much better now."

"Good."

I spun my fork in the pasta, sopping up some of the sauce and capers. It was not crap. It was the best food I'd eaten since Dolma's. I cut a triangle-shaped bite off my chicken and tried that. It was tender and moist and not blue, which was a step up from any of the poultry in my house.

"Clementine, will you have sex with me tonight?"

I finished chewing my chicken and took a sip of wine. I had an empty stomach and a few glasses and a joint in me. My decision-making skills might not have been tip-top, but what do you expect of a girl who fucks her shrink?

"I have a constant need for approval," I said, "so you have to tell me it's great."

"It's great," he said.

"You haven't tried it yet."

"You're right. It could be crap."

20 Days

It was crap.

I woke up with a dull thudding in my temples, a serious case of dehydration, and a crushing weight on my chest, which turned out to be Miles's arm.

He had the most hairless body I'd ever been with. There were only a few wisps in the required places: under his arms, on his groin. Even his thighs were smooth. Light brown, soft hair only appeared below the knee, like it just couldn't be bothered to climb any higher. He had apathetic follicles.

The sex had been terrible the night before, and no amount of ego stroking could fool either of us into thinking it was anything else. We had fallen asleep out of sheer embarrassment. When your eyes are closed, you can pretend you're not thinking about him lying on top of you, floppy and limp as a giant gummy worm, trying to shove it in with his hand because surely, surely, it would get hard then.

Maybe, I thought, he won't wake up and look at me. Maybe he will have died in his sleep.

"Hi."

Damn.

"I have to pee," I said.

I got up and locked myself in the bathroom. A man with dignity would take the opportunity to throw on his boxer shorts and sprint out into the hall clutching his tie and undershirt. But Miles wasn't a man with dignity. He was a therapist. He would want to talk about it. He would want to tell me about his feelings and for me to tell him about mine. There would be hugging. If I didn't already want to kill myself, I would then.

Safe inside my tiled sanctuary, I did pee, and just to extend it, I stayed on the pot and read the back of both the shampoo and conditioner bottles on the edge of the tub. Rinse and repeat for best results. Then I brushed my teeth, which was over too quickly, so I flossed and inspected my gums for obvious disease. When that was done, I washed my face and thought about popping a zit on my chin that was still in the infant phase, but then I figured it might not heal in time for my death. I wanted to go out with good skin. I dabbed some cream on it instead. I didn't have a watch, but I figured I'd been in there seven minutes, maybe eight.

I turned on the shower.

When I opened the bathroom door, wrapped in a towel and with comb marks in my wet hair, Miles was still there, dressed in yesterday's work clothes and sitting at the table. He'd helped himself to a bowl of cereal and was reading one of the magazines I kept to disassemble for my work. I didn't like that he'd touched my materials. It was like having him paw through my underwear drawer.

"All right," I said, "but next time, I'm going through those filing cabinets in your office."

"What?"

Losing Clementine 113

He looked up from the copy of *Architectural Digest*. His hair was damp on top, and I pictured him patting down his cowlick in the kitchen sink.

"You went through my work stuff. I'll go through yours."

He looked down at the article in front of him. "It's a magazine."

"It's my materials."

"I'm sorry," he said, flipping it closed and pushing it across the table toward me. "I didn't know."

"Yes, you did."

He pressed his lips together and made that small fake smile that means you're being called an asshole. "I apologize."

I opened the fridge and pulled out a loaf of bread. My mother had kept bread in the fridge to keep it from molding, which had the unfortunate side effect of turning it into dehydrated carbojerky. But you had to hand it to her, the bread did not mold. I put two dried slices in the toaster, unwrapped the towel, and used it to wring the drips out of my hair.

Miles watched and chewed cereal.

"I think we should talk about last night."

I looked into the toaster. The little coils were red hot, but it would be another minute before my food was done. That's what I got for cooking.

"You know, I really don't want to."

"I think it would help."

"Help what?"

"Help us get past it."

"We are past it. Time is funny that way."

"You can't joke your way out of this."

My toast popped up. I stood at the kitchen counter naked and spreading half-liquefied butter from the glass covered dish that lived next to the stove, no doubt growing dangerous levels of bacteria. I added orange marmalade and smeared it all the way to the edges.

Miles waited while I chewed, which is something they don't tell you about fucking a therapist. They'll just let that silence hang forever until you fill it with something they can write down in their little notebook.

"You couldn't get it up. What do you want to talk about?"

"I've been having a very stressful time in my practice. I've been worried about you. I smoked some pot."

"You just wanted to give me your list of excuses?"

"I don't want there to be any uncomfortableness between us."

I'd already felt the uncomfortableness between us when he'd tried to shove his limp dick into my cootchie. I didn't want to feel that uncomfortableness between us again, either.

I ate more toast, decided I was thirsty, and went fishing in the icebox for orange juice, which I drank out of the carton.

"You used to use a glass," he said.

"I'm economizing."

"Do you have any tea?"

"Yes, but I don't have a teapot or cups."

"What happened to them?"

"I threw them out the window."

Miles put on his concerned therapist face. "I'm not going to ask you why, but if you want to tell me, that's okay."

I didn't want to tell him, so I ate more toast and drank more juice and pressed my butt up against the edge of the kitchen counter. That would probably leave a mark.

"Did you ever think about your breakfast being redundant?" he asked.

"No."

"I mean because you eat orange marmalade and drink orange juice."

Losing Clementine 115

"Yeah," I said. "No."

"Clementines are a variety of orange. Did you know that?"

"What are the odds I didn't?"

"Why are you so hell-bent on picking a fight with me?"

Fair question with an obvious answer. Because I wanted him to leave.

He didn't wait for me to answer. He got up from the table and brought his bowl to the sink next to my left hip. He stood very close to me but without touching while he rinsed the bowl and left it upside down in the bottom of the drain. He dried his hands on the tea towel hanging from a drawer pull and finally looked at me. We were the same height and stood there eye to eye.

"Can I come back sometime?"

"As my shrink?"

"Can I come back as your shrink?"

"No."

"Can I take you to dinner then?"

"Possibly. I'll call you."

"Today?"

"Yes."

He headed for the door, patting Chuckles, who had curled up in a chair, on the way out. The phone rang as he was going. I answered it, and we didn't say good-bye.

"I found some stuff. You can have it if you want it."

I looked at the microwave clock. Aunt Trudy would be on her fourth cup of coffee, standing in the kitchen with the avocado green wall phone and wearing her swimsuit. She wore the same one every day and washed it once a week.

"I'm in the process of simplifying at the moment. What stuff?"

"Your mother's and father's things. If you don't want it, I'm putting it out in the garbage now. The trash men haven't come yet this morning."

"I'll be there this afternoon."

I turned up "Soul Man" on the radio and swayed in the driver's seat on the way to the cemetery. The station went into some old Ray Charles, and things got even better. This was definitely one of the things I was going to miss when I died.

The entrance and exit of the main drive were split by a green, green grass median and a guard shack. I couldn't imagine why you'd need to guard a cemetery. Perhaps it was to prevent zombie corpses from escaping. I pulled up and rolled down my window.

"Here to see a man about a horse."

The dark-skinned, uniformed man pressed a button and waved me through without looking up once to check for zombies.

I took the winding drive past neat rows of tombstones and more green, green grass cut neater than John Waters's mustache, following the discreet and somber signs to the office, which was marked by an equally discreet and somber sign. A small concrete pad to the side had spots for three cars, all of them empty. I wondered where employees parked.

The building was the same red brick as the guard shack with shiny black shutters and a shiny black door with a gold knocker, which I whacked twice for attention and once again for the fun of it. I was dressed in uniform—paint-splattered jeans and a tank top. It was peacock blue that day. The man who opened the door was also in what was no doubt his uniform—dark suit, white shirt, and discrete and somber tie.

"My name is Clementine Pritchard," I said. "I have an appointment."

"Of course." He held out a too-smooth and soft hand to shake. "I'm Charles Weiner."

It was Weiner like wee-ner, not wy-ner, which was too bad for him.

"Please come in."

He held open the door, and I stepped into the waiting room. My foot sank into the mauve carpet up to my ankle. The plush pile was padded from below with enough foam to keep the princess with the pea happy, and someone—possibly Mr. Weiner— had recently vacuumed. The lines were still visible, and the whole room—decorated with dark cherrywood and Japanese prints of cranes—looked clean enough to perform operations.

"We can step into my office," Mr. Weiner said, already leading me down a short hallway.

I *squish, squish, squished* in the carpet behind him.

His office was decorated with the same claw-footed cherry furniture as the anteroom with the same mauve carpet and beige walls. No cranes, though. Just a large picture window behind his desk that looked out onto carefully sculpted rolling hills full of dead and rotting corpses.

I took the guest chair.

"How may I serve you today?" Mr. Weiner asked, settling himself in the slightly larger executive seat. He spoke in a low, soothing tone that gave the impression he was used to guests falling to pieces in front of him.

"I want to buy a plot."

"Is this for a family member?"

"No, it's for myself."

He spun silently on the chair's swivel and selected a brochure from a stack to his right. "It's very important to plan ahead. I congratulate you. So few people do, and it makes it so much easier on the family when the time comes."

"I'm going to need it soon."

He blinked. Perhaps I had stepped outside his cemetery sales training.

"I'm dying," I clarified. "Soon. So I'm going to need something in a little less than a month."

He smoothed his discrete and somber tie. "Yes, of course. I'm so sorry to hear that. Illness is always difficult. We will do everything we can to ease the process."

I appreciated that and said so.

He turned the brochure around to face me on the desk and opened it. The pages were printed on heavy, matte cardstock that made me want to touch it and take it home to add to my materials.

Using a gold mechanical pencil with the lead withdrawn as a pointer, he went quickly through all the special features I could expect as a long-term resident of Stony Brook Cemetery, none of which I expected to be able to appreciate. At the back of the brochure was a map. He used his gold pointer to highlight the areas where there were still vacancies.

I asked if any of the vacancies were on a hill, and he said yes. I asked if any of those were near any trees, and he said yes.

"I'd like to see that one then."

I followed him back out of the office—*squish-squish-squish*—and around the building. In back, a white golf cart was parked. I called shotgun, and we rode along the quiet, winding roads deeper into the garden of the dead.

Along the way, we passed a man on a riding mower with a ball cap pulled low over his eyes and a white paper painter's mask over his nose and mouth. Mr. Weiner used this as a visual aid to go along with his spiel on the excellent maintenance I could expect in my years of decay.

The grounds undulated like the rolling, snakelike back of a

dragon, so much so that I began to suspect they'd carved the land that way on purpose. I tried to imagine the sort of equipment that would take but didn't get very far before we came to a stop on top of one of the dragon-back ridges next to a large tree.

I asked what kind of tree it was.

"Bigleaf maple," he said, patting the crackled bark. "All of the trees at Stony Brook are native to Southern California, unlike the palm tree. Did you know the palm tree doesn't naturally grow here?"

"Yep."

I wandered over a few feet to the very crest of the hill and looked around. We were slightly higher than the other hills, and I could see the wrought-iron and brick-fenced edges of the vast cemetery and the houses and shopping malls beyond its borders, including a new Target under construction. Just below us were the rows of white headstones, denser at a distance and then getting sparser as they approached the hill. I knew from the brochure map that many of those empty spots were spoken for by the not-quite-dead. On my hill there were no headstones at all. Mine would be the first, like the inaugural flag planted on foreign soil.

"I want this spot right here," I said, pointing down at my work boots.

"It's a lovely plot. Would you like to come back to the office to sign the papers?"

I didn't answer for a moment, just took my time looking around at the view from my spot.

"All right then," I said finally. "Let's go."

I wrote the check in full before I left the office and climbed back in my car, but instead of turning right toward the exit, I turned left and wound my way toward the southern and older part of the cemetery. I pulled off onto the shoulder of the black asphalt road, got out, and made my way to another tree, this one a western sycamore with a smoother, lighter bark than my maple.

I stood in front of two matching headstones.

Beloved Mother
Kathleen Pritchard
1944–1985

Beloved Sister
Ramona Pritchard
1974–1985

The stones were a soft gray and two feet tall with straight sides and arched tops. I stood there and looked at the dozen words until they didn't look like words anymore but ancient, cryptic scratches. Then I got back in the car and drove away.

Aunt Trudy had left the front door unlocked. I opened it and walked along through the entryway and kitchen and out the sliding glass door to the pool, where she was lying on her usual chaise. Her sunglasses were very dark, and I couldn't tell if her eyes were open or closed. She had a Band-Aid on her nose. The light peach of the plastic contrasted with the dark tan of her skin.

"What happened to your nose?" I said, instead of hello.

"Cancer. Doc cut it off this morning."

I sat down across from her. Bob was floating on a turquoise inflatable raft in the middle of the pool. His hairless skin looked buffed and polished. He waved, and I waved back.

"Ain't nothin' to worry yourself over," Aunt Trudy said.

I wasn't worried. Aunt Trudy had been having cancer cut off of her for ten years with no ill effects other than half a dozen scars. The one on her nose would be a doozie.

"You doing what the doctor told you to?"

"Never trust doctors," she said, swinging her brown, wrinkly legs to the side and getting up from her chair. "All that schooling makes them dumber than an inbred chicken."

I watched the droopy butt of her swimsuit disappear into the relative dark of the kitchen. It smelled like Banana Boat Dark Tanning Oil even after she'd gone.

Two minutes later she was back and carrying a shoe box that looked forty years old from a brand I'd never heard of.

"Here. Them's the things I kept separate when we cleaned out your mother's house. Lord knows why. Must've thought they were important at the time."

I set the box on my knees and took off the lid. The inside smelled like dust and mothballs and old, decaying paper things. On top, folded in half, was my parents' marriage license from the state of California. I unfolded it and looked at it for a moment. My mother's handwriting, which I had forgotten I knew, was loopy and feminine, her signature a series of bubbles. My father's was narrower and leaned hard to the right, as if it was running off the page.

There were other official things: thirty-year-old bank statements for closed accounts, a copy of the title for the car my parents had owned when I was small, my sister's birth certificate. I looked at each piece and put it in a pile next to me. There were no photos. Not a single one. At the bottom of the box in the corner was a gold band. I picked it up and held it between two fingers.

"Your mother's wedding ring," Trudy said. "She wasn't buried in it, seeing as how she'd stopped wearing it."

My mother's hands had been much smaller than mine. I had big hands just like I had big feet. I remember her telling me I was just proportional, which was only a little helpful when I towered not only over the boys but all the female teachers and some of the men, too. I tried to slip it on. The thin gold band wouldn't go past my second knuckle.

"Too bad you don't have one of those," Trudy said.

"I used to."

I put the ring back in the box and piled the papers neatly on top of it before replacing the lid.

"Like I said, too bad."

Trudy had liked Richard. Everyone liked Richard. Even I had liked Richard most of the time.

"Trudy, leave that girl alone."

I hadn't known Bob was listening.

"I'm just sayin'," Trudy huffed.

"Well, don't," he said, dipping his hands in the water and using them as paddles to make his way to the side nearest the chairs. "She's big enough to run her own life."

When Bob got to the edge he held on to the ladder to keep from floating away again. "You trying to find your dad, Clementine?"

Trudy's head snapped around at that. "Tell me you are not playing in that wasp nest!"

I didn't look at her. "Trying," I told Bob.

He nodded, and Trudy made a sound like a strangled chicken.

"Trudy, put a sock in it," Bob said.

I knew there was a reason I'd always liked him best.

"I didn't know him very well. I hadn't been around long when he run off, and we didn't mix much when he was around."

Trudy lay back on her chaise and crossed her arms over her crepe paper chest. She was done with us both and preparing herself for the time to say, "I told you so."

"Mostly," Bob went on, "he talked a lot about a car club he was involved in."

"Hooligans," Trudy interjected.

Bob and I ignored her.

"He loved that car. Not his everyday car, but the hot rod he bought. Pretty sure your mom and him had a row over that."

"Damn shameful use of money was what it was," Trudy said. "Him acting like a teenager when he had two kids to support."

"It was sweet." Bob let out a low whistle. "'56 T-Bird convertible, canary yellow. He'd take it out to Van Nuys Boulevard and show it off with the rest of the club. They had a name." He scrunched up his bald forehead while he thought. "Pumas, maybe? Something to do with cats."

"How do you know all that?" Trudy demanded.

"Me and him went once."

"You didn't tell me that."

"I did so."

"You did not."

"Hell, Trudy, it was thirty years ago. You wouldn't remember what I told you."

19 Days

"You didn't call."

"Got busy."

"Can I take you to dinner?"

I let the question hang for a minute. I had three dozen magazines spread out across my worktable and a few on the floor. My hand was cramping around the X-Acto knife. I'd been at it for ten hours and had eaten nothing but toast and the last of the orange juice. Chuckles, who'd been sprawled out on top of a stack of three-year-old *W* magazines, yawned. He opened his jaw so wide I got a direct view of his scaly tongue and deeply ridged palate. He was the only person I'd seen all day, and he wasn't actually a person.

"Pizza?" I asked.

"Pizza," he agreed.

"Gribaldi's?"

"Affirmative."

"One hour."

I hung up the phone and capped the pot of glue. I leaned

my hip against the table and peeled the thin dried membrane of adhesive from my fingers. It had built up all day like another skin, copying even my fingerprints.

The back of the buffalo was filled in with the lightest human flesh tones I could find in six years' worth of *Vogue* magazines, a saddle-shaped spot of filleted Eastern European teenage models. The darker skin for the rest of the back was proving much harder to find. When and if Jenny came back, I'd ask her for more *Ebony* and *Essence* magazines. The ones I had were full of skin indistinguishable from that in *Vogue*. I cut them out, held them up against the buffalo's back, and then wadded them all up and threw them away. Not enough contrast. Not near enough.

By the time Miles pushed the buzzer downstairs, I was out of the shower and dressed in one of two pairs of jeans I owned not speckled with paint. I pushed the button to let him in, unlocked the front door, and went back into the bathroom. I had been attempting to work the directional nozzle attachment on the blow dryer while holding a brush at the same time, which is really only possible if you happen to be a multi-armed Hindu god. I kept aiming the hot air at my knuckles, which had turned the color of boiled lobsters, and my hair was not appreciably improved. Chuckles, who made no distinction between the blow dryer and the vacuum, was hiding under the bed, and I was considering giving it all up as a bad job.

"Are you almost ready?" Miles called from the entryway.

I turned off the blow dryer, gathered the tortured strands in a clip at the nape of my neck, and smeared cream concealer across the zit still on my chin. It was unreasonable that in my twilight days I should have to deal with clogged pores.

We ordered bottles of cold beer and two small pizzas because there is beauty in a simple pizza margherita, especially if the basil is torn, not chopped, but it's a fool who argues against the pizza Diablo with spicy sausage and hunks of jalapeño. Sometimes the answer in life is not one or the other but both.

Miles used napkins to dab spicy sausage grease off the piece on his plate, because when you're not dying you have to do things like that. I, on the other hand, was considering asking for a little straw to suck the pooling neon-orange fat right off the top, sort of the way fancy restaurants sometimes give you straws for marrowbones. Let no meat by-product go unsucked.

Gribaldi's, staunchly Italian, was on Hollywood Boulevard just at the edge of Thai Town, which only makes sense in Los Angeles. The ethnic neighborhoods had been morphing and joining and morphing again since Wilshire Boulevard was a dirt road. West Hollywood, for example, the once and current home for recent Russian immigrants with their root vegetable diets and black-scarved babushka grandmothers, had now also turned into a gay meat market. The Russians and gays go along side by side with a minimal amount of fuss. I love that about L.A. It's one of the things no one ever tells you about the place.

So next to the fourth-best place in the city for dry curry and a twenty-four-hour Laundromat was this pizza, which is not an easy thing to find. Good pizza was the only thing other than subways that I missed about New York. Not that I would imply Gribaldi's was New York–caliber pizza. But it was good for a city that did better with dry curry and borscht and illegal taco trucks and all other things decidedly un-European.

Our table was covered with Magic Marker and ballpoint pen graffiti and even some of the old-fashioned, scratched-in-with-a-car-key kind, which gave you something to read while you chewed. I preferred the philosophical scrawls. The one under my beer said, "You are doomed," which was a good bit funnier than "Janice was here."

I looked behind me. The to-go line was out the door, and I counted three babies with mohawks, which were the new "it" accessory, displacing nervous Chihuahuas in handbags. Bonus points if your baby wears an ironic T-shirt. A woman in shredded stockings—on purpose, not like her cat went nuts and she didn't have time to change—bumped into my chair on her way out. Miles was the only person in the place wearing a tie, which in the language of hipsters could've made him cool but didn't quite.

I finished off a slice of Diablo and went for a basil-scented palate cleanser. Miles took a drink of his beer. He was only halfway through and falling behind.

"So when did you decide to buy a cemetery plot?"

It got hard to concentrate on the pure, milky flavor of the dolloped mozzarella.

"Excuse me?"

"I saw you bought a plot and was wondering if there was a reason you decided to do that now. It's the same cemetery as your mother and sister, isn't it?"

Anger started in my gut and spread like a Southern California wildfire in August.

"I will kill you. I will kill you and shove your balls down your throat so that you choke on them."

"Clementine—"

"Don't you speak to me, you snooping bastard."

"It was on the kitchen table."

"Inside my bag inside an envelope, which was sealed!" My voice carried, and people in the to-go line stared.

"I was concerned about you. I was looking to see if you had any medications. I saw the return address on the envelope, and I just thought—"

"Fuck you! Fuck you and that lying bullshit." A little bit of spit flew out of my mouth and landed on his grease-free pizza. I leaned across the table. "That could've been a bill. That could've been anything, and whatever it was it wasn't fucking yours. What else did you do? Count the condoms in my nightstand?"

"I am not your ex-husband."

"What?"

"I am not your ex-husband."

"My ex-husband didn't snoop."

"Your ex-husband left you, and you've never resolved it. That's why you're pushing me away. You're trying to reenact that with me. You're transferring your feelings about that relationship onto this one to play them out again."

I felt my cheeks flame red. He'd screwed up, but, of course, it was my head that was really the problem. Nothing—nothing!—could possibly be wrong with him, the shrink who fucked his patients. I wanted to tear his guts out with my bare hands and hang him by his own intestines.

I did the next best thing. I slipped a hand under each half-eaten pie and flipped them both across the table. The margherita grazed his left arm, leaving a blood-colored war wound of sauce on his sleeve, but the Diablo, true to its name, landed grease and all on his crotch, taking his beer with it. I was only sorry the pans were no longer searing hot. Foamy, piss-colored liquid *glug-glug-glugged* out across the scarred table and dripped onto the floor, and the restaurant went quiet enough to hear it.

I knocked my chair backward on my way up and out, while Miles just sat there, clinical and calm, with pork fat soaking through his pants.

The to-go line parted as if Moses had commanded it, and I walked through the empty space out to the street and to my car, fantasizing the whole way about turning his ass in to the medical licensing board for sexual misconduct.

I was fastening my seat belt when I thought of Richard and missed him so much tears dampened my bottom lashes. Richard wouldn't have done that. Why hadn't he been the one to show up at my door?

I wiped my nose on the back of my hand and told myself they were angry tears, so I could start the car.

Van Nuys is one of those places where no one chooses to live or wants to go. It's what happens when your other options are too crime-ridden to be considered. Compton, maybe. Or Watts. It's the sort of place that makes you sigh and say, "Well, I guess it could be worse."

The tears had dried, but my stomach still had that tight feeling that signaled either an emotional meltdown or food poisoning. I did the opposite of reflection and concentrated hard on not concentrating on my insides. Instead, I stared out the windows and took note of everything. Jane Goodall studying the chimps.

It was just after eight o'clock, and things were getting started along Van Nuys Boulevard. Potbellied, white-haired men sat outside with their potbellied women on folding lawn chairs. As many as could fit were crammed around tables outside the hole-in-the-wall diner that, if the sign was to be believed, specialized in pie. Classic cars in varying states of refurbishment were parked in the supermarket's lot with their hoods up and their windows down.

New arrivals filed past me until the line of hot rods waiting to get in started to block traffic, and an LAPD cop on a motorcycle pulled up alongside and turned on his public address system.

"You are creating gridlock. Please move. You are creating gridlock. Please move."

One or two cars pulled out of the line and made their way

around the block, and the cop moved on, too, apparently calling it victory enough.

The sun was sinking, and the crowd was growing and changing. Motorcycles and choppers were showing up, some of them lined with glowing lights. The short-haired, middle-aged men were being joined by skinnier, long-haired guys in Harley vests. They brought along their women, too, one of whom stopped to light a smoke next to my window. Her hair was dyed the same flat black as a few of the scragglier cars pulling in. It matched her T-shirt, which advertised beer. She'd ripped out the sleeves and the neckline, so it drooped over one shoulder and left her arms, tattooed in full sleeves, out in the open. When she brought her ciggie up to take a puff, the red spider's web over her elbow stretched and contracted.

I started to wonder if my father, the accountant, had had a secret life.

By the time the cigarette was done and my companion had moved on, the crowd was morphing a third time. A loud hiss and puff of air like something out the back of a fighter jet made me jump in my seat. A white car to my left that was longer than most yachts and piloted by a kid straight out of East L.A. rose up on its back tires like a proud jungle cat, a steady *boom-boom-boom* coming out of its speakers. Coming down the road from the opposite direction a smaller version done up in purple sparkles like a drag queen started bouncing up and down, its shiny wheels and thin tires threatening to pop with every impact. The white yacht rose and lowered in response.

Wild Kingdom, I thought. Mating dance.

Dusk was closing in fast and flirting with dark, making the underchassis lights on the cars glow bright. I got out, shoved my hands in my pockets, and headed toward the parking lot. On the way, I got hit up by a guy passing out business cards for custom paint and a woman selling coupon books for a drug recovery shelter. From the looks of her, I guessed she might need to go back soon, but everyone else gave the impression of sobriety. If they were drinking, they were keeping it hidden. It was too bad. After that dinner, I could've done with another beer.

Every spot in that part of the lot was taken up by some piece of automobile love. Ninety-five percent American steel. Five percent British. Not a Japanese model in sight. Not even a bike, which were exclusively Harley or so tricked out it was impossible to know what they had once been.

The thick-bodied Hispanic boys from East L.A. stood next to newer models with flashy paint. Flames were so ubiquitous they didn't even count. Some hung with their boys, while others brought girlfriends and kids. The two white groups—the bikers and the old-school classic guys—mostly came in pairs and talked to other pairs of their same species. It was clear where my interests lay.

I snaked my way through the crowd and around slow-moving cars still trying to find their spot in the parade. Every time the light at the nearby intersection changed from red to green, a thunder of engines revved, and the one or two grocery shoppers just trying to make their way to the store for onion bagels winced and reconsidered.

I shoved my hands deeper in my pockets and cursed myself for not bringing a sweater.

Speakers competed with one another, creating a din of sound that only turned into a song when you got close enough for its decibels to drown out all the other decibels around it, like microclimates of sound. I moved from Snoop Dog to the Beastie Boys to the Doors doing "L.A. Woman."

I stopped there and pushed up against two couples, both easily in their sixties. The tallest of the bunch sported a belly that made him look sixteen months pregnant. I wondered if his back hurt.

"Nice car," I said, which was about all I knew to say. I'd bought the Corvette in a manic fit a few years before after not getting off the couch for a week.

"Thank you." His voice was deep, not Barry White deep but well into baritone range. He had a silver beard and would've made a good Santa Claus. "'56," he told me, nodding toward the open hood with his chin.

The engine shone in the overhead parking lot lights as if someone had rubbed it with a cloth diaper. I wondered if he ever drove it.

"My dad had a '56 T-Bird," I said. "He used to cruise here back in the seventies."

His woman, who had short curls clipped tight to her head, smiled. "Oh yeah."

"Some of these boys date from then," Santa Claus agreed. "Not me. Bertha, here, cruised it, though. That woulda been with her first husband."

Bertha was all agreement. "Oh yeah."

"He was in a club," I said. "Might have been the Pumas."

"Sorry, sugar," he told me. "I was back in Arizona up until '85."

I looked at Bertha for a little help, but she was all out of agreement. I smiled and nodded and moved on.

At the end of the row, I passed a cluster of choppers, got a couple of approving looks, and made a one-eighty down the next line of showpieces. I passed up anything that looked newer than the 1960s and got my crotch sniffed by a docile, light-gray pit bull while waiting for a Stingray to pull out.

I stopped at a Mustang and two Corvettes much nicer than mine but didn't get any further than I had with Kris Kringle. No one had heard of the Pumas, and while everybody agreed a canary yellow '56 T-Bird was a sweet ride, nobody, not even the guys who had cruised back in the day, remembered one. Although one guy wanted to know if it was all stock, and if so, where my father sourced his parts. I told him if I ever found the man, I'd ask.

I was close to giving up, close to freezing to death, and close to losing my hearing by the time I'd snaked down the second row. But in the last spot next to the exit sat what I'd have called a station wagon except it looked like it had been made before they were called that. It wasn't a van, but the long back section of the cab was closed in with panels instead of windows. The front end was long, too, with big rolled wheel wells that came up as high as the hood. It was painted cherry red with orange and yellow flames coming off the grill. The man standing beside it wore a palm-tree–festooned Hawaiian shirt over khaki shorts with white knee socks and an old-fashioned driving cap on backward. Nothing is impossible in L.A., but the two children at his side—a boy and a girl in matching sweatshirts with the hoods pulled up—were young enough that I was going to guess it was grandpa's night out with the tykes. And not a single one of those things was the most interesting part. The most interesting part was a sticker on the lower passenger side of the windshield that said "BobCats."

I had to wait for a break in the line of cars inching out onto the street before darting across. He saw me coming and didn't look like he knew what to think about that. I tried to be less enthusiastic, less hopeful, just generally less, and to keep it away from the kids in case he got jumpy.

"Is that the name of your car club?" I asked, pointing at the sticker.

"Yeah." He said it like you say it when the phone rings during campaign season and someone who mispronounces your name asks if you're home.

"Were you guys around in the late seventies? Like 1978, maybe?"

He relaxed a little, and the kids started to lose interest in me and went back to trying to scrape petrified gum off the asphalt with the heels of their tennis shoes.

"Oh yeah. We're one of the oldest clubs out here. Not many hung together from the old days. But we kept doing shows and stuff even when they closed the boulevard down."

"My dad was a member back then."

His shoulders dropped the last few inches, and we were friends. "Yeah? What was his name?"

"Jerry Pritchard."

He shook his head. "Sorry. Don't remember him. It was a long time ago."

"He was an accountant," I pushed. "Worked at Parker, Combs, and Jimenez back when it was just Parker and Combs."

"Sorry," he said again.

"He had a '56 T-Bird. It was yellow."

His face cracked open, and he pointed at me like Uncle Sam in a recruitment poster. "Now that I remember. What did you say his name was again?"

"Jerry Pritchard."

"Guess my memory just isn't what it used to be. Then again, I never was good with names. How's he doing?"

"That's what I'm trying to find out." I gave him the white-washed version of my story.

"Too bad, kid. Well, I hope you find him. Wish I could tell you something, but it's that hot rod I remember more than anything. It's too bad he sold it, too."

My guts came loose from their moorings and sank into my lower intestines. My only lead was about to be severed.

"He sold it?"

Losing Clementine   135

"Sure did. I remember cause there wasn't one of us guys didn't want to buy it. He wanted a lot, though. Too rich for my blood. You should've seen the interior. It was that old-fashioned sea foam green they used to use. I think that's probably the color the paint used to be, too, but he kept it yellow. Went good with the green, I guess, but I'd have painted it back to the way it was."

"Why'd he sell it? Do you know?"

"Said he was going out of state. Didn't want to take it with him."

18 Days

I rolled off the bed and fell two and a half feet to the floor sometime after 8 A.M. but before 9. I'm not sure if I did it on purpose or not, but when I landed, my elbow jammed into my ribs and my head bounced a little off the hardwood floor. It didn't hurt as much as you would think. I landed on my left side facing the gap under my bed. There were boxes under there I'd never unpacked after leaving Richard. The corners had collected so much gray dust it looked like fur, and the cardboard was sagging and going soft like we all do with age.

I felt the light change through the day as much as I saw it. I felt the sun come through the open window and felt it move across my feet, warming them, and then up to my ankles and my calves before the bed blocked it from going any farther, and then the earth turned some more and the rays no longer came straight through the window. I kept lying there with my elbow in my ribs and my head on the boards looking at the furry boxes. It got brighter and then darker and then quite dark staring under there. I had to pee, but I pretended I didn't. I wasn't hungry or thirsty. I didn't want to be anything at all. I didn't want to exist.

I didn't think I could go another eighteen days. Eighteen days seemed an interminable period of time.

This was how I found my sister.

She was lying on her side in her bedroom. She was farther away from the bed, though. Closer to the center of the room. She was sticky and wet like I was; although I was wet, I realized, because sometime during the day I'd peed myself. Ramona had bled out.

There is no such thing as instant death. Not unless the bullet severs the brain stem. Doctors and police officers tell families that story because otherwise they have to tell them the truth, which is that you lie there in the process of dying and in horrible pain while your heart keeps beating and your nerves keep feeling and your brain keeps spinning until your circulatory system spews out all the blood it can, and there's no more oxygen to get to your brain. Then you die. It takes a while. I learned that in a high school health class. An EMT had come to give a lecture. Ramona and my mother had been dead for two years then. For two years, I'd believed their deaths had been instant and painless.

They had not been.

I had sat glued to my seat, the kind with the chair and the desk all in one piece, while the EMT talked. I'd thought I might vomit. I didn't, but I didn't go to my next class, either. I asked to go to the school nurse, who let me lie on the vinyl examining bed with a cool washcloth over my eyes. I told her I had a migraine.

Ramona had had a cold. It wasn't a bad cold, but it wasn't a fake cold, either. And she had been staying home from school for two days. She was old enough to stay home by herself and not so sick that she couldn't. On the first day, my mother had gone to work and left Ramona with some cough syrup and some sandwiches and the television. On the second day, she stayed home, too. She was having a "black day." That's what she called them, her sad days. Mostly she stayed in bed on black days. I would make our lunches and our dinners and see that Ramona's and my teeth got brushed.

I packed my own lunch that day and went to school. Sometime after 10 A.M., our mother went into Ramona's room with her father's pistol. He'd left it to her in his will because she was the oldest child. She shot my sister twice. One bullet went through Ramona's chest, right where her small left boob was. The second shot went through her stomach.

Then Mom went into her bedroom, sat down in the small *foufou* chair that made up half of her vanity set, and shot herself in the head. She put the gun in her mouth and angled it up a bit, so the power of the blast ripped her cheeks open and blew out the back of her skull. She probably died a lot quicker than Ramona. She was probably already gone while my sister was still beating and feeling and spinning, but pretty soon Ramona died, too.

I found them both at three-thirty when I came home from school. The blood was dark and congealed by then. I thought a mugger or a rapist or a hobo had done it and went screaming out of the house to the neighbor across the street. I didn't look for cars and was almost plowed down by a Plymouth.

That night I went to stay with Aunt Trudy and never went back inside the house again. I wonder sometimes what it would've been like if I had known when I was running out that I would never, ever again cross that threshold or see those things or breathe that air. I wonder what I was doing when my mother shot my sister. I know I was in algebra class, and we were having a quiz. Which problem exactly was I doing when the bullet left the barrel? When Ramona finally pumped out the last of her blood and her oxygen? Did I get that problem right?

Losing Clementine 139

I didn't go back to class for a month, and I eventually changed schools. Someone went and got my books and my work from the teachers. I like to think it was Bob, but I don't remember. It's like someone cut the film of my memory from the time the police came until weeks and weeks later. I was in suspended animation, except I'm pretty sure it was painful. Like now. It probably felt a little like now.

I was almost twenty before I started having black days, too.

It had gotten dark in my apartment. I couldn't see the boxes or the dust. Chuckles had come and gone a few times. Once he'd meowed. I hadn't fed him, and he was hungry. Now he came back and sniffed my foot. I hoped he wouldn't eat my face off. I'd heard that could happen even if you were alive—if the animal was hungry enough and you were trapped and couldn't get away, like maybe you'd had a stroke and were paralyzed.

This was like a stroke. I stayed where I was with my elbow in my ribs; although, I couldn't feel either of them anymore. Chuckles went away, and I must've fallen asleep.

17 Days

I threw the clothes from the day before in the Dumpster. I showered and put on fresh work clothes, which meant they were covered in glue and paint and smelled of solvents but had nonetheless been through a complete wash and dry cycle and were, therefore, considered clean.

I found some men and women in a *National Geographic* who had the walnut-colored skin I wanted. Some darker, some brighter. Highlights and lowlights that from a distance made up the movement of muscle. I cut pieces of them out with my X-Acto knife, and I applied them to the back of the buffalo on the canvas. If I had time, I thought I might do a whole series of animals.

I worked fast and ate Twinkies. Twinkies are the sort of thing you can eat a lot of because they don't taste like anything except eventually of chemically altered lard. Still, you can push right past that and keep going.

After my shower, I'd gone online and ordered groceries to be delivered for the first time. I should've started doing that years before. It was a revelation. I almost couldn't believe it when the kid with the shaved head actually showed up at the door carrying the bags of food. And by food, I mean junk. But still, there he was holding exactly what I had decided I'd wanted a mere two hours before. It was like magic. It must've been how Benjamin Franklin felt the first time his kite got hit by lightning.

I ate the butt end of a snack cake and shoved the cellophane wrapper over into the pile of cellophane wrappers. Chuckles, too, had scarfed his breakfast before demanding and receiving a refill. The sun came through all the windows like God rays, and dust motes danced in the light like fairy sparkles. I tore into another magazine on the hunt for more flesh to strip. Everything seemed to be happening at time and a half, even the banging on my door.

"It's open," I yelled, unwilling to stop cutting out the dark, thin thighs of a preschool-age child from the background of a shantytown.

Carla came in. Her nearly shaved head shone in the reflected God rays, but that was the only shining she was doing. The invisible crown she usually wore had slipped, and the film of impassivity across her face had dissolved.

"You could not be contacted for comment."

"If you're going to come to my studio, I'd appreciate it if you didn't speak in non sequiturs like the goddamn Cheshire Cat."

Carla's long straight skirt whished around her thin ankles as she crossed the hardwood floor. She laid a newspaper next to my pile of wrappers and picked up one of the pieces of cellophane, the inside smeared with stuck bits of sponge cake.

"How many of these have you eaten?"

She pawed through the pile, which crinkled under her hand, and started counting.

I shrugged and pushed the cellophane out of her reach.

"What do you want?"

She dragged her eyes away from the wrappers and pushed the newspaper closer to me. It was neatly folded the way business-men on subways hold their papers and open to the front of the arts section. There was a photograph of me taken the year before at a museum event next to a photograph of Elaine Sacks, which, judging from the shrunken state of her crow's-feet, had been taken much longer ago than that.

Plagiarism at the Taylor?

I picked it up, and my glue-coated fingers stuck to the thin newsprint. The article took most of the top half, leaving nothing but a narrow column on the right for a write-up of the philhar-monic's financial woes. I sat down on the blue stool pulled up to the worktable and read the entire thing, including the photo captions. My name was all over it and so was Jenny's. She was quoted. I could not be reached for comment. Carla had talked in art-speak about aesthetic trends that could be seen across the work of many artists during a given period. Elaine denied all knowledge of me and my work, implying we'd hardly met. The vandalism got prominent mention but wasn't attributed to me, nor did the reporter say that Elaine's cheating, copycat ways had led the unknown perpetrator to his or her crimes.

When I was done, I folded it up and handed it back to Carla—also without comment.

"I've been asked to resign in two weeks. Mr. Taylor thinks two weeks is an appropriate time frame," she said.

I no more cared about what John Taylor thought than I cared when he took a shit.

"Thanks for letting me know."

Carla's skull looked even more perfectly formed than usual. It was smooth all around without any of the usual lumps and bumps, and it sat on a neck at least 25 percent longer than an average neck. It was longer today than before. I was almost certain of it. In fact, everything about her was elongated: her hands, her fingers, her legs, her feet. I couldn't believe I'd never noticed how much like a Steven Spielberg alien she looked.

"So I guess you win," she said.

I blinked.

"I win what?"

"You got what you wanted. I've been punished."

It's strange when you discover someone is attributing to you feelings and motives and a whole level of involvement you don't have. "That's not what I wanted."

I got up from the stool, taking the cutout leg with me to the canvas. I spread glue over the paint, placed the paper, and brushed more glue on top of it, careful not to cause any wrinkles or bubbles. Carla watched. When I was done, I set the brush down and took a quick step back to make sure I was happy with it.

"The gallery would appreciate it if you would say something publicly to make it clear this is a dispute between you and Elaine and not with us."

I wasn't happy with the leg. I stepped forward and peeled the piece off the canvas with the sharp end of a sewing needle, rotated it three degrees and pressed it back down.

"No," I said.

"No, what?"

"No, I won't make a statement."

Carla sat down on the blue stool and leaned both elbows on the worktable. She looked as if her head was wearing out her neck and she might like to lay it down someplace, maybe right there. She was in danger of getting paint, glue, and Twinkie crumbs on her shirt, but I figured she'd been around enough artists' studios to know that on her own.

"Why not?"

"It's not true, and I don't want to. Besides I'm on a deadline."

"We're not responsible for what our artists do."

I was not in the mood to argue the point. In fact, I was more in the mood to throw some teapots out the window, and I was fresh out of teapots. So I asked her to leave—just like that, and it was very satisfying.

The advantage other major cities have and the reason L.A.'s museums will always be in a state of turmoil is that we are so damn unwilling to share. Every billionaire wants a building with his name on it in which to hang his pictures and only his pictures, and they all think they have a collection worthy of isolation. None of them do, of course, but it doesn't matter. Rather than enriching the holdings of the public museums, whole edifices have risen following the death of each megalomaniac, each building holding a thousand mediocre paintings and two or three good ones. This has made art patronage inefficient for the masses. The only upside is for the artists. With those acres and acres of white walls multiplying exponentially with each funeral, museum directors have had to do something.

I parked in a loading zone and stood in front of the two-story plate glass windows that fronted the lobby of the Walton Museum of Art. I sign all my pieces with my first name, and there it was across the window, just as if I had written it. The C alone—the only really legible part—was a story and a half, and the T's crossbar stretched forty feet. Below, in red, it said:

Only in art can that be the years not of birth and death but of the retrospective's scope. They weren't bad years as far as years go, but I didn't spend much time thinking about them or looking at the work I'd done. Mostly because it was painful. I'd do it all differently now.

This particular stretch of West Los Angeles is populated by silver, mirrored skyscrapers that buzz with lawyers during the day and empty of all but the Hispanic cleaning crews at night. Twenty-four-hour traffic on the 405 two blocks away hummed overhead while street-level gridlock inched and honked along. I walked around the other side of the building, which took up a whole city block, and entered through the gate.

The courtyard with its bamboo garden is open to the public and at lunchtime is populated by paralegals with brown bags eating their ham and cheese while their bosses order the octopus salad from white-clad waiters in fancy restaurants. The courtyard is nicer, and I have a feeling the paralegals know it. The bamboo canes stretch almost to the roof of the three-story building, getting narrower and narrower the higher they climb. Any slight breeze sways them and bangs them together like wind chimes. It's the only noise that really drowns out the freeway.

I skipped the gift shop and took the outdoor staircase to the second-floor exhibition space. The signature and tagline from the front windows were repeated on the freestanding white wall that greeted visitors. I slipped in past the guard, despite not wearing an ENTRY FEE PAID sticker, and started the tour.

The curator had arranged things more or less chronologically, so I was zoomed back in time twenty years. I'd used more paint then and fewer magazines or other modern media. I'd cut heavy black mat board into silhouettes and made years of work that looked like Indonesian shadow-puppet shows.

I didn't know as much then. My technique wasn't as good, and that needled me. I was making just enough to keep the lights on and food in the pantry.

This was the first time I'd seen the exhibit. You'd think someone from the museum would've called me for a consult or something, but they hadn't. I was invited to the closing-night party. There was going to be a DJ and a cash bar. I'd get free drink tickets if I were going to be around then, which I wasn't. The exhibit would be open another two months. I hoped someone else got to use my drink tickets.

I wandered into the second room and watched other people look at my work. There was a young couple, maybe even still teenagers. Students, I guessed, from nearby UCLA. Maybe art majors. Or philosophy. Something that scared the shit out of their parents. She wore cutoff denim shorts with long threads dangling from the unfinished hems and shredded, opaque tights underneath. He wore a black scarf despite its being summer and had tied it just so. Very Parisian. Very gay. They held hands and looked at things slowly. A middle-aged woman with short, cropped gray hair sat on the bench in the middle of the room. I sat next to her. She wore glasses with large red frames that matched her clogs. I'd have bet anything she donated to PBS and NPR both. She didn't move around at all, just stared at the one or two pieces in front of her with much less absorption than the kids. Maybe her feet hurt. Maybe she'd given up pretending to take art that seriously. I could respect either of those things.

This room went up to the late nineties. I was using a lot more color and had obviously been spending way too much time thinking about Basquiat. I'd even experimented with words—cutout words—in the pieces. Not all of them made sense even to me. It was a little William Burroughs that way. I'd been doing a lot of coke back then, which meant three-quarters of the work had been done at four o'clock in the morning with blackout curtains pulled shut against the impending dawn. Coke did interesting things during my more manic periods.

I scooted closer to the woman and followed her line of sight.

Detroit No. 4

I remembered that series. I'd done a dozen of them. All with lots of blazing reds and oranges, with black and brown paper and newsprint. The destruction of manual labor, of industry in the U.S. Everything looked like it was burning, which it was supposed to. I'd cut a story out of the *Times* on plant closures and stuck parts of it all over the place, layering a bit of thinned paint over it, so you could just, if you tried, make out some of the words. I'd gone in with permanent marker on some of the paper and drawn right on it, colored in sections with it. It didn't look as good as I remembered.

I stood up, crossed right in front of the woman, maybe even blocked her view, to squint at it a little closer. I hadn't seen *Detroit No. 4* or its siblings since I sold them ten years before. The black wasn't as black as it used to be. I got closer to check.

Nope, definitely not.

It bugged me. It looked old, faded, dying. It made my palms and the bottoms of my feet itch. Had the damn thing been hanging in front of a window?

I flipped open my bag and dug around. I kept all sorts of things in there for emergencies. Scissors and baggies and even one plastic glove for any crap I wanted to pull out of the gutter and take home to Jenny for storage. I also had a permanent marker. It was big and fat and smelled like it would get you high, which was always the sign of a good art supply.

I took it out, yanked it open, took a good whiff, and leaned in close to make the touch-ups. I concentrated hard, my other hand holding the piece steady. It wasn't as big as some of my later work, and I didn't want it to wiggle.

The thing about art—the thing you must understand if you ever buy a real piece of it—is that it never belongs to you. Not really. It's always going to belong to the artist. I don't care what your insurance company says, which is exactly what I said to the guard who bum-rushed me.

Thank-fucking-God, I'd pulled my marker up from the canvas when he hit me. If the tip had left a wiggled line like a stock market crash down-down-down to the bottom corner, I would've kicked him to death, I swear it.

"Don't resist. Don't resist."

The guard, who was young enough to be someone I'd babysat, was straddling my hips and had his forearm across my neck. I don't know if they taught him that in museum guard school, but it was a shitty plan. I brought my elbow back to the floor and punched him square in the nose. He made a yelp like a coyote pup and put both hands to his face. I was struggling to sit up and looking for a nice fleshy spot for another blow when the whole museum goon squad came running in, their orthopedic shoes slapping on the marble floor.

"Vandal!" the woman in the red glasses shrieked, pointing at me in case things weren't clear enough. "Vandal! Vandal!"

I was really starting not to like her, and if the goons hadn't dragged me off the floor and out from under Officer Friendly by my armpits, I might have let her have it, too.

Two guards had my wrists and were pinning them behind my

back, up between my shoulder blades. Junior, one hand still on his nose, bent down to pick up my bag and paw through it.

"Take out my ID," I said to him. "Read it. I'm Clementine Pritchard. That's my painting."

"That painting belongs to the museum," said one of the guys behind me, this one closer to my age.

"Actually," I said, "it's on loan."

I couldn't help it. Authority makes me lippy. He squeezed my wrist tighter and pushed it up higher until my shoulder ached, and I wanted to bite someone.

The kid fumbled with my wallet like zippers were new to him before getting it open and my driver's license out. He squinted at it and then held it up for the others to see. There I was at the DMV two years before, looking a little haggard and pissed off, probably a lot like right then. My name and address were right next to the photo, clear as a California day.

I thought I felt the field level out, but that could've been my imagination.

"Is she really Clementine Pritchard?" the woman asked.

The guard on my left scowled at her and didn't answer. I tried to blow a piece of hair out of my face.

"What do we do?" Junior asked.

"We follow protocol. This doesn't change anything."

"She is Clementine Pritchard!" the woman exclaimed. "Oh, I just love your paintings. I have been here three times this week."

Without closing it up, the kid shoved my wallet back in the bag. "We should call the director."

"Fine." The two guys behind me shoved, and I skittered forward.

I wanted the hair out of my face, so I could see. But the guards were too busy giving me Indian burns on both wrists to let me do any grooming. Through the veil of black tresses, I saw the kid in the gay scarf flash me a thumbs-up. I gave him a chin bob back.

"I'm sorry I called you a vandal!" the woman shouted as they steered me out of the exhibit.

"This is a very unusual situation."

The museum's director was wearing a dark gray suit, a white shirt, and a light gray tie. When they say everyone looks better in black-and-white, they mean photos. He looked a little sallow, nothing a blue sweater couldn't have fixed.

I didn't know what to say to that. Things had been pretty unusual around me for a while. It sort of depended on your perspective.

"I called the Shipleys, who kindly loaned us the painting."

I had told the creep it was a loan.

"And they've been very understanding. They've decided to accept your"—he paused and made a flittering hand gesture—"touch-ups as an improvement by the artist."

"They are. It was fading. You should tell them to stop hanging it by the window."

He gave me a closed-lip smile as if he were indulging a child. "I think I'll let them make their own call on that one."

He leaned back in his chair behind the long, shallow blond wood desk. It was entirely free of ornament and clutter, an homage to modernism if I ever saw one. I leaned back, too, and laced my fingers across my stomach. Larry, Moe, and Curly had long since been dismissed. The whole thing had taken several hours, during which I'd been locked alone inside the employee break room. They'd taken my bag, so I didn't have any change for the candy machine, which sucked.

I hadn't been invited up to the office on the third floor until my identity was verified and several phone calls had been made, one of which was to the Shipleys on their window-filled estate.

No harm, no foul, I thought. I was starting to wonder why we were both still sitting there, eyeing each other with polite interest.

He leaned forward. I didn't. His hair was thick and full and the sort of dark brown they always show on do-it-yourself hair color commercials. It was so perfect, in fact, that it made me wonder if it wasn't a very, very good wig.

"I'd like to turn a negative into a positive here."

I bounced a knee. I feel about corporate-speak the way I feel about authority. Bitey.

"I'd like," he went on, "to add a nice footnote to tomorrow's news story."

Ah. That's why I hadn't been turned out on my keester.

The brat in me didn't want to play ball, but the grown-up considered the circumstances. It would, after all, be my last show. I sucked on the inside of my cheek.

"We can get you some supplies," he said.

"I don't work on an empty stomach," I told him.

A secretary brought me a menu from one of the octopus salad places nearby and then went to call Jenny, who, it was reported back to me, would come with everything I asked for. I asked if she'd seemed surprised.

"Not really."

I ordered half a chopped salad and grilled prawns, which each turned out to be the size of a baby's arm. I got my bag back and fed quarters into the machine for a diet soda, and by the time I'd polished off the side of toasted bread, Jenny was there with brown paper grocery sacks in either arm.

"I was on a date," she said.

"And I feel bad about that. You want dinner?" I asked, pushing the menu toward her.

"I ate on the way."

I took a swig of diet soda. "Would I have approved of him?"

"No."

"Why not?"

"He's an artist."

"A species not to be trusted," I agreed. I dunked the last bite of bread into the leftover salad dressing and shoved it into my mouth and, before chewing, said, "Let's do this."

The museum had been closed for over an hour. The sun had set while I'd been held up inside. The grid of streets below had quieted. When red turned to green, there was no one waiting to go. Jenny and I walked alone back to the exhibition space. A guard stood out front. I didn't recognize him, which was nice for both of us.

He showed us to the final room of the exhibit, two rooms past where I'd made it. There was a large blank wall that had been freshly skinned, a process museums use to allow artists to paint directly onto it. The guard stepped away, and Jenny and I stood in front of it. It was bigger and whiter than I'd thought. Even I felt small.

Jenny sat the bags down, and the clatter echoed in the empty room.

"Why are we doing this again?" Her normal voice sounded like a shout bouncing around the hard planes.

"I forget."

"Maybe we can just leave." She'd dropped down to a golf whisper.

"A soldier doesn't flee the battlefield," I golf-whispered back.

"It's called desertion. Happens all the time. If it didn't, there wouldn't be a word for it."

"Aren't you supposed to be inspiring me to have confidence?"

"Sorry."

"It's okay."

"You're going to rock this."

"Uh-huh."

"You're the man."

Was it my imagination or was the wall getting whiter and bigger the longer we stood there?

"Desertion, you say?"

"You're a soldier. This is a battlefield."

"Did you bring everything?"

She looked down into the bags at her feet. "I think so."

I held out my hand, and she handed me a charcoal pencil like I was a surgeon being handed her scalpel. And like the first cut, I touched the lead to the wall, took a breath, and started to sketch. It wasn't long before I had to send Jenny in search of the guard and the guard in search of a ladder.

When she came back, she sat down cross-legged on the floor, cutting out leaves from all the clippings I'd saved over the years, every bit of press I'd ever received. I'd kept them the way a mother would, stashed in a shoe box that became two that became three that eventually became a plastic filing box when Jenny brought some order.

There are some artists who do little of their own work, who have assistants who paint and draw and sculpt for them. You might purchase a piece by Tom, and all he did was spout some babble at the beginning and sign it at the end. Those artists run their studios like businesses. They are the CEOs of Artist, Inc. They work the press to keep their brand solid, they work patrons like stock investors, and they work their assistants like assembly-line workers trying to keep up with the demand created by the first two.

That would be fine except it's shit.

When you buy my piece, you buy my piece. Mine. I did it.

Jenny and all my assistants before her—a proud lineage of recent art school graduates with poor job prospects—stretched and treated my canvases, mixed my paints, and washed my brushes. They answered my mail, bought my groceries, and generally tried to keep me from collapsing in on myself too often. Some were more successful than others. Some lasted longer than others. But not a damn one ever painted a stroke. Frankly, it made me a shitty boss, but it made me a good artist, even if I was a slow one. So fuck the rest of that shit.

Until that night.

I only had one night. Tomorrow, I'd already told the museum, I had plans. So I was selling out like William Shatner. Jenny was cutting, and I was drawing. And her name wouldn't be anywhere on it.

I climbed down off the ladder, having finished adding a series of lizards that morphed into birds as they rose higher.

"Come here."

She looked up. Her hair really was as blond and as flyaway limp as a woodland fairy's. As always, it was falling out of the ponytail and hanging in her face, and it made me say what my mother had always said to me:

"How do you see like that?"

"Like what?"

"With your hair in your face."

She shrugged and tucked a particularly problematic lock behind her ear.

"Come take this," I said, holding out the charcoal pencil.

She stood up and brushed small slivers of newspaper trimmings off her shorts before taking it and starting to put it back in one of the bags.

"No," I said and pointed at the bottom of the weeping willow—a long, dangling, melting, abstract version of a weeping

Losing Clementine   155

willow that I had drawn eight feet tall, leaning so far to the left it looked like it might fall. It wrapped inside the corner of the wall so it folded in half like a book on its way to closing. "Sign it."

Jenny froze as if I'd handed her a gun and told her to shoot a whole litter of golden retrievers. Who were all Seeing Eye dogs. For disadvantaged children. She looked at the wall and then at me and for a second I thought she was going to cry and run away, which would've been a big problem considering all the paper leaves I needed her to cut out.

"I can't," she said finally and tried to hand the pencil back to me. I wouldn't take it.

"Yes, you can."

"But it's not right."

"You're doing the work."

"Assistants don't sign things."

I opened my mouth to argue the point, to make clear logical statements as to why that was twenty-seven kinds of utter bullshit, but all I really managed to do was sigh, because some things are so obvious that you can't explain them without tripping over your own words. So I did what any good authority figure would do. I dictated.

"Sign it," I said. "I command you."

She stood there, unsure.

"Go on," I said. "Time is wasting."

She took a step toward the wall, crouched down on one knee, touched the lead to the paint, and looked up at me one last time just to make sure before signing her name in clear schoolgirl loops very different from mine.

She took a step back and looked at it.

"Now get back to work," I said, deliberately avoiding any sort of hugging moment that might have led to swelling orchestral music. "Those leaves aren't going to cut themselves."

Twenty minutes later, just as I was dipping my brush into a muddy green and brown mixture of paints and touching the bristles to the wall for the first time, a reporter and a photographer walked in. Both were wearing jeans and looked like they'd been pulled away from a family dinner or a child's T-Ball game, which they probably had.

It was five o'clock in the morning by the time Jenny and I finished. We were stupid with tiredness, jittery and almost nervous from lack of sleep. The guard let us into the break room—or as I thought of it, my cell—and we bought packages of powdered sugar doughnuts and Bugles with our pocket change.

I waited until she had white powder on her cheek to bring it up.

"You called that reporter at the *Times*, didn't you?"

She took a swig of Sprite, the morning soda of choice, to wash down the masticated carbs. "Yes. Are you mad at me?"

"I might be if I thought about it more, which I haven't."

"I guess I should've asked your permission first."

She wadded up a wrapper and held it in her hand.

"You should have."

She looked up at me. Her hair was no longer in a ponytail so much as in a general mess that suggested a ponytail might have once existed there.

"I'm sorry."

"Okay."

"That's it?"

"That's it."

16 Days

The ad on a classic car enthusiasts' Web site was for a canary yellow '56 T-Bird with pale green upholstery. There was a photo taken on a grassy field and a red banner across the ad that said SOLD. It listed a contact phone number. I called it.

It rang and rang and rang and no one—not even an answering machine—picked up. I hung up and typed the number into an online reverse directory. The address was forty miles outside of Fresno.

An hour later, I'd packed a knapsack for a possible overnight and poured extra kibble into Chuckles's bowl. He pretended not to notice. I told him not to throw any wild parties while I was gone and reminded him we needed to talk about his future plans.

Fresno is a little more than halfway between Los Angeles and San Francisco as far as mileage goes, and a whole world away by any other standard. It's in the middle of the San Joaquin Valley, where all the water used to drain into a lake that no longer exists. Everything wet has been diverted to the farms that surround it. Grapes and oranges, garlic and almonds. Even kiwifruit, which I have trouble imagining growing at all. Any fruit that grows hair is the gift of a friendly alien race. There's even hay and cotton, though the south gets all the credit for that.

I turned off the 5 well before Bakersfield and watched as civilization thinned out and road signs got larger and more interesting. A helpful tip-off that a fast-food restaurant was only twenty-two miles ahead got me a little excited and not just because I had to pee. The road was flat and straight and the rows and rows of irrigated farmland trancelike. Combined with my lack of sleep, it was all I could do to keep my eyelids from snapping shut.

By the time I approached the address, it was still only early evening, and the sky had just barely started to hint at the dusty purple and salmon pink of velvet Elvis paintings. The weedy shoulder of the highway had been blackened for the length of two football fields, and I could smell the acrid soot. Fire is so common during California summers it has a season of its own. The landscape is opposite that of the rest of the country. It's during summer that everything turns brown and dies. Instead of the remains being covered with snow, they catch hold of some careless cigarette butt and ignite. Not until fall and winter bring rain does everything sprout green again.

I had turned off Highway 99 at an intersection too small to have so much as a gas station. I went another few miles before finding a stand of neglected single-story homes all clustered together in the middle of open farm country like cows in a thunderstorm. Some of them were brick, but most had aluminum siding that was well past its warranty date. Large mismatched awnings shaded the windows, and the yards—front and back—were surrounded by chain-link fences. More of the fencing blocked off

Losing Clementine 159

gravel driveways with gates that were chained and locked. Each of the gates had signs that read NO SOLICITING/NO TRESPASSING. The only things not fenced off and guarded were the mailboxes, each stencil-painted with a number.

I pulled off and parked at the edge of the road. When the crunch of loose gravel under my tires quieted and the engine powered down, there was nothing to hear. No birds. No kids. Nobody watering the weedy brown grass. I rolled up the window and watched. Closed up, the inside of the car smelled like stale french fries from a pit stop an hour ago.

Call it city-girl paranoia, but something was wrong with a place that didn't move a twitch in all the time I sat there watching and waiting. It had the stillness and ill will of a military base long abandoned for being too close to a nuclear testing site.

I got out and walked across the road—no need to look both ways—and stood in front of the gate across the driveway of my target house. There was a dusty brown Cutlass circa 1980 parked behind the gate with its long nose nearly touching the garage door. There was not, however, any way to knock or ring a bell or for any visitor at all to announce her presence except, perhaps, by shouting, which just felt wrong. I put my toe into one of the diamond-shaped holes just below the NO TRESPASSING sign and boosted myself up onto the fence. I threw my other leg over and landed on the gravel drive.

The growl and the bark and the roar that came at my back sounded like a tyrannosaurus. My spine stiffened, and my pee muscles clinched. I was afraid to turn around and afraid not to, and there wasn't enough time to consider my options because it was on me in less than a second. When I did turn, I was pressed up against the gate looking into the open jaws of a German shepherd. The mouth was so big and gaping and full of yellowing teeth that I couldn't see the rest of its body. It had come darting out from under the Cutlass like a greased weasel, and I knew I was going to get bit. The question was only how bad. I tried to scamper back up and over the fence, but I was afraid to turn around again, and my hand slipped on the top. The sharp twisted wire at the apex of one of the diamonds sliced through the skin of my forearm as neatly as a butcher's knife but with a much higher risk of tetanus.

The creature's jaws lunged at me, catching my jeans and scraping against my shin underneath. They clamped down on the tough fabric and yanked, pulling me the rest of the way down off the fence. I heard the denim rip.

"Jasper!"

The front door flew open, and a man in a ball cap charged out onto the small cement stoop. He did not come any closer.

"Jasper, cut that the hell out!"

Jasper let go and sank into his shoulders, giving him the scary hunchbacked look of a hyena. A growl rumbled around in his chest like one of the hot rod engines that had got me into this mess in the first place.

I took a gulp of air that rattled my rib cage as if the bones had come loose from their moorings and for a horrible moment wondered if I had peed myself. I couldn't tell by feeling. The adrenaline rushing through my system like five eightballs mixed up my nerves, and there was no polite way to look down between my legs to check.

"What the fuck is the matter with you, woman? You trying to get yourself killed?"

It was so ironic I wouldn't have known how to answer even if I could speak, and I wasn't sure that I could. I was still looking at Jasper, who was obeying his master but giving the impression that either of them could renege on the current arrangement at any moment.

"What do you want?"

The bottom fell out of my brain, and for a minute I couldn't remember what I wanted. "We don't buy nothin' around here. Can't you read the damn sign?"

He was older than me, but I couldn't tell by how much. I got the feeling people aged differently out here. It was hot out, hotter than L.A. by a lot, and there was nothing to provide shade except for the big plastic awnings over the windows, which came down so far I couldn't imagine you could see anything from the inside. Nonetheless, Jasper's companion wore jeans and a long-sleeved plaid shirt buttoned all the way up to the very top of the neck. The ball cap, like the awning, blocked too much and made me even more uneasy, if such a thing were possible.

"Did you own a '56 T-Bird?"

He shifted where he stood, and it was impossible to tell if it was curiosity or unease. "Why you asking?"

"It's an unusual car," I said. "My dad owned one once. I'm trying to trace it."

"I don't have it no more. Sold it more than a year ago." He turned toward the door. "Jasper, come."

Jasper was a lot easier to read. He wanted to turn away from me about as much as he wanted to leave a two-inch-thick rib eye.

"Did it have a tear in the seat?" I hollered after him. "The passenger-side seat?"

"Not anymore. I fixed it. How did you know that?"

I ignored his question in favor of my own. "Where did you get it?"

"That ain't any business of yours."

I nodded my concession of the point. "I'm only asking because I'm trying to find my dad. I don't know where he is or if he's even alive, but I know he owned a car like that. So maybe whoever you bought it from bought it from someone who bought it from him."

"I bought that car thirty years ago. I can't help you."

I took a step forward to stop him, forgetting about Jasper, who scrambled up to an attack position and growled a reminder.

"Jasper, down."

"What year? What year did you buy it?"

His shoulders dropped and he looked on the verge of an audible sigh.

"I'd just bought this place. So it must've been seventy-eight."

"Just after school started?"

"What?"

"September? Did you buy it in September?"

"Mighta been."

"Do you remember anything about the man you bought it from?"

The street and all the surrounding houses remained still and silent. Not one person had so much as pushed back a drapery.

"It was a couple."

"Pardon?"

"I bought it from a couple." He raised his voice, as if the problem was that I might be a little deaf or a lot dumb. "Husband and wife. They was moving to the Midwest somewhere, and his old lady didn't want to take it with them. Made over twenty thousand dollars on it when I sold it, too. Man was a dumbass selling that car for less than it was worth. I talked him down, but he shouldn't-a let me do it."

"He had his wife with him?"

"Yeah, she was the one so keen on selling."

"The Midwest, you said?"

"Kansas, maybe. One of them real flat places. I remember

thinking it was good he was selling it out here. Cars don't last long in them middle states. All that salt they put on the roads in the winter corrodes the metal something awful. Never buy a classic car that's been livin' out there. It won't last you."

It hadn't occurred to me that Mom might have known he was leaving, might have insisted he sell the car before going, taken her cut.

"Thank you for your time," I said and took a step back.

I turned to climb back over the padlocked gate, and Jasper gave one last bark in case I had any fancy ideas.

"Wait a minute," the man called out. "I can open the damn thing."

I waited for him to cross the wide lawn and thought all the things I'd never thought as a kid. Had it been my father's choice not to write or send birthday gifts or had Mom told him not to? What about when she died? Did someone tell him? Why did she lie to me? Why act surprised?

Up close the man's neck was burned red with white creases where the skin folded. He smelled like engine oil and soap, and when he bent over and pulled a lump of keys out of his pocket to unlock the gate, his shirt sleeve pulled up and showed a tiny bit of gold watch on his wrist. Jasper had trotted up to him and was sitting at his foot, panting under the sun. I knew how he felt. After only a few minutes, I felt the prickly pink of sunburn threatening.

The man unlocked the gate, and I went through, then turned to say good-bye.

"She had pretty red hair."

"Who did?"

"The woman. I got kind of a thing for redheads. I just remember cause it looked natural like. Not that bottle red that don't look nice."

"Oh," I said.

"You color your hair?" he asked.

"No," I said. "I don't."

"Good. It never looks nice."

I nodded, unsure of what to say. This John Frieda side of my new backwoods friend was unsettling.

"Come on, Jasper."

He locked the gate and walked back up to the house with the German shepherd behind him. Once he was inside with the door shut, the silence was so complete it pressed down on my eardrums. No birds. No people. No cars. No nothing.

I walked back to the car and started the engine.

I'd inherited my hair color from my mother. "As close to black as it could be without being Chinese," Aunt Trudy used to say.

I had no idea who the redhead was.

I drove on to Fresno with my brain spinning out, my thoughts pooling on the floor like an unraveled roll of toilet paper.

I stopped at the first chain drugstore I found and went in for gauze pads, ointment, and liquor. I ripped open the packaging right there at the cash register and squeezed the oily, clear gunk onto the cut on my arm, which had pulled away from itself on either side like a rip in a couch. The skin around it was an angry red.

"You gotta be careful," the girl behind the counter said. She was round, Hispanic, and not a day over sixteen. "That could get nasty infected."

I only needed it to hold together for another two weeks, sort of like having a rental car. As long as it runs, right?

I put on too much of the ointment, pressed a gauze pad to it, and then—with the help of the counter girl, who told me she was thinking about going to college to become a nurse—applied four strips of no-ouch medical tape.

Losing Clementine 165

"Why not be a doctor?" I asked, stuffing the trash back in my plastic sack along with a not-so-great-but-as-good-as-they-had bottle of tequila.

"Doctors are assholes."

"Especially shrinks," I agreed.

"Yeah," she said and nodded, even though I was willing to bet the closest she'd ever gotten to a shrink was a school counselor, which was probably close enough.

Three stoplights later I found a chain hotel/motel with a big red sign on the building that said $119/NIGHT POOL AND FITNESS CENTER in white letters. I took a front parking spot, a complimentary newspaper, and a Chinese take-out/delivery menu from the front desk.

In my room, I turned on the Discovery channel, sat on the unwashed comforter with the busy floral pattern so useful for disguising bodily fluids, and unwrapped my complimentary plastic cup. I poured the tequila into it one shot at a time. I could've drunk from the bottle, but I'm a lady.

Three shots in I ordered kung pao shrimp and egg rolls and watched beavers mate until both the beaver and the food came.

15 Days

Tequila does not go with duck sauce. I don't care what anyone tells you.

It was 10 A.M., and I had a cold, wet, industrial-grade washcloth pressed to my face and the back of my head resting on the tub. The lights were off, and the blackout blinds were drawn. I was, I decided, prepared to leave my room and go in search of a hangover cure just as long as the world agreed to turn off the sun for the next twenty-four hours.

By 11 A.M., I was in a chain diner that served breakfast all day and separated its booths with frosted glass dividers. While I'd waited for a table, two kids in matching green soccer uniforms complete with knee-high socks had run around pretending to score goals. One of them stepped on my foot in cleats. I cried out louder than was necessary just to get their mother's attention. It hadn't worked. She had no sympathy left for bystanders. Then my table was ready.

I ordered coffee from a woman with long, yellowing, unpainted nails that reminded me of witches and glittery eye shadow she was at least sixty years too old to wear. She brought the whole pot. I wasn't sure if that was normal or I just looked that bad, and I couldn't see through the divider to check on anyone else's table.

The coffee was the kind you don't want to drink black but is all right with enough cream and sugar. I tasted some and then added more cream every few sips as I made room in the cup. I no longer wanted to vomit, but it was unmistakably true that my skull had been cleaved in two somewhere over my right eye. I drank more coffee and talked myself into moving enough to pull my cell phone out of my pocket.

I called information and winced when the operator picked up. I kept my eyes closed for the entire call. Things were better that way. "Anywhere in Kansas . . . Jerry Pritchard . . . None? . . . Thank you."

I hung up. It was a long shot anyway.

"My husband was from Kansas City. Lit out of there so fast, you'd think somebody set his pants on fire."

Oh, good, I thought, a chatty waitress.

"I've never been to Kansas," I said.

"Ain't in Kansas. Kansas City's in Missouri, which don't make a damn bit of sense, but there you go. You know what you want yet?"

"Mexican scramble."

"Bacon or sausage?"

"Sausage."

"White or wheat?"

"White."

"Buttered?"

"Dry."

"Got it."

She walked away, and I drank more of my cream laced with

coffee and artificial sweetener. Then I called back the operator with the too-loud voice.

She must've been in the bathroom because a guy picked up.

"Jerry Pritchard in Missouri," I told him. "Anywhere in Missouri."

He came back with three numbers. I made him wait while I dug in my bag for a pen. I didn't have one. I didn't even have a lipstick. I told him I'd call him back. He offered to put me through to the number of my choice.

"Are you kidding?" I asked. "I didn't even think this would work."

Then I hung up, which is when I noticed my heart was pounding. I liked it better when I was just looking. I liked it better when the universe wasn't throwing me a bone. I liked it better when I didn't have to think about what I'd say when the asshole picked up the phone.

"Hi, remember me? The fruit of your loins?"

I probably wouldn't say that. *Loins* is a gross word.

I drank more coffee because caffeine would certainly help lower my heart rate and tried not to think so damn much. I wished I had some of my pills to take. I wished I had some pot.

I'd plugged his name into a search engine a few times a year for ten years. You'd be surprised how common names are. Nothing that was clearly him had ever popped up. There were a lot of things that might have been—a Rotary Club listing, 5K race results. I'd thought, for a while, that a man in Texas who blogged about conservative politics might have been him, but he turned out to be lifelong military, which couldn't have been right. Cyber-stalking strangers, squinting at Facebook photos for a family resemblance, all of those things felt safer.

My waitress came back ten minutes later with a pile of bright yellow eggs flecked with diced tomato and green onion and oily, reddish chorizo. Next to it, lying like felled logs, were good ol' American sausage links with toast triangles piled on top. She set the plate down in front of me, and the eggs wiggled a little wave.

"Hey, you know anything about a little town about forty miles from here off Highway 99?" I asked. "It's not even a town. It's like a neighborhood or something. Maybe twenty-five houses all by themselves."

"Creepy quiet?"

"Yeah."

"Don't be going down there, honey. That's them Word of Our Savior people. Gonna go all Branch Davidian one of these days."

"It's a cult?"

"You better believe it. You go down there you're likely to end up wearing brand-new sneakers, drinking poisoned Kool-Aid, and going to meet your maker on the big spaceship in the sky. The county sheriff don't even like going down there."

"Great."

"They all run into their houses and pull down the blinds like you're gonna bite 'em or something. Got a neighbor that was trying to sell magazines door-to-door. That's who told me. What a waste of time that racket was. You want any hot sauce with that?"

"Yes, please."

She came back a minute later with hot sauce, the check, and four aspirin that she dropped next to my coffee cup.

"Been there," she said.

Always nice to know you really do look that bad.

Outside, the sky was bright and the sort of pure light blue that people paint nurseries. I sat in the car with a napkin and the pen I'd used to sign the credit card slip. I looked at my cell phone and then out the windshield for a while. An old woman with a cane in one hand and her husband's arm in the other stared at me as they shuffled and clomped past on their way to pancakes. They were both wearing dress pants, and her purple rayon blouse was tied at the neck with a big bow. I hit the speed dial. Jenny's voice mail picked up. I didn't leave a message. I was supposed to be the boss, the grown-up, the one with answers. I wasn't supposed to ask her what I should do.

Quick like pulling off a Band-Aid I dialed information and got the three numbers. I wrote them on the napkin and then tossed it in the glove box. Yesterday's white plastic sack from the drugstore was still in the passenger seat. I changed the bandage on my arm just to have something to do that wasn't thinking, then turned the car south, turned the radio up too loud, and headed home.

Hours later, showered and curled up in bed, I gave my full attention to the yellow legal pad on my lap. I'd been practicing this letter in my head for a year. I wanted to get it down now. There would be a lot to do at the end, and this wasn't the sort of thing you rushed. I would probably need to do several drafts.

Dear Richard,

I'm afraid things have gotten bad. I guess that's an understatement.

I tried all the medicines. I swear I did. I tried them until I couldn't remember if I'd eaten breakfast, until my face got puffy, until I was nauseated and dizzy, until I couldn't poop and I couldn't fuck.

The black just gets you, you know? It sneaks up behind you and drags you underwater. It holds you down there for as long as it wants until suddenly it lets go and you come shooting out like a cork. You'd think it would be better, having the highs to go with the lows, but it's so much worse. It makes you crazy. It makes you feel crazy, always waiting for the next swing. It scares people. It scared me. The black gets blacker and the highs get higher and you can't poop and you're all alone inside your head, and it's so fucked-up in there. You just get crazier and crazier like a train picking up speed, and you know something bad is going to happen.

It was time to jump off the train, Richard, before the brakes failed and somebody got hurt.

But it was good while it lasted, huh? Remember that time right after we got married when we had that crappy little apartment with no closets and the homeless guy that would sleep by the dryer? We were watching Wheel of Fortune because we were too poor to pay for cable, and we heard water dripping. We checked all the faucets, but we couldn't find it until you looked up and saw it coming out of the ceiling. Remember? And the whole thing just made this big crack, and it started to gush, just whoosh right into the living room like Niagara Falls. We were screaming and running around, carrying the TV outside with the plug dragging behind us, trying to save everything. You were great. You were great the whole time, and none of this is your fault. None of this is anyone's fault.

There is not one thing anyone should have done differently or should have seen coming. There was a cosmic spin of the genetic wheel, and I just lost is all. It just happened, and it could have been anybody and turned out to be me. I'm sorry I lied to you about being a different kind of sick, but I didn't want you to feel like you had to rush in and save me. I knew you'd want to, but you couldn't. It would've hurt both of us too much for you to try. But having this is like having a cancer. You just have this ticking time bomb that finally goes off. It's nobody's fault and everybody tries. When it's real cancer, everybody tries. There are medications like poisons, and your face gets puffy and you're nauseated and you're dizzy and you can't poop. And sometimes still it doesn't work. It gets so bad that everyone sees how much it hurts and that it's not going to get better. They have mercy on the patient in the bed, and they turn off the machines. They give them painkillers and make them comfortable, and when they go, everyone says it's a mercy.

It is a mercy, Richard.

Except, when you're sick in the head, nobody turns off the machines when the pain gets too bad, even when everyone knows it's not going to get better. They just keep pumping in the poison and telling you to talk about your pain like that's going to make it better, and eventually you just run out of things to say. It's the same pain all the time. All the time.

I just needed some mercy.

I'm sorry. I hope you understand and can forgive me someday.

Please visit Ramona's and my mother's graves if you can.

All my love,
Clementine

14 Days

I sat at the kitchen table. The sun was well on its way to precisely overhead. I had showered and then straightened my hair products, throwing out the ones I wouldn't be needing anymore. I wiped out the sink with a wad of toilet tissue and then went to the fridge for breakfast and spent some more time throwing out expired condiments. It occurred to me it would no longer be prudent to purchase unripe fruit. I made toast and then ate a Twinkie when the toast proved woefully inadequate. I made coffee and stood at the counter while it dripped. I did not look at my computer. I did throw a glance at the unfinished canvas across the studio.

I hated it. I hated everything about it, which was normal. Each piece has an emotional life cycle that plays out in my head. Inspiration, excitement, doubt, loathing, hope, determination, acceptance. I was hurtling through doubt and planting my feet firmly in loathing, which wasn't as upsetting as it used to be early in my career. I didn't know that was normal then. It took a few years for me to see this always happened and a few more to discover it happens to every artist. We all hate everything we do at one time or another. Eventually, we forgive ourselves for sucking so damn bad and go on because there's no other choice. They should teach that in art school.

I still didn't want to work on the piece of crap. Not at all. Never again. I would've thrown it out the window if it would fit through the opening, which it would not. That was too bad, because work was the last excuse I had not to sit down at the computer, and I didn't even have that.

I went to the desk in the corner that used to be Jenny's, a small wooden thing simple enough to have been made by Shakers, and opened the single center drawer. I took out the large spiral-bound book of checks, each with a stub attached for record keeping. It was half-empty, with just those little receipts left, all filled out neatly and completely in Jenny's looping hand. I wrote out a check for her to cover the night at the museum, put it in an envelope, added a stamp, and walked it down to the mailbox.

When I came back in, the computer glared at me from the kitchen table. There was no more avoiding it. I opened the browser and typed each of the three numbers I'd received into the cross directory. One came back Springfield, which a trip to the mapping function told me was down by the Ozark Mountains, spitting distance to Arkansas. I hadn't known Missouri had mountains and frankly remained skeptical. The other two numbers had the same area code and corresponded to two addresses in two different suburbs of Kansas City, Missouri. Chalk one up for the diner waitress.

I got up and poured another cup of coffee I didn't want, just to have something to do. Then I picked up the phone and dialed the first K.C. number as quickly as I could. My stomach felt like it was being pulled through a keyhole, and my brain dumped too much adrenaline into my bloodstream, which was not helpful. After two rings, a mechanical voice of the female persuasion picked up.

"The number you have dialed is no longer in service."

I was so relieved I wanted to laugh. It was the heady feeling of relief you get when they don't pick you from the jury pool, and you, unlike the rest of those suckers, are free to walk out into the sunshine. I knew it wasn't rational, but feelings aren't supposed to be.

I stood up and walked around the kitchen, just to work off some of the nervous energy, disturbing Chuckles who was making out with my ankles. Before the euphoria got out of hand, I dialed the last number and had only one ring to get nervous before an older woman picked up.

"Hello?" she said.

I hung up.

Shit.

I should've said something, asked some brilliant question that would let me know if I had the right number or not. Something really smart, like "Is Jerry home?"

Shit.

I couldn't call back. She had caller ID. She had to have caller ID. It's not even optional anymore. I had it, and I hadn't asked for it.

Shit.

I sat down in front of the computer's cross directory one more time and searched for a neighbor's address and phone number. Better prepared, I called that.

"Hello," I said when a man, who sounded middle-aged and possibly stoned, answered. "I'm calling from the IRS. We're investigating your neighbor, accountant Jerry Pritchard. Do you know Mr. Pritchard?"

"Whoa. The IRS is doing an internal investigation? Seriously?

Does this mean I'm not going to get a refund this year? Cause I told him those deductions were kosher."

I could feel my plan veering off the road and rumbling across open country, bumping over rocks and ruining the suspension.

"Is Mr. Pritchard your accountant?" I asked, cradling the phone against my shoulder and madly typing "Kansas City" and "IRS" into my search engine.

"I wouldn't call him my accountant. I shovel his driveway, and he does my taxes. I mean, he works for you guys. What more do you want? Dude has a bad back anyway. Couldn't leave him stranded in his garage not being able to get to work when the snow blows in, could I? That's not why you're investigating him, is it? He told me he couldn't take any money for doing it, and I didn't give him any. I would've shoveled his driveway anyway."

Hit after hit rolled up on my screen. Kansas City was one of the IRS's largest hubs. I clicked on an archived news article and read the stub. Brand-new facility. Almost twenty-eight acres. Just shy of four hundred million dollars. About a bajillion employees.

I rubbed the heel of my palm into my eye. Every accountant in four states must work there.

"You there?" the man asked.

"Thank you for your time," I said and hung up.

Smooth, Clementine.

I got up, found the pretty glass apothecary jar of prescription pot, and crumbled some into a rolling paper. When it was good and tight, I scrabbled around in the same drawer for the translucent purple disposable lighter and sparked it.

I held the smoke in my lungs and closed my eyes until it was time to breathe again. Then I let it out between my lips in a swirling jet stream.

Repeat.

Repeat.

Ahhhh.

I picked up the phone again, scrolled through the search results, and dialed. Twenty-eight acres of accountants somewhere in the Midwest. Twenty-eight acres of clean, gleaming floors and modern light fixtures. I pictured long, long hallways and men in ties at identical desks in huge rooms, rooms like football stadiums. I was transferred and transferred and transferred again, hopscotching my way from phone to phone across that grid of desks until it finally rang, and he picked up.

"Good afternoon. Jerry Pritchard speaking."

I looked at the clock. It was well into the afternoon there, two hours ahead of me. If I were there I'd be two hours closer to dying. He was probably thinking about going home. Thinking about what his wife would make for dinner. Maybe Salisbury steak. They probably ate a lot of Salisbury steak in a place like Kansas City. Maybe he was thinking about stopping at the store on the way home. Milk, eggs, butter, salt.

"Hello?"

He sounded older. Old. I hadn't been picturing him old. I'd been picturing him frozen in amber like a museum specimen. He wasn't the man who had left more than thirty years ago.

"It's Clementine," I said.

He didn't say anything.

"Clementine Pritchard."

"I . . . I don't have anything to say." His voice faltered and jumped, skipped like a warped record.

"How are you?" I asked.

"I don't want to talk to you."

He said it like a doctor might say, "I'm sorry. You have cancer," except he skipped the "sorry" part. I took another drag on the joint, because I had it burning there between my fingers. I hoped it would soothe me, but it didn't. I wished I hadn't called, and

I was going to cry, which made me feel like a little girl again. *Wham*. Just like that I was ten years old again, and the feeling of helplessness and dependence made me even angrier. Fuck him. Fuck him. Fuck him some more.

I went right for the big guns. "Mom is dead. Ramona, too. Did you know that? Did you know they died?" Take that, asshole.

"I can't talk about this. I'm at work."

Fuck him and his work.

"I want to fly out there," I said.

"No, no. You can't. That's not a good idea. I have to go."

I heard the click and the line go quiet. I hung on, though, just in case he picked up again. I hung on until the second click and the dial tone beeped in my ear.

Then I booked the tickets.

13 Days

The skin around my eyes had the texture of crepe paper. High-end crepe paper maybe, but I had some vague recollection of taut smoothness more like an inflated party balloon than a roll of colored streamers. I leaned in closer to the mirror, because who could resist getting a good look under the bright bathroom lighting. I stood back and then leaned in again.

Near.

Far.

Near.

Far.

Crap.

I shoved my feet into flip-flops and went out the front door wearing nothing but a white towel wrapped around me like a very short terry-cloth party dress. I knocked on my neighbor's door, didn't wait the customary ten seconds, and knocked again.

He answered the door looking like something Caligula would've wanted around for parties. His hair was dishwater blond and curly. The tan, I suspected, was augmented. He had biceps that stretched the armholes of his fitted gray T-shirt, which was tucked into the waistband of jeans that, if we can be frank, hugged his package like a stripper's thong.

He smiled. He had dimples. Of course he did.

"Did you lock yourself out?"

The lisp gave him away and broke the hearts of women all the way to Santa Barbara.

"I have old eyes. I need bangs."

"You are beautiful, as always, but you're lucky I specialize in crisis makeovers. Who's the boy?"

Brandon stepped aside so I could come in. He had lived next door for two years and had really prettied up the place. His decorating was okay, too. He was a hairdresser/dancer/sometime bartender.

"No boy."

"Bullshit."

He steered me over to his dining room table, pushed me into a chair, and then grabbed it by the two front legs and rotated it to face him. It was quite the manly show of strength, and I felt like I should fan myself with something.

We were in front of his bank of windows, which looked out on more or less the same view I had. The layout of his place was the same as mine, but it looked entirely different. His wasn't a work space at all, which left an extravagant amount of room for tables and chairs and sofas. He'd used double-sided bookcases to block off his bedroom area, which was three times the size of mine.

"Every woman gets a haircut after a breakup. Fresh start."

Losing Clementine 181

He kept his shears in a zippered black leather case, which he set down on the polished wooden table and unzipped. He took out his comb and spritzed my hair with water.

"Fun and wispy or china doll serious?" he asked.

"China doll."

"Oh, my. Some boy." He combed a hank of my hair down over my eyes, so I looked like Cousin Itt.

"There may have been two."

He paused in the middle of his separating and combing. "Two boys?"

"It's possible."

"Well, china doll it is."

The sound of shears through hair is a very specific sound, and I'd always hated it. Something between a crunch and a scrape. *Shrrrap. Shrrrap. Shrrap.* He combed and spritzed and trimmed, and when he was done he steered me into his bathroom, which had much kinder lighting than mine. My shoulder-skimming black bob now had a triangular segment of fringe that peaked at a perfectly straight part and widened out across my forehead, stopping just barely above my eyebrows. I looked as if I needed a scarlet silk kimono and a cigarette holder. I looked as if I had secrets and men, plenty of both.

"I love it and you," I said, turning and kissing his cheek, and I meant it. "How much?"

"Not a dime. This crisis is on me."

I went back to my own poorly lit bathroom, glowing with transformation.

I took a black dress out of the closet. It was sleeveless and cut high in the front and plunging in the back. I dropped it over my head and wiggled so it slinked down my body. I took down the shoe box into which I'd thrown little clutch handbags and other rarely used accessories. On top was a white silk spider mum as big as my fist with wisps of white feathers sprouting out in all directions. I blew bits of fluffy gray dust off of it and took it into the bathroom.

With the alligator clip, I pulled back a lock of hair and attached the big showy flower over my ear. It was almost enough to distract from the stubborn bits of paint staining my cuticles.

A photographer snapped my picture in the living room. I hadn't seen it coming. It was like being ambushed. I blinked in the dim light, trying to get my stunned pupils to readjust.

"What the hell was that?" I asked my host.

Annabelle shrugged and took a sip of the rose champagne bubbling in her flute. I had a matching glass and was one good-size sip away from draining it.

"The *Times* society section sent someone."

"He should have a bell around his neck."

Annabelle has a way of laughing at your jokes that makes you certain you are much funnier than you really are. It's a sharp political skill, which she deploys often on her husband's behalf. She is older than me and looks younger, thanks to some very subtle surgery. It was her house that I and several hundred of my closest friends were milling about in.

The house sat up in the Hollywood Hills on one of those impossible grades where you have to drop your car into first gear to make it up the driveway and everything at the top costs at least five million dollars. That night there were valets to meet guests by the side of the road. Four Hispanic men in orange vests and black pants grabbed keys and drove off into the residential neighborhood, running back uphill for the next car. They did it again and again until sweat dripped into their eyes and they had to wipe it away with the backs of their hands before going on the next wind sprint.

All the blinds were open, making each windowpane glow yellow against the navy sky and matching monochromatic hills. Voices had trickled down the driveway as I'd walked halfway up the hill, cursed, pulled off my high heels, and made the rest of the trip barefoot. The calm, modulated buzz made it clear even from a distance that this party would never get out of hand. For a moment I wondered if I could just watch from outside, looking into the glowing panes getting brighter and brighter as the sky darkened. I wondered if one of the uniformed waiters would bring a drink to me out in the bushes and maybe a blanket to sit on.

Inside, Annabelle was talking, and I wasn't listening. She was wearing a silky, bright printed dress that dropped into a deep V in the front and swished loose around her knees. Her skin had the same dark tan as Aunt Trudy's with none of the wrinkling and speckling. I wondered if she had it sprayed on with an airbrush gun, and if so, did she do it naked?

My brain dropped back into the conversation.

"I see someone I must go say hello to," she said. "Kiss me."

I went for her cheek, but she caught me on the lips and then slipped off, leaving a trail of vanilla perfume behind her.

"Clementine."

I turned, saw who had spoken, and then did drain my glass. "Director."

He stepped sideways to slip between guests and made his way around a white couch and an end table holding a reproduction Ming vase.

"You look very nice this evening," he said.

"Thank you."

Apparently keeping me locked up in the employee break room put us on friendly terms.

"Your piece was brilliant. Did you see the story in the paper?"

"No, not yet."

"I'll send you a copy. It's very complimentary. Lots of great photos. Almost the whole front of the arts section."

It already seemed like a long time ago.

"I think it worked out for everyone," he said.

"Please excuse me," I said. "I see someone I have to say hello to."

Without leaving a wake of vanilla behind me, I slipped out the sliding glass doors onto the wide flagstone patio that surrounded the pool. I was still barefoot, having dropped my shoes by the front door when I came in, and the stones were warm under my feet. The air had given up its afternoon heat much more quickly than the stones, and propane lamps stood ready to be lit at the first sign of a shivering guest. To my left was one of several bars, and I made my way to it, holding up my empty glass. By the time I got there, the bartender had pulled the champagne bottle with its white napkin bib out of the silver ice bucket and was holding it aloft, waiting to pour.

I brought the full glass to my lips, but before I could take the first sip, a young man stepped up beside me. He had the first three buttons of his white dress shirt open.

"I saw you talking to Director Kirby," he said.

It's an advantage to have an accent, in his case a musical Irish lilt. It keeps you from having to start by saying something interesting.

"Actually, he was talking to me." I finished tipping the glass into my mouth. The champagne was lip-puckeringly dry. I liked it. Maybe too much.

The air up here was clean and still and the night darker above the ambient glow that kept Los Angeles from ever really getting dark. I looked up. You still couldn't quite see the stars, but I imagined it might be possible on another night. I took another sip.

He ordered a gin and tonic, which in my opinion tastes far too much like gin.

"Then you have an excuse," he said. "I'm William."

"Clementine," I said and took his hand, which was no bigger than mine. Nothing about him, in fact, was bigger than anything on me. I was looking down at the part in his hair.

"Men must stare at you all the time," he said.

I cocked my head and felt my bangs shift and tickle my forehead.

"You're a six-foot-tall doll come to life. Even"— he looked down—"barefoot."

Men should tell all women they're beautiful and stop. Details always ruin things. The small girl feels too small. The tall girl feels too tall. And no one wants to be told she looks good in glasses. I had the sudden feeling my limbs had been stretched another foot and that perhaps I should duck to avoid ceilings.

"And you're a leprechaun," I said.

He threw his head back and laughed in the way you're supposed to at your own expense, just to show you're a sport.

"I had that coming," he said.

He did, and we fell into silence. I waited for him to wander away like you do at parties. My stomach growled. I kept an eye out for a waiter.

Out past the pool there was a wide landing strip of grass that ended abruptly where the top of the hill dropped into a ravine. A white movie screen had been set up to one side, and pillows the size of coffee tables were spread out on the manicured lawn. A few young women, who reminded me of ponies, stretched out lanky brown limbs on the cushions and laughed. I felt as if someone should come by to rinse down their withers and feed them sugar cubes. Someone, metaphorically, no doubt would.

William watched them, too. And I watched him watch them. He was about their age, young enough to still be in college or just graduated from college. Maybe he was on his postgrad world tour, backpacking through the Hollywood Hills.

He took another sip and turned away from the horse barn.

"So are you here because of your abiding love of independent documentaries?"

"I'm here because Annabelle let me sleep on her couch for three months when I moved to L.A. from New York, which turns out not to be the sort of debt that's easily paid in a mere fifteen years." That should've given him some idea of how old I was.

Annabelle was throwing the party in honor of a friend's husband's new movie. Before this, the husband had been a sous-chef in one of those red-hot-for-five-minutes fusion restaurants near La Brea. Now he was a director. The wife did and still does work for Disney, which provided the sort of dental insurance and 401(k) necessary to support a spouse with career ADD.

The film was about genocide in Darfur, which was probably more timely when he started shooting than when he finished. Rumor had it George Clooney was in it, and that the director's wife had arranged that.

"Tom and I were in film school together at USC," he said.

In L.A., that was a throwaway brag. USC is to film school as Harvard is to law.

"If you're a cinema brat," I said, "how do you know Kirby?"

"He's my dad."

That was the funniest thing I'd heard in days. I put the back of my hand to my mouth and snorted, which turned into a guffaw, which sent champagne up into my nasal cavity, which made my eyes tear up, which made him laugh, which is funny in an Irish

Losing Clementine 187

accent, and soon my cheek muscles ached and I had a stitch in my side and people were staring.

When we settled into snickers, William wiped his eyes. "It's true. I mean sure he's a kiss-ass wanker now, but twenty-five years ago, he was stud enough to knock up my mum on holiday."

That answered the question of his age, but the trials of a single mother were less amusing. We both settled into a postgiggle valley of conversation.

"So," he went on, "I didn't much know him until I came to the States. He sent checks for my schooling but never came for a visit or anything. Then I showed up in Los Angeles, and we started having lunch on campus."

I imagined PR-conscious Kirby trying to smooth things over with his long-lost love child. I wondered if he'd gotten William any coverage in the *Times*.

We hit the low point in the valley. "So," he said, breaking the quiet, "what do you do?"

"I go looking for appetizers on a toothpick," I said. "Thanks for the giggles."

I snagged a couple of pork *shumai* from a passing tray, left my empty glass on an inlaid sofa table, and turned my attention to finding the bathroom. The one I found was occupied, so I wandered up the stairs, which were tiled and curved along with the wall. At the top, I could see down to the crowd below. I leaned over the railing and watched Annabelle glide from group to group. Her husband was standing in a corner, talking seriously to the one man in the crowd wearing a suit.

Annabelle and I had had a fling during my couch-surfing months. It was the midnineties, and everyone was doing something to show they were cool. I had been Annabelle's something. As far as I knew, her husband didn't know. She had been a painter for a while. That's how I'd met her. Now she was a wife and a patron, which suited her better but still seemed a letdown.

I pushed off the rail and continued down the hall.

I put my hand on the levered doorknob and turned. It moved less than a quarter inch and stopped. Locked. I hadn't yet removed my hand when the door pulled back, and Elaine Sacks looked out at me.

We both froze. Her curly hair was pulled back in a loose knot that let small ringlets curl around her face. She looked like the cover of a Jane Austen novel, which is false advertising if I've ever seen it.

"Sorry," I said, which came out over her words, "Congratulations on the Walton show," so the whole thing was "*Garble-garble*—ations on the Walton show."

It took a second to know what to do with that.

"Thanks," I said.

She stood for a moment as if there might be more to say. Then again, maybe she just couldn't get around me.

I stepped aside, and she slipped out and quickly down the hall. I watched her go. I couldn't believe I hadn't punched her. I couldn't believe Annabelle had invited her. I couldn't believe Elaine hadn't screamed about her painting and the gallery window and the article in the *Times*. It was an unexpected retreat, and I didn't like it. It was unsettling.

I went into the bathroom and looked in the mirror to see what she saw. The giant flower looked ridiculous, like I was posing for a Hawaiian Tourist Bureau poster. I took it out and tossed it in the trash can, tucking the ends of my bob behind my ears before lifting my skirt to do my business.

Back downstairs everyone was drifting out to the pool, and a projector had been set up. I picked up another glass of champagne from a waiter and stepped off the flagstone patio and into the grass, which felt soft and tickly on my bare feet.

"Clementine." I looked down, and Irish Eyes was looking up at me. He patted the empty spot beside him. "I've been saving it for you."

I doubted that, but the long-limbed fillies were all still grouped together several rows ahead, so what the hell?

I gathered my skirt under me and sat, careful not to slosh out any of my drink. The bottoms of my feet were so dirty they looked like they'd been fingerprinted. A waiter slid over and offered us paper cones of popcorn, which, because it was Hollywood, had been sprinkled with some kind of herb.

I scanned the crowd. Elaine was sitting on a chaise by the pool talking to an older woman I didn't recognize.

"Where's your dad?" I asked.

"He's always the first to leave a party."

The outdoor lights dimmed, the projector flickered on, and everyone but me clapped. My hands were full of champagne and popcorn. The ground was too uneven to set the flute down, and I had to use my lips and tongue to fish out the kernels.

I sat cross-legged, while William lounged back on his elbows, one leg out straight, the other bent and lying flat on the ground like a homoerotic underwear ad. The screen flickered with images of burning Sudanese villages and militia members riding camels and horses. A well-known black actor was doing the voice-over. William put his hand on my bare back. On-screen, the body of an old woman was being wrapped in brightly colored cloth for burial. William used the tips of his fingers to trace circles on my skin. Goose bumps popped up on my arms. Girls in flowing skirts and rubber flip-flops went in search of firewood while the narrator's voice warned of the rape and torture—as though those were two different things—they faced. William let his fingers drift under the fabric, and I felt the panel of my underwear dampen. Aid workers were being interviewed.

William tugged on my arm, and I leaned over.

"Want to get out of here?" he asked.

12 Days

His apartment turned out to be a bedroom with a hot plate and a stand-up shower near Hollywood and Highland, where the stars get down on their hands and knees in cement.

"I have a refrigerator, too." His lips were still pressed to mine, and his breath and words went straight into my mouth.

And so he did. It was the sort of fridge that comes standard in dorm rooms—two feet tall and just big enough to hold a six-pack and some yogurt. His had a microwave balanced on top of it. There were dirty socks on the bed, and I was lying on them with both of his hands up under my dress.

The truth was I had liked this better at the party. When we were talking, I could feel mature and urbane. Now I wondered if he had noticed that my butt was dimply and my upper arms were losing their elasticity. I was not a long-legged filly. I was more like glue fodder.

For obvious reasons, I'd soaked my brain in two manhattans after leaving the party and before lying down on a pile of unwashed laundry. I was drunk enough that when I closed my eyes the room would spin, so I left them open while he pulled down my underwear and settled himself between my legs. His tongue was warm and soft, and he used it gently at first as though he was asking permission.

I looked up at the ceiling and then over at the dresser while he worked. There was a stereo and a pile of CDs. I squinted in the dim light to read their spines. Tupac was heavily featured. Next to that were a few bottles of liquor, including the three wise men, Johnnie, Jack, and Jim. A photo of William with a blond pixie of a thing was framed on the nightstand. I was guessing not his sister. On the far wall hung a large flat screen television worth more than everything else in the room combined.

"You're not into this."

I looked down. When had he stopped?

"I suppose I'm not."

"Is there anything I can do different?"

"Age twenty years." That was out of my mouth before I could stop it. "Sorry."

He rolled over on his side and rested his head on his palm. "It was worth a try, yeah?"

"Yeah," I agreed.

Poor kid was still in his dress shirt and trousers, which were fitting snug in the crotch.

"You want to spend the night?"

Oh God, I really did not want to spend the night. The booze would soon start to leave my bloodstream and leach out through my pores, leaving me all too aware of my surroundings. The air smelled of something that could have been microwave burritos mixed with cigarette smoke, and I was about to have to use the bathroom, which I wasn't looking forward to. Seeing it all in the smog-diffused sunrise was more than I could bear.

"Can I have a glass of water?" I asked. "Can I have three?"

He fetched a cold bottle out of the minifridge, which did not, as it turned out, contain any yogurt. I opened it and drank. The bathroom was not the horror show that it could have been. There were no cigarette stubs in the toilet or pubic hair in the sink. Used condoms did not lie gushily on the floor of the shower. It did have the moldy smell of poor ventilation, no window, and the approximate square footage allotted airplane lavatories. I peed and washed my hands and straightened myself, all without facing my reflection.

When I stepped out, he was stretched out on the bed with the television on. Jon Stewart was behind an anchor desk. We watched it together while I finished two and a half bottles of grocery-store-brand water, which was the kind I bought, too.

Each gulp brought more and more sobriety until I was pretty sure I could stand on one foot and touch my nose.

My shoes were on the floor, and I slipped them on. Barefoot at Annabelle's was one thing. Barefoot walking down the sidewalk in this neighborhood was another. William walked me to the front door of his building and kissed both cheeks good-bye.

Cars were parked nose to tail on both sides of the street, and the sidewalk was cracked and uneven where tree roots had broken through. The buildings were close together, all stucco with the arched doorways and tiled roofs of L.A. architecture. Some of them were pretty, even in their worn, decayed states. Vacancy signs were posted in upper-floor windows, and the grass had been worn to the sandy, unfertile dirt below.

I was less than a block off the main roadway but walking deeper into the neighborhood. I'd circled twice before finding parking. Sounds of traffic and late-night commerce faded as I walked, and quieter residential noises, fewer and farther between, took over. A car door slammed on another block. Two voices argued then laughed as I walked past a group of shirtless men smoking on a porch. My shoes *click, click, clicked* on the concrete like the sound effects in a monster movie before the ominous music starts to swell. I tried not to think about that.

I found my car, drank the last of my bottle of water, and climbed in.

I was close enough to the freeway to see the entrance sign when the yowl of the siren startled me. I glanced down at the speedometer. Ten miles per hour over. *Crap.* I looked in the rearview mirror. He was right on my tail, lights flashing, turning the siren on and off so it yelped like a wounded puppy instead of the long blare of an emergency chase.

I pulled over, turned off the engine, and fumbled for my driver's license and registration. I wiped my sweaty hands on my dress, which had no doubt picked up the aroma of microwave burrito. When he got to my window, I handed him my identification. He read it and my registration and took them both with him back to his car.

I waited. The dashboard clock read 2:14. I dug in my purse for a petrified piece of gum and crammed it in my mouth. I checked the rearview mirror again. No movement.

2:20.

2:29.

2:34.

My body didn't know whether to get less nervous or more nervous as time went by, but sitting still was becoming unbearable. Would it be considered a sign of aggression to knock on his window? Could he have had a stroke sitting in his cruiser? What were the odds he was in desperate need of CPR at the very moment I was tapping my thumbs on the steering wheel?

It was after the thirty-minute point that worry began to morph into anger. It crept up the back of my neck and flushed my cheeks. This was not how I wanted to spend the time I had left. I put my hand back on the keys still dangling from the ignition and checked the rearview mirror one last time.

He was stepping out of his car.

My annoyance did not abate.

"Ma'am," he said, when he got back to my window, "have you been drinking tonight?"

Trick question.

"Not so that it's a problem," I said.

"Would you step out of the car, please?"

The breathalyzer read 1.0, only 0.2 over the legal limit. I felt pretty good about that under the circumstances.

"You're going to have to hire a lawyer," Richard said. "Your insurance is going to go through the roof. You'll probably lose your license."

"Technically, I already lost it." I held up the piece of paper I'd been issued in lieu of my real California ID.

"Jesus Christ, Clementine. Why couldn't you have just stayed wherever the fuck you were?"

"He was young enough to be my kid. He had a studio apartment with no kitchen. It smelled like burritos."

The vein in the side of Richard's neck bulged, and he didn't look at me. "That was fast."

I leaned my head back against the seat. Sunrise was no more than an hour away. I was so tired my eyes itched, and moving my arms seemed like too much work. Richard took the on-ramp too fast, and my shoes rolled around on the floorboard.

"What's fast?"

"You were just in bed with me a week ago!"

"It was two weeks ago. Stop yelling."

"Out of one bed and into the other."

"Hey, screw you. You going to tell me you've stopped sleeping with Sheila out of respect for our little fling?"

Richard didn't say anything.

"That's what I thought."

We drove in heavy silence down the freeway. Even at this undefined hour, too late for night but too early for morning, cars were in every lane. Where were all these people going? I wasn't complaining. I liked how the city was always in motion at all hours, no matter what.

"You cut your hair."

I jerked my head up off my chest. I was asleep enough to drop my head and awake enough to know it.

"What?"

"You cut your hair. I like it."

We were nearing my exit.

"Is that ex-husband-speak for 'Sorry I called you a slut'?"

"I didn't call you a slut. I wouldn't say that. I just like your hair."

He was wearing sweatpants, flip-flops, and a giveaway T-shirt advertising a software company. His hair looked like he'd been running his hands through it the wrong way, and there was just enough product left in it from the day before to make it stick like that.

When he pulled up to the curb, I unbuckled my seat belt. "Tell Sheila I'm sorry I woke her up."

"She wasn't there."

"Okay."

He didn't say anything else, and I didn't, either. Maybe she was on a trip. Maybe she'd taken to pitching a tent in the backyard. Maybe she'd entered a fugue state. It wasn't my business.

I gathered up my shoes and climbed out. He rolled down the passenger-side window, and I leaned down to look in.

Losing Clementine 197

"You could've been hurt," he admonished. "You could've hurt someone else."

"I was barely over the limit. I wasn't impaired."

"You've never been a very good judge of that."

"Are we still talking about booze?" I asked.

"No," he said and rolled up the window.

11 Days

The phone rang, and the number showed the call box on the front of the building.

"Son of a bitch," I told Chuckles. "They're early."

I picked up the receiver and punched the access code to unlock the door.

The buffalo piece was on the floor. The animal was filled in, what you could still see clearly of it. I'd slept until noon the day before, taken a taxi to get my car out of impound, and then come home to work. I'd taken the widest brush I could find, like a housepainter's brush, and dipped it in bright red paint thinned to make it translucent. Then I'd made the animal bleed. All afternoon and evening I'd paced around it, adding gore, creating a scene of pain and destruction. The bucking outline of the animal that before could've been a defiant leap was now a death throe, and I was happy with it. It leaned against the wall, and a fresh, primed canvas with its first coat of paint was on the easel.

I hadn't showered since before going to Annabelle's. I was

wearing jeans and a black tank top I'd found on the floor. I had red paint settled into my nails and the wrinkles of my hands up to my elbows. I had it on my pants and a smear across my boobs. I even had some in my hair from when I'd pushed it out of my face.

I'd stopped yesterday only to eat a little dinner and to answer the e-mail of a man from Silver Lake who wanted to meet Chuckles. He was supposed to come by at noon. By then I was planning on looking a little less as if I'd recently dismembered a body. Chuckles, who was on the verge of going feral, was going to be brushed, probably with my own comb, as I had no idea where Jenny kept his—or frankly if he even had one of his own. She could've been using my toothbrush to groom between his toes for all I knew. I had, in a moment of grandeur, imagined giving him a bath, but the mania dissipated, and I decided to just spray him down with room deodorizer instead.

But it was just after eleven, and all I'd done was add a coat of orange paint to my fingers. There was nothing to do but man the battle stations and hope for the best. I ran for the bathroom and lathered up to my elbows, leaving a sink full of sunset-colored bubbles. I sniffed my armpits, detected telltale, day-two musk, and added more deodorant. I snagged the Spring Fresh spray off the toilet tank, found Chuckles sunbathing in a pile of dust and crumbs on the kitchen floor, picked him up, brushed him off as best I could, and squirted his belly with the cold aerosol, which had the unintended consequence of pissing him off no end.

He turned his squished face to mine, yowled, and used his back feet to disembowel my bare bicep. Then, like a porcupine shooting quills, he let loose enough white fur to assemble a new, better-tempered cat, which stuck all over my black tank top.

By the time I got to the door, still clutching him, we were

both furious, and one of us was bleeding. At least I could lie and say it was paint.

"Hey, there. I . . ." The words died in my mouth.

Elaine Sacks was standing in the hall with her hands shoved in the oversized patch pockets of her tunic. She'd showered and was probably wearing perfume that didn't come from a poop-stink-no-more can.

"You can't have Chuckles."

It was the first thing that came to mind, and he reiterated the point by slamming his back jackrabbit feet into my gut and launching himself out of my arms, making for the space under the bed without a single paw touching the floor.

"What?"

"You didn't answer the ad about the cat?"

"No."

It would've been a lame prank, signing Paul to the bottom of an e-mail about a soon-to-be-orphaned animal.

She was wearing black leggings underneath a button-down gray top, which was long enough to have been a dress. Her brown curls were pinned back in a low ponytail, and she wore black ballet slippers, all of which made her look more fragile, vulnerable, and feminine than I preferred to think she was. I preferred to think of her as not unlike Chuckles on a bad day except taller and with less shedding.

"Can I come in?"

"Why?"

I was genuinely asking.

"I thought we could talk. There are some things I want to say."

The ground underneath me felt unsure. I wanted to check for traps. I turned my wrist as though to look at a watch that wasn't there.

"I have company coming in an hour."

"I'll be quick," she promised.

I turned and walked back inside, leaving the door open for her. I threw a drop cloth over the buffalo, which wasn't yet completely dry. I hoped it wouldn't hurt it.

She saw me, and I didn't care that she saw me. The other pieces, the ones that never went to the show, were stacked up, too. Those I left out in the open in defiance.

She stood in the entryway, unsure of what to do with herself. I pointed to the kitchen table, which was covered by my computer, newspapers, mail, and other debris that needed a place to land. She pulled out one of the chairs and sat down.

"Do you want anything to drink?" I asked.

She shook her head, which was just as well. The only things I had were water and soda from the grocery delivery boy.

I sat down several feet away from her on one of the stools pushed up to the kitchen island.

"So talk," I said.

She crossed her arms across her flat chest.

"First I want to say that I know you were the one who did what you did at the Taylor."

"How do you know that?" I asked.

"Everyone knows that."

I didn't say anything. I let the room go quiet and just sat and watched and waited for what she'd say next.

"The insurance covered it."

I laughed. I couldn't help myself. "Well, great," I said. "At least someone called State Farm. That just settles it all then."

"I'm trying to put this behind me. I'd like for you to, too."

"Why should I?"

"What?" she said, dropping her arms to her sides. "Property

crimes, destroying art, running a smear campaign in the paper wasn't enough?"

"I didn't have a damn thing to do with that article. I didn't even talk to the reporter. If you read it, you'd know that. And none of it changes the fact that you stole from me."

"Artists create similar work all the time. Cultural zeitgeist influences us in unconscious ways. Whole schools of artists—"

"Oh, shut the fuck up."

I slid off the stool, went to the fridge, opened it, didn't know why I'd done that, and slammed it again. "Save your tired-ass art school bullshit for the buyers, Elaine. You've been watching me for twenty fucking years. When I changed materials, you changed materials. When I went primitive, you went primitive. When I signed with the Taylor, you signed with the Taylor. Now I'm quitting, so what the fuck are you going to do for the rest of your career?"

She couldn't have looked more surprised if I'd smacked her square in the face with a cast-iron frying pan, which considering our relationship wouldn't have seemed that surprising to me.

"You're not quitting. You went and tagged your own exhibit. That's even more publicity. You're not quitting."

I wondered if I could get her to say "You're not quitting" again.

"It wasn't about publicity."

"It's always about publicity." She recrossed her arms.

I looked at the clock on the wall. I needed to change, find the cat, and possibly shove some tranquilizers down his throat.

"That's why you are where you are," I said, and for a moment I felt sorry for her because she would never see it.

"They want you back at the Taylor after you do those"—she pointed at the pile of paintings on the floor—"at the Contemporary."

She put her elbows up on a bare spot and spun a pencil I had lying on a stack of papers. We were both quiet. Everything began to make sense and not in a good way.

"Carla asked you to make nice, didn't she?"

"Yes."

"What do you get out of it?"

"If you come back, I can stay."

"She said that?"

"She implied it was in my best interest."

"You're doing a piss-poor job."

"I get that impression."

There was, I had to admit, something nice about being wanted.

"I'm not coming back."

"Why not?"

"I told you, I'm quitting."

"You can't quit. You're still working." She nodded toward the buffalo under the sheet.

"That's different," I said. "That's for me."

"We all say that. We're like junkies, all of us. We can't let go of it." She leaned back in her chair. She was more relaxed than I'd ever seen her. I still hated her on principle, but we were no longer lionesses circling each other in a cage. I wasn't sure when that had happened. I tried to remember the last few sentences, but still couldn't pinpoint it.

"I'm hungry," she said, looking around like there might be something edible within reach. "You want to get lunch or something? We could call a gentleman's truce long enough to eat."

"Why would we do that?"

She cocked her head. "You're an interesting woman, Clementine. Don't you want to see what happens when we stop spitting at each other? We can always start up again afterward. It's just a temporary truce."

"You're going to poison my food, aren't you?"

Her face broke in half, and she laughed so hard I thought she might never stop. It's bad form to laugh at your own jokes, but watching her I couldn't help myself.

"I've got an appointment," I said. "I can meet you in an hour."

"I have to run some errands anyway. Where do you want to meet?"

"Dim sum?"

"I love dim sum."

"Everyone loves dim sum. They put coke in the dumpling wrappers."

She smiled.

Paul showed up at noon. I managed to wrangle Chuckles out from under the bed, but he'd never been a lap cat and saw no reason to start making exceptions then. I tried giving him a stern look, but that hasn't worked on any cat in recorded history. Mostly it just encourages them to throw up on the carpet.

I asked Paul, who was seated on the couch, if he'd ever owned a cat before.

Oh yes, he said, many of them.

How many?

He was evasive. It was so hard to keep track.

I asked him if he had any other cats at the moment.

Oh yes, he said, many of them.

How many?

"Oh, you know how they can just multiply on you."

"What? Like in *Gremlins*? Did you feed them after midnight?"

He blinked at me. I guess he'd never seen the movie.

Losing Clementine 205

I thanked him for coming and told him we'd be in touch. I was pretty sure he smelled like urine.

"See?" I told Chuckles when he'd gone. "I told you. Kitten hoarder."

Chuckles turned his back on me and disappeared inside his covered litter box. There was scratching, which I took to be his form of social commentary.

If this kept up, I'd have to share the poison with him the way the Egyptian pharaohs did with their cats.

"How did it go?" Elaine asked.

"He smelled like pee."

She shrugged like this could happen to anyone.

She'd already been seated when I walked into the cavernous Dim Sum House. We were at a table meant to hold eight, which was the only size table they had. A white pot of tea hot enough to sterilize surgical instruments was in the center. Elaine had poured some into our little handleless teacups, and it had sloshed out onto the tablecloth, which always happened to me, too.

"I haven't had tea in a while," I said. "I threw my cups out the window."

"I once threw a VCR out a window," she said. "In college. It belonged to a guy."

She didn't ask how the cups had offended me. I appreciated that. Manic episodes were hard to explain.

Small Asian women in matching black pants and red vests pushed steaming metal carts around the crowded dining room, which was large enough for a regulation football field. They pushed the carts up to our table and began opening the round silver containers to display their wares. English was limited. "Shrimp" or "Pork," they would sometimes inform us. Other times it was up to your experience and best guess. It didn't much matter. Everything was good except the chicken feet, which were easy to spot. Most everything else was dumplings. When you made your selections, the dim sum girls would put a stamp on your bill indicating the charge for each item. This was impossible to read by anyone except the waiters, who wandered around the floor bringing more tea and spicy chili sauce and totaling receipts. You couldn't spend more than thirty dollars on a meal whether you were feeding two people or the full retinue of eight.

We chose four different dishes to start.

"So what are you going to do next?" I asked.

"You mean now that I don't have you to copy off?"

"That's exactly what I mean," I said.

She either let it go or accepted it as fact.

"I'm doing a series of nudes," she said.

I concentrated on picking up a barbecued pork bun with my chopsticks. After decades in L.A., I should've been better with them, but they were so damn inefficient. The bun was sticking to the little piece of parchment paper protecting it from the metal serving dish. No amount of chopstick wrangling could free it.

"I'd like you to pose for me," Elaine said.

I gave up and used my fingers.

"What?"

"I'd like you to pose nude for me."

You'd think, having been in the art world since I was eighteen and having known a number of lothario painters, that someone would've asked me this before. They hadn't.

"Did Carla ask you to ask me that, too?"

"Nope," she said and picked up a sweet taro ball filled with bean paste. "I just thought of it."

"Now that would be good publicity for you."

She smiled and put half the ball in her mouth. It took her a second to chew it. Those things have a gummy texture that gets in your teeth and hangs up in your throat. They're not for everyone.

"It would," she agreed. "But it would also be cool. You're retired now anyway." She took a sip of the no-longer-volcanic tea to wash down the rest of the bean paste. "What do you care?"

I had to admit it might be satisfying. I tore off a quarter of the pork bun and put it in my mouth.

"Let me think about it," I said.

The woman pushing the dessert cart drifted past. Hers was the only see-through cart, and inside were mostly gelatin-based items, many of which were layered and multicolored like a box of crayons. Several had paper umbrellas stuck in them. Never, not once, had I seen anyone order anything off of that cart. It was the saddest job at Dim Sum House.

"You've got time," Elaine said.

"Less than you'd think."

10 Days

I spent the morning drafting another online ad.

> Whole house sale. Everything must go. Furniture,
> kitchen appliances, clothing, dishes, and more.
> Must see to believe. 10 A.M. tomorrow until it's
> gone or I get tired. Whichever comes first.

I read it to Chuckles, who'd found another pile of dust and
crumbs to lie in. We had another appointment with potential
adopters in a couple of hours, this one off-site, so he was getting ready. Maybe he'd roll around in paint or fall in the toilet
later.

I posted the ad and walked over to the easel with a piece
of toast between my teeth. I had a cup of coffee in one hand
and a charcoal pencil in the other, and I started to sketch.
The buffalo, which was still under canvas against the wall,
felt like a rough draft, just a way to get where I wanted to go.

I took my time drawing the body of a cow on the new canvas. Then, coming out of the forelimbs and the back where the chest and neck and head would start to appear, I drew human parts. It morphed into the torso of a cowboy complete with shirt and hat and maybe, for whimsy, a cigarette. Maybe the Marlboro Man. I sketched and sketched and changed my mind and drew a new line here and there, and then I set the charcoal down on the table and walked off toward the shower. My coffee was long cold, and I left it on the table, too.

Chuckles was in the passenger seat and yowling in his box. He tried to stick a white paw through the grated front at a stop-light, and I reached down and touched the soft fur. We still had each other for a few more days. He could lie in all the crumbs he wanted. He got a few toes through a hole and let me pet them. We were like prisoner and girlfriend holding our hands up on either side of the bulletproof glass. I could see him looking up through the air holes in the top of the crate, and something in my chest squeezed. I loved him. I really did. I loved that squished-up face and that he never cared that I was crazy. I liked having a warm body in the apartment. I loved him like he was people. I loved him like he was Jenny or Richard. And this was so much harder than anything else I'd had to do so far.

I took a deep breath.

"So those are your new people," I told him. "You be nice and don't scratch too much furniture. It looked expensive." My throat was gumming up and a knot like a giant rubber band ball was forming. Hot tears gathered on my bottom lashes and dripped down my cheeks. "That brown chair in the corner was crap, though, so have a go at that. Okay?"

Meow.

"Yeah?" I laughed, just one chuckle through the snotty sobbing. "I love you, okay? Don't forget me."

The door to my studio was open and Brandon was backing in, carrying the last two of his dining chairs from next door. His table was already pushed up against mine in the middle of the floor. His was a rectangle and mine a circle, so the arrangement looked like a banjo. He placed the chairs in the remaining spots and shrugged.

"Not exactly *Architectural Digest*, but at least we'll all fit," he said. "I'll bring flowers."

"Thank you."

I had menus spread out across the top of my worktable, lying over stacks of cut-up magazines and propped up against pots of gesso. I was marking them up with a black Sharpie, trying to pick my favorite dishes from each restaurant. It was harder than I thought it was going to be. Food tasted so much different now. I had missed out on a lot over the years.

Brandon read over my shoulder for a minute before bumping my arm with his. "Why didn't you tell me sooner?"

I turned my face up to his and kissed him on the cheek. It's easy to love people you need nothing from. "There was nothing you could do."

"I would've been a better neighbor," he said.

"You're a perfect neighbor. You cut my hair for free and bring me furniture."

"I have loud sex."

I smiled and circled the fried chicken.

"Really? I never noticed."

He crossed his arms and affected a pout. "I don't know how to take that."

"Don't be late for dinner," I told him. "I'm counting on you for eye candy."

He left, and I called Jenny, who was picking up the food. "Do you have a pen? Write this down."

The boyfriend, Ray, didn't stay, which saved me the trouble of asking him to leave. He came up with Jenny to help carry the bags. He had black hair and dark skin of indeterminate origin, which made him her physical opposite.

"I saw you in the *Times*," he said.

I made a noncommittal noise.

"I don't do art on command or commission," he said. "I think a piece done that way should be more rightly called a craft. Don't you think?"

I put my hands in my pockets and cocked my head. "I think I was in the *Times* and you weren't, so I don't really give a damn what you call it. But since you were trying to be insulting, I think you should apologize to Jenny. It was just as much her craft as mine." I nodded toward the kitchen. "You can leave the food over there."

The red blush bloomed out from under Jenny's collar and rushed up her neck to her cheeks.

"No offense," Ray said to me.

I didn't reply, and he didn't make the apology I'd asked for.

He left the paper bags on the counter and left without kissing Jenny.

Shortly after, Jeremy, my favorite professor, came and brought his new husband, Mark, and two bottles of wine, a red and a white. Jeremy beamed at me through his round, black-framed spectacles.

"W-w-w-will you show me what you're working on later?" he whispered.

I promised him I would.

Jenny was in the kitchen plating appetizers, and I took the wine in to her and set it on the counter. Her hair was falling out of the clip again. I refilled my glass from an already open bottle of very good pinot grigio and fixed her hair.

She looked up and blinked.

"Don't worry. I'm not hitting on you," I told her. "And that steak tartare is for Chuckles."

I picked up a lobster dumpling topped with crystal clear threads of shark fin and left her standing there holding the take-away box from a high-end Chinese place downtown.

Brandon came in without knocking, holding a bouquet of flowers that looked like something out of Lewis Carroll. Dusty purple cabbage roses as big as your fist with cattails and something pink and furry that might have been an artichoke but wasn't. He set the whole thing down in the middle of the table.

"Where's my drink?" he asked no one in particular.

Mark handed him a glass and shook his hand. I raised an eyebrow at him. He either didn't see or pretended not to.

Annabelle was late, no doubt on purpose. She wore a strapless black jersey dress that went all the way to her feet, letting only her tan, painted toes peek out. We hugged and kissed and kissed again. She smelled like vanilla as always.

"Where's the husband?" I asked while her arms were still around my waist.

"Work," she said. "We're better off without him."

She was the last. Richard wasn't coming. Maybe I was being punished. Maybe he, too, really did have to work. Maybe it was Sheila.

I shooed Jenny out of the kitchen and picked up serving plates to carry to the table. The light was low. Marvin Gaye was playing. People wandered to their seats carrying their glasses. Annabelle and Jeremy were laughing. Jenny smiled at them. I could tell she wanted badly to fit in.

I'd ordered all my favorite foods from all my favorite restaurants. This was it. Not my last meal but what a last meal should be. I set down the corn fritters with spicy aioli and the watermelon and mozzarella skewers drizzled with syrup-thick balsamic vinegar. I stayed standing while everyone else settled into their chairs and conversation naturally fell away and eyes came to me.

"As some of you know by now, I'm very sick."

Jenny looked down at her plate, and Jeremy put his fingers to his mouth.

"Sick with what?" Annabelle asked.

Half the table threw her a look for interrupting.

"Cancer," I said. "In my brain. There's no use fighting it anymore, so I'm discontinuing treatment and throwing myself a party instead."

The corners of mouths and eyes twitched downward. Everyone looked as though they'd all been fired. Jenny for the second time.

"I have, in my own way," I continued, "been throwing it for three weeks. I've done what I wanted in just the way I wanted, and I'm going to go right on that way until it's time to stop. So stop looking at me like that. It's depressing. I have right here all my favorite people, all the best wine, and all the best food. So cheers, motherfuckers, cause there's nothing left."

I held up my glass to toast.

Nobody knew what to do. They sat there with corn fritters cooling in front of them, waiting for someone to take the lead. Marvin seemed to get louder in the silence, and a stone formed in my stomach.

Then there was a scraping of chair on polished concrete, and Mark stood up and raised his glass. After a moment, Jeremy stood up and Jenny and Brandon and Annabelle.

"Cheers, motherfuckers," Mark said.

"Cheers," the others echoed.

We drank, and then we ate. And the more wine we poured the easier things got. We ate roasted marrowbone and crispy pig ears, frisee salad with bacon and poached egg, barbecued ribs, macaroni and cheese, and fried chicken with hot sauce. I said I didn't want to talk about being sick, so we argued about art and who was good and who wasn't. Jeremy asked Jenny what she thought. Annabelle asked to see Jeremy's work, and someone brought up sex because someone always does.

"All art is about sex," Annabelle said.

"All of everything is about sex," Brandon hollered across the table.

Everyone laughed, and Mark called out a "Hallelujah," which made Jeremy blush.

Marvin gave way to the *Best of Motown* and then to Ray Charles, who is the best of everything. We polished off another bottle of wine, and I dropped it into the recycling bin, which threatened to fall over and tip out all the other bottles.

After dinner, I made everyone help clean up, and when they left, everyone wrapped their arms around me an extra long time. Jeremy told me not to give up, and Jenny looked as if she didn't know what to do with her arms. After they had gone, I went to bed in my underwear, feeling tipsy enough to give walking my full and undivided attention.

Chuckles hopped up on the bed. He had a tiny bit of tartare stuck to the fur on his chin. I touched it with the tip of my finger. He pulled his smooshed face back, stuck out his tongue, and licked it off. Then licked again and moved on to licking other parts just in case there was something else he'd missed.

"Good night, Chuckles."

9 Days

I woke up looking at my alarm clock. It was notable, I thought, to be down to single-digit days. It was energizing and looming and too soon and too far away, and all of those feelings were strangely remote, as though they were happening in a movie. I empathized with that character but soon would get up and go home, leaving my popcorn bucket and half-full cup of soda behind for someone else to clean up.

I got out of bed. I had a big day ahead of me.

At ten o'clock, I opened my studio door and, failing to find anything convenient and heavy to prop it open with, ran a loop of duct tape around the door handle and secured it to the wall. I marked everything that wasn't for sale with blue painter's tape: all the art and supplies, enough dishes and clothes to get me through the next week, my bed, the litter box, and just in case you were thinking about it, my toothbrush.

By ten thirty they had started to trickle in. I got college students moving into first apartments and hipsters either broke or finding authentic angst by living as if they were. I sold the sofa to a Swedish couple living in the States for two years and unwilling to purchase nice furniture they'd only abandon. I had to assume IKEA was closed or possibly destroyed by fire. A middle-aged man in starched jeans bought my toaster. Other customers browsed but not him. He went straight for the toaster and snatched it up as if there might be a run on them. I sat on one of the blue stools at my worktable, which someone had tried to buy out from under me but I had refused to sell. I had to sit on something, and I'd already lost the couch. I counted change and sketched in a notebook and barked at people who tried to peek behind the drop cloths I'd draped over my paintings.

"Not for sale!" I snapped. For a while, I did it in a fake Chinese accent, which is the sort of thing you do after four hours of watching people paw through your things.

One woman chose the dress I wore to Annabelle's party.

"You may want to have that cleaned," I said, as I reached for the cash.

She changed her mind.

An older woman in comfortable shoes was interested in my cookware, some of which, including a Bundt pan, I didn't know I owned. We perused my cabinets together with an equal sense of discovery and newness. Either some of that stuff had been wedding gifts or I was robbing Bed Bath & Beyond in my sleep.

"So," she asked, after we'd agreed on a price for an assortment of pots and pans and a never-before-used cheese grater, "are you moving?"

"No," I said. "I'm dying."

"Me, too!" She exclaimed it with great joy, as though she'd just discovered we both collected Beanie Babies or had attended the same Weight Watchers meetings. "I'm going to use these to cook up all my favorite foods. Everything fried and with cheese."

She held up the grater.

"Good for you," I told her, and we waved good-bye.

People came and went in waves. There were lulls in between, and when another lull hit at four o'clock, I decided I was done. I'd sold enough, enough to make it easier on whoever came and cleaned up afterward. Richard, maybe, if he wanted the job. I sold the dining room set out from under my computer, and then the laptop itself. I'd sold the television, my nightstand, and half the clothes. The small kitchen appliances were all gone and so were most of my books. I'd made a little over a thousand dollars in cash, which was interesting in the way that the average temperature in Antarctica is interesting. Nice to know, but it's not really going to be applicable.

I picked up the landline, which had a bit of blue painter's tape stuck to it, and dialed Elaine's number.

"Let's get naked."

Elaine gave me an address in Topanga, which is a squiggle on a map where I don't go. L.A.'s urban sprawl is limited only by the surrounding mountains. Topanga sits on its wild edges. There's one main road both in and out that winds in tight S-curves through what is mostly state park land. Mule deer that hop like rabbits and have ears like donkeys live there, along with quail and rattlesnakes and spiders the size of dessert plates. Topanga has creeks that fill up, flood, and wash out roads; boulders that fall from the sky; and once every few years wildfire rushes through to blacken the ground and eat all the houses. Joni Mitchell lived there along with a few of the Doors and some people Hollywood kicked out during the Red scare. It had a nudist colony for years; although I hear they sold the land and bought pants. Most Topanga residents are vegan and smell like patchouli. It is, in short, far more dangerous than South Central ever dreamed it could be.

It also gets dark fast there. The sun dips below the mountains and the wooded, narrow roads have no more lighting than the headlights of your car. Something scurried in the underbrush, and I remembered that one of Charles Manson's victims lived here. I drove slowly, squinting as I approached each small road sign marking a narrow turnoff. I took one of the roads and slowed further as my tires bounced across a steel and wooden bridge not more than eight feet long across a dry creek bed. I started to gain elevation and began to pass driveways with gates and arches that led to houses too far off in the woods to see.

Half a mile in, I saw the Asian-inspired, squared-off wooden arch I'd been told to spot. I turned on my blinker, signaling to the prowling mountain lions, and bumped onto the gravel driveway. Two ruts with a grassy strip down the middle guided my tires toward her house and studio, which, now that I was off the road, glowed like a campfire lantern in the near-full dark.

"I come in peace," I said when she opened the door.

"That's good. No one can hear me scream out here."

I followed her inside. Obviously she knew that bit of Manson trivia, too.

"There's a city just over those mountains," I told her. "We have indoor plumbing and takeout."

"Actually," she said, "I like it here."

The inside of the house looked like below deck on a sailing boat, all polished wood surfaces and built-in furniture. The recessed lighting bounced off the oak and made it glow like light passing through honey. A flat-screen TV hung over the fireplace, and through a doorway on my right, I could see chef-quality kitchen appliances.

My television, when I'd had one, had been two feet deep, full of vacuum tubes, and powered by a rat on a squeaky wheel. Probably I could've replaced it if I'd cared enough, but this was another level entirely.

"Where did all this money come from?"

It was out of my mouth before the full rudeness of it registered.

"Trust fund."

"I thought those were an urban legend," I said, "like people who have their kidneys stolen and wake up in a bathtub full of ice."

I looked up. Even the ceiling was wood. There was a lot of art. Paintings and photographs on the walls, a little of everything, none of it hers. Mostly thirties- and forties-era stuff. Sculptures, too. Small-scale abstract pieces on the coffee table and tucked into bookshelves, built-in, of course.

It was such a crapshoot, wasn't it? How differently her life must've gone from mine. I'd never thought about it before. We had the same job, showed at the same gallery. I never thought our lives—our day-to-day, taking-out-the-trash lives—would be so different.

"What did your father do?" I asked.

"Engineer by trade. He had some aerospace patents, started his own company."

"Did your mom stay at home?"

"Until she died."

"Died of what?"

"Ovarian cancer."

"My mom died, too, when I was a kid."

"I didn't know that," she said. "I'm sorry. What did she have?"

"A gunshot wound."

She opened her mouth and then closed it again.

"It's okay," I said and pointed at the dispenser on the door of her refrigerator. "Does that make crushed ice?"

"Yes. Do you want some?"

"Do you have Coke?"

"With a cherry and a bendy straw?" she offered.

"Absolutely."

She made my drink and pointed out a glass door to a small outbuilding twenty yards away. Lights were on inside it, and a flagstone path through a bed of gravel lit with ankle-height lanterns marked the way.

"I laid a robe out for you in the bathroom. Just come out when you're ready."

The bathroom was down the hall. It had a modern claw-foot tub and a hammered copper sink basin. I opened the cabinets underneath, but this wasn't her private bathroom. There were no toiletries or medicines, only spare toilet paper rolls and hand towels. I peed and washed my hands. The soap in the dispenser smelled like honeysuckle.

I took off my clothes and folded them up in a pile on the marble tiled floor. It was good, I thought, that the bathroom mirror was hung high, and I couldn't see anything in it from the nipples down. Otherwise vanity might have stopped me. The robe was white and fluffy like you might get at a high-end spa. I put it on and took my Coke with me.

Out on the flagstones, I shivered and hurried to the studio.

Inside, Elaine was setting up her materials. She had a handful of heavy, fibrous pieces of paper, off-white and with raw edges, alligator-clipped to a drawing board and set up on her easel. They were each two feet tall, and a hell of a lot more expensive than anything I'd have used for sketching.

She pointed to a stool ten feet away. "Make yourself comfortable," she said. "Whatever position you prefer."

There was track lighting above us with most of it pointed over her drawing space and my modeling space. It was like having a soft spotlight shining on you. It was warm in there. I didn't really need the robe.

"I'm not usually so easy to get naked," I said.

Losing Clementine   221

"Everyone's nervous the first time."

She was barefoot and wearing an embroidered peasant blouse over moss-green hiking shorts and was at a quarter profile to me. It was easy for her to shift her gaze to me when she needed without either of us having to stare directly into the eyes of the other.

"I'm not nervous," I said.

She waited.

"Okay, I'm nervous."

My stomach felt like I'd swallowed a handful of jumping beans, and I was thinking about how, after years of meds, I'd put on weight and my butt was dimply. I took off the robe quickly and tossed it toward the worktable, but only part of it made it and then the whole thing slid off onto the floor.

"I'm not going to ask you not to draw my butt fat because if someone asked me not to draw their butt fat, I'd probably decide the butt fat was the most interesting thing."

"You won't even be recognizable when I'm done," she said.

I'd perched myself on the edge of the model's stool, one foot on the rung and one on the floor. My hands were on the seat behind me, my elbows straight and locked. "If I'm not recognizable, you'll have to talk about me a lot so people know I posed for you."

She smiled with teeth. "You know I will."

8 Days

"What the hell happened to all your stuff?" Richard demanded when I opened the door.

He was wearing long cargo shorts and a gray T-shirt. He hadn't shaved in a couple of days, nor, I suspected, had he showered before showing up at my place that morning. He had a Dodgers baseball cap pulled low over his eyes and didn't look like he'd slept.

"I sold it," I said, letting him in.

"Why?"

"It wouldn't fit in the economy-size pyramid my slaves are building to guide me into the afterlife."

He did not think that was funny. In truth, it wasn't one of my better jokes, but I still thought I should've gotten points for trying.

"You haven't called me about your appointments," he whined. "I told you I wanted to go."

"There hasn't been a good time."

"It's never a good time. It doesn't matter."

"You have a life."

"Sheila and I broke up."

Well, there. Now we were getting to it.

"That's too bad," I said, because that's what you're supposed to say, and those sorts of things just come out like farts and sneezes.

"Thanks."

"What happened?"

Chuckles came over to rub the length of his body on Richard's sneakers and then roll over on top of his foot to display both his shaggy stomach and his preference for my ex over me.

Richard bent down to scratch the cat's undercarriage as directed. "You know how sometimes you fight about something, like who's running up the electric bill, but you don't even care about the electric bill?"

"So you broke up over an electric bill because you wanted to break up and that's the best you could come up with?"

"Pretty much. She thought I was insane."

"You are insane."

"I was going to ask if I could sleep on your couch." He looked at the empty and slightly cleaner spot on the floor where the couch had been. "Guess not."

"I sold it to a Swedish couple," I said. "IKEA was closed."

We stopped at a taco truck, which was doing a brisk early lunch business with the construction workers who'd torn up a particularly inconvenient section of Santa Monica Boulevard. While we waited for our order, we listened to traffic, and I sipped a tamarind Jarritos and thought about how much time I'd spent hearing traffic in L.A. and how I'd never really noticed it before.

"You notice how L.A. is a city of sound more than smell?" I asked.

"What?"

Richard had a can of Diet Coke and was wiping condensation off the sides with a napkin. The truck gave out the sort of napkins you buy at the grocery store and use in your own house rather than the kind that come out of dispensers at diner tables.

"Some cities are all about the smell. New York is all about the smell. L.A. doesn't really smell much, but it has this low-grade ambient noise all the time. Mostly cars."

"The Santa Monica Library smells like piss," said one of the workers waiting for his order. He had on an orange vest and was wearing long pants and sleeves despite the heat.

"I'm not saying there are no smells," I said. "I'm just saying smell doesn't define it."

"And when the tide goes out, the beach smells like rotten fish," his buddy offered.

They were missing my point.

"Everybody says the ocean is supposed to smell clean and refreshing," Richard said.

"It doesn't," the first guy said. "Except sometimes at night. Then it's okay."

I was glad when the cook pushed their order through the window and they moved off. Conversation vultures.

Our order was up next. We each took our double-layer paper plates loaded with tacos to the salsa bar. I picked the one that looked spiciest and dribbled it across all four of mine, already loaded up with chopped raw onion and cilantro with sliced radishes and a side of lime wedges. Each taco was built on small corn tortillas that, like the plates, were doubled up for better engineering and stability.

"*Cabeza* means 'head,' you know."

"I know," I said, squeezing my limes and tucking in for a bite of my head taco. Each one was about three bites for a total of twelve bites of heaven. All for under five bucks.

Richard had ordered *carne asada,* which is what he always ordered and is fine if you don't know enough to order the *cabeza,* which isn't brain but more like cheek that's been stewed and stewed until it's so tender you don't need teeth. The *carne asada* is usually tough. My superior taco selection allowed me to save on chewing time.

"At least I don't have to feel guilty anymore," he said.

"About what?"

I had a nearly empty plate and was down to eating the bits of fallen meat, which left orange stains on the paper. I chewed on the stray radish slices. Radish was key to a good taco.

"About us, what we did."

I folded my empty plate in half and tossed it into the trash can along with my napkin.

"Jesus Christ, Richard."

"What?"

"You broke her heart and fucked up her life so you wouldn't have to feel bad about sleeping with your ex-wife?"

"No."

"Yes."

"No, she broke up with me. Technically."

"You're such a tool."

"What the hell?" He threw up his hand, forgot he was still holding half a taco, and spilled meat and onion across the sidewalk.

An hour later, we were standing in the showroom of a funeral home the cemetery had recommended. The carpet under our feet was dark teal with heavy, matching drapes, and the wallpaper was a camel color that alternated satin and matte stripes. All the artwork was framed in ornate gold and featured the French Revolution, when presumably coffin sales were way up. The saleswoman, who wore a lady suit and sensible shoes, had gone to fetch brochures and left us alone with a roomful of empty caskets. Some of them were on display racks that tilted at a forty-five-degree angle so you could appreciate the tufted satin and the little pillows that came with them.

I reached in and tested the cushioning, which really gave Richard the heebie-jeebies.

"Do you think all this fluffy stuff would be, I don't know, claustrophobic?"

"Normal people don't pick out their own coffins."

He was refusing to look directly at them, as though they might become aggressive.

"Who else is going to do it?" I asked. "You? Besides, it's part of the package deal."

The options boiled down to either metal or wood, with large gradations in price. The steel was economical, but I was leaning toward a bronze finish. You only die once, right? I would, however, probably skip the customizable embroidery on the inside of the lid lining, which felt just a little too much like having your shirts monogrammed.

He dodged the question. "I don't think it's healthy. Have you told your doctor you're doing this? Aren't you supposed to be doing positive thinking exercises?"

"I don't have a doctor," I said. "I've discontinued treatments."

He looked a little as if someone had let the air out of him. "Tiny, you have to try."

He hadn't called me that since we were married and still liked each other. I'd all but forgotten it.

"I did try."

And I had. Boy howdy, had I ever.

"There has to be something, some experimental treatment in Spain or something."

If I'd said there was, he would have, in that moment, picked me up and sprinted to the airport. He would have carried me himself, like a knight on a white horse, which was why I'd married him in the first place. When it had turned out he wasn't a knight and didn't have a white horse and that I wasn't capable of being rescued, we had both been let down.

"Want to see my plot?" I asked.

"What plot?"

"My burial plot."

"No!"

The saleswoman, just coming through the door with the brochures, jumped at the outburst and then pasted on her best conciliatory smile. It looked experienced. Probably more people argued in funeral homes than you would think.

"Hey," I asked, "can I lie down in one of these?"

"Only the ones that are displayed level."

"Are you serious?" Richard asked. "Clementine, you are not getting in a casket."

I was already kicking off my shoes.

"It's one of the benefits of shopping with us," the saleswoman explained, using the same calm, quiet voice that seemed to pervade the entire death industry. "When you order online, you don't get the full sensory experience."

"You can order online?" Richard's voice got high and loud.

"Yes, from Walmart." She looked as though this saddened her, but I couldn't tell if it was because of the competition or the fact that you could pick up your loved one's final resting place along with dog shampoo and a new bathmat on sale for $6.99. "We don't recommend it."

While they talked, I hoisted a leg over the side of the bronze casket I'd been admiring, then pulled the other leg in and scooted down. The lower half of the lid was still closed, so my legs disappeared inside. It was long enough, for which I was grateful. Pants, for example, have always been difficult to get in my size.

"Get out of there!"

Richard had turned around.

"I want to try it."

I did want to try it. It felt important. If I didn't try it, how could I know everything would be okay? That was the point of waiting thirty whole days. Everything would be done. No mess would be left. No one would have to sweep up after me or find me after school with my blood sprayed across the wall. It would be neat. The casket had to fit.

"Get out."

Richard had crossed the distance between us in two steps and wrapped a hand tightly around my bicep. He was stronger than I remembered, or maybe it was just because he'd never done something like this to me while we were married.

"Get out."

He was trying to yank me or lift me, but the angle was against him. The skin on my arm was starting to chafe and burn from the twisting friction, and my upper body was pulling too far to the right considering that my legs were trapped under the lid. If he kept it up, I was going to end up facedown on the floor with two hundred pounds of metal on my back.

"Richard."

"Sir, please," the saleswoman said.

We had gone beyond the bounds of normal family funerary disputes.

"Let go of me!"

He dropped my arm and stepped back. "Get out. Get out now. I don't want to see this."

And then he turned and walked out, leaving the saleswoman and me alone with the caskets.

We didn't talk about it on the way home.

I borrowed Brandon's inflatable mattress. Richard put it where the couch used to be.

We still didn't talk about it.

In an unexpected show of loyalty, Chuckles slept with me.

And we didn't talk about it.

7 Days

I had one week left to live, and I spent part of it in the security line at LAX. It's fashionable to hate LAX, much as it's fashionable to like Wes Anderson movies. I'm unfashionable. I'd stepped past the nun collecting coins for charity, gotten my boarding pass from the automated machine, and shown my ID to the first of several TSA agents, all in under ten minutes. The main downer is that the airport cops ride Segways, and none of them will give you a lift. For their unkindness, the universe makes them wear stupid bike helmets. Feel free to mock.

It was a three-hour flight to Kansas City, and I spent it watching network sitcom reruns, edited for my protection, on the back of the headrest in front of me.

Kansas City is not a hub for anywhere or anyone, and when we got off the plane, there seemed to be hardly anyone else there. My fellow passengers quickly dispersed like molecules going into uniform solution, and I was left alone in my own bubble of space.

I walked outside to grab a taxi. No cars lined the circular drive. No one honked, and no traffic officer attempted to bring order to chaos. A minivan two doors down was discharging a woman and two children, each with a rolling suitcase. A few people walked to the lot across the drive, which was a quarter full. It was twenty degrees hotter than L.A. It was hot the way the Valley gets hot but with the sort of wet, sticky air that attracts mosquitoes. I went back into the air-conditioning, quizzed a middle-aged black man with a mop, and used the courtesy phone to call a taxi.

It took forty-five minutes to drive into the city, not because of traffic but because the airport is sequestered in the middle of open fields far away from anything. I sat in the back sipping a bottled Sprite I'd bought and waited to see something more than freeway off-ramps and billboards advertising riverboat casinos. When the skyline finally came into view, it was compact, but L.A.'s skyline is compact, too, not like New York's, so I wasn't judging. We took an exit and turned away from the biggest and tallest of the buildings.

The downtown was that particular type of downtown that still has a few cafeterias and owner-operated men's tailor shops in between FOR RENT signs. The weathered brick and a few art deco signs told you it might have once been a swinging place, and maybe it would be again if enough people decided it was worth doing. It had good bones but also too many broken up sidewalks and chain-link fences that collected Styrofoam trash, too many vacancies and cracked storefront windows held together with tape. People didn't walk around outside much, which was a shame. Maybe it was the heat.

The IRS building was massive. It had been a main post office in another life, a building already the size of a train station, with three huge wings built on in addition. Almost thirty acres of accountants, *tap-tap-tapping* out their calculations, *scratch-scratch-scratching* out the numbers. Rows and rows and rows of them all the way to the horizon. I imagined them moving in lockstep like a German army of human adding machines.

When we stopped, the taxi fare was outrageous. I paid it the way you pay auto repair bills, knowing you're being robbed and impotent to do anything about it. My driver could go home now. He didn't have to work for the rest of the day.

I walked inside. It felt surreal going to see my father at work, the way you might if you were a child, which I was the last time he saw me. I don't know what I had thought would happen when I got in. I think I thought I would simply stop one of the human adding machines and give them my father's name and be shown to his desk. Row 28, column B in one of the football-field-size adding rooms. But just inside the door was a desk of guards and a metal detector. It looked like airport screening, and I wondered if I should take off my shoes.

The guards asked me my business, and I told them, leaving out the part where I was unexpected and just how long it had been and that I wouldn't recognize Jerry Pritchard if we shook hands at a cocktail party. They walked me through the scanner—my second of the day—and searched my bag, which was full of small travel bottles and clean underpants because if you have shampoo and cotton undies you can go anywhere and do anything for an almost unlimited period of time. Then one of the guards looked up the extension to call my dad and tell him I was there.

Surreal turned to nerves when I realized he could just pick up, listen to what the guard had to say, and deny me admittance. He wouldn't even have to do it to my face.

I tried not to sweat watching the guard holding the phone to his ear. He had hands the size of dinner plates with ballet-slipper-pink fingernails on deep dark skin. I waited and he waited and

Losing Clementine 233

we both waited together, and still he held that phone up to his ear with a hand that nearly swallowed the whole thing, and nobody said anything.

Then he hung up.

"Not answering," he said.

My heart stopped beating and my lungs stopped expanding and my cells stopped dividing.

"Lakisha, would you take this lady upstairs to see her daddy, please?"

I took a breath, and the oxygen was such a shock to my system I felt lightheaded and had to put my hand on the counter.

Lakisha was doing a crossword puzzle in the newspaper. She put her pen down and pushed away from the desk. "What room?" she asked.

"Three-oh-two."

Lakisha and I walked together through the old post office part of the building. They had left the marble floors and the dark wood and the brass P.O. boxes, which might have been nice if I'd been paying attention. I followed half a step behind my escort and tried very hard to look like a normal person.

Lakisha and I went up to the third floor and down the hall, and we stopped in front of door 302. She opened it and held it open for me to go in first. The room was not the size of a football field. It was the size of my studio and without any charm of the old P.O. boxes downstairs. It was full of cubicles, all in beige, with walls so high I couldn't see how many were full, but there was room for no more than ten people.

I followed Lakisha down the row. She had wide hips and a protruding rear end that rolled when she walked, which was a strange thing to notice at a time like that, but I did. She stopped halfway down and spoke to a woman sitting in her cube. The woman had decorated her space with dream catchers and drawings of Celtic knots and scantily clad fairies.

"Jerry around?" Lakisha asked, nodding at an empty desk with the chair pushed away and spun around as if it had just been abandoned, perhaps in haste.

The woman's nameplate said SUSAN.

"Yeah. He went to the break room for a candy bar. Should be back soon."

Her computer screen was a spreadsheet of numbers. Beside it was a framed photograph of a dog.

"This is his daughter," Lakisha said. "I'm gonna leave her here."

Susan looked at me in a way that made me think she knew something was wrong and that she might open her mouth and my good luck would be for naught. But she didn't. She just nodded, and Lakisha walked away, and I smiled with my lips pressed together and stepped over to my dad's cubicle to wait.

He didn't have any personal photographs at his desk. No dream catchers or fairies, either. He had a word-a-day tear-off calendar and a rubber band ball the size of an orange. He was neat. He drank diet soda and brought his lunch in a soft-sided pail with a shoulder strap. Blue. No logo. That was it. That was all the information I had.

I shoved my hands in my pockets and leaned against the divider and tried not to make eye contact with anyone else while I watched the door. It was quiet. No one was talking on the phone or playing a radio. Keyboards clicked. I felt awkward, as if my limbs had all been attached in the wrong places. I wondered if I should've worn a dress and then got mad at myself for feeling like I needed to impress him. I felt clammy. I wished I had something to do.

I recognized him when he walked in. I didn't think I would,

and I didn't know if I recognized him or if I recognized some-thing of myself. He was simply familiar. And old. So much older than I was prepared for. He had lost most of his hair, although what remained was still brown. He wore rimless glasses, black dress pants, and a black-and-tan-checked shirt. He shuffled a little when he walked and carried two candy bars in his hand.

I was staring. How could I not be staring? I don't know if that's what pulled him up short, this stranger at his desk staring, or if he, like me, saw something he recognized, but he stopped at the end of the row all the way down from me and stared back. I thought he might run, but he didn't. He took a glance around and then came toward me with that shuffling gait. He stopped at Susan's desk and offered her a candy bar.

"I thought you might want one," he said to her.

"Awww, thank you. Hey, you going to introduce us to your daughter? This isn't the one from California."

He looked at me and then away.

"She lives in California, too. This is Clementine," he said.

Susan nodded at me. "Pleased to meet you."

I tried to smile but wasn't sure if I managed it.

The silence that followed must've seemed unbearably awk-ward and quiet to everyone else, but I couldn't hear it over my heartbeat.

Jerry stood there not so far from his chair and looked down at the candy bar in his hands. He tore it open, tore it until the wrapper was split halfway down, and then he broke it in two and offered the top end to me.

"I don't know if you like chocolate."

I took it. "I like chocolate."

"I was just about to go home," he said. "I like to come in early, so I can beat the traffic."

This was it, I thought, the part where he runs. Here's some

candy. Have a nice life. My stomach spun like a washing machine, and I tried to prepare myself for it. I told myself it would be easier now that I was an adult, but I knew that wasn't true.

"Do you want to come home with me?" he asked.

I almost didn't hear him. I was so wrapped up in the script I was writing in my head. His deviation made me stutter.

"Yeah, okay, yeah."

"Okay," he agreed and nodded, looking at his chair. "I should call Charlene and tell her you're coming."

Charlene. I tasted the name on my tongue.

He picked up his phone and pushed a button for a line before dialing. Charlene picked up quickly.

"We're going to have company for dinner," he said. "Clementine is here . . . No, I don't . . . Yes . . . Don't worry about it. That's fine . . . I'll pick it up on the way home . . . Yes . . . Me, too . . . All right then."

"Clementine is here," he'd said. I wasn't a complete surprise. She knew of my existence, anyway, even if she hadn't been planning on dinner guests.

He hung up and looked at me for the first time since seeing me across the room. He didn't make eye contact. He hadn't worked his way north of my chin. I was still staring, though. He looked so much like Ramona. There she was: a little bit of my baby sister walking around in the body of an aging, balding IRS worker. If that didn't beat all hell.

"If you're ready," he said to my chin, "my car is in the garage."

"I'm ready," I said.

I followed him out. He carried his lunch pail over his shoulder. The doors to all the offices were closed, and I never saw a giant calculating room like the one I'd imagined. We passed people in the hallways, other workers, none of whom said hello to Jerry, and Jerry said nothing to me. He walked with his hands

Losing Clementine 237

in his pockets, and when we got belowground and walked out through a tunnel into the parking garage and the hot, wet air wrapped around me again, I stopped at the first trash can I saw and threw up.

I was glad I hadn't eaten much. The candy bar came up undigested, and I fished in my bag for what was left of my bottled Sprite. Jerry waited, not saying anything and not looking, either because it was disgusting or because he was giving me some privacy.

"Sorry," I said, when I was ready to keep going.

He drove an American-made hybrid and listened to NPR. There was no trash on the floorboards or stuck in the door pockets. Nothing hung from the rearview mirror or was tossed in the backseat. It could've been a rental it was so impersonal. The radio station was on when he started the engine, and he left it on.

"How long have you worked here?" I asked.

"About thirty years," he said. "I'm going to retire in twenty-two months."

It was like having a conversation in an elevator with a complete stranger.

We wound our way through the surface streets toward the freeway, which was nearly vacant by L.A. standards. We got on and headed east.

"So," he said, "what have you been up to?"

I laughed. I couldn't help it. It was such a casual question, so small, so inadequate. I laughed so hard my sides cramped and my cheeks ached and when I touched them they were wet. I had been so unaware that I was crying I thought for just a moment that maybe I'd been cut and had begun to bleed. I touched my cheeks again and looked at my fingers just to be sure.

Jerry gripped the steering wheel and leaned closer to the windshield as if willing us to get home faster.

"What have I been up to?" I said when my wind came back.

My nervousness had been pushed aside, replaced with incredulity and curiosity and indignation. It felt like being a teenager: wrong-footed, frightened, and cocky. Maybe I had to age all over again, I thought, go through all those stages again with him. It was a sobering thought. I didn't have time for that, and I sure as hell didn't want to die a mouthy brat with acne.

I took a breath and tried to grow up.

"I'm an artist. I live in L.A. I was married, and now I'm not. I don't have any children."

"I'm married."

"I heard."

"She's a nice woman," he said, "a nice, nice woman."

"Mom was a good woman, too," I said.

He said nothing. He said nothing long enough for us to listen to three-quarters of the hourly news brief on the radio. Roadside bombs in Qandahar. Unemployment rates increased. I waited. I wasn't going to fill the gulf. I wasn't going to let him off the hook. The traffic report came on.

"She tried hard," he said, "your mother, she tried hard, and she was a good woman."

"She shot Ramona. Did you know that?"

"Yes, I knew that. It's the worst thing that ever happened in my life."

It should've been that one of those things could not have been true, that she was a good woman and that she'd shot her child, but they both were. It was one of the strange, scary, great truths of my life.

"They weren't really in your life anymore," I said.

"Why . . ." He stopped and considered and went ahead anyway. "Why didn't she kill you, too?"

I looked out the window at the freeway going by. It was more

Losing Clementine 239

billboards and exit signs, like there was nothing else in the damn place but billboards and exit signs.

"I was at school. Ramona was home sick that day."

We were both quiet. Chance is hard to accept, the randomness of your existence or your death. Sometimes it's easier to believe greater forces are at work protecting or punishing you.

"Your mom," he said, "she had bad days sometimes."

"Yeah."

"She'd just get really sad, and she couldn't function right."

I wanted him to stop talking. I'd come all that way but not to hear what he had to say about this. But I didn't know how to make him stop.

"Sometimes when someone is that sad, they do things that don't make sense to other people."

That was my greatest fear, and more than twenty years of therapy hadn't been able to allay it. What if I got so sad I did something that didn't make sense to other people? What if I did what she did? What if I was dangerous?

I was crying again, but this time I knew it. I didn't try to explain, because it's normal to cry when talking about your dead victimized sister and your crazy dead mother. I let him believe the lie of the cry all the way to the restaurant where we stopped to pick up dinner.

The building had the look of having been something else before, without the remodeling budget to cover it up. The parking lot smelled liked smoked meat, and the inside looked like a Taco Bell. I followed Jerry up to the counter where he paid for two large white plastic sacks of food his wife had called ahead for. I picked them up. Each weighed at least five pounds, and it occurred to me that there could be more people waiting for us at his house than just his wife.

We only had a few hours of daylight left, but still the sticky, hot air hadn't relented. It was the sort of heat I'd have expected in the Deep South. It was the sort of heat that made people irritable, caused marital disputes and petty crime. I wished I'd worn shorts.

We made our way into the planned, looping residential streets full of cul-de-sacs and with no recognizable grid. Churches seemed to guard the middle ground between residential and commercial. Jerry lived behind a Baptist church of modest size with a blacktop basketball court in back and a parking lot in front, but I'd seen all kinds of churches as we drove, more denominations than I could have named. It felt oddly egalitarian, even for a nonbeliever like me.

The neighborhood wasn't new, and it wasn't old enough to be charming. The houses were all split-level and looked like school milk cartons. Each had a driveway that led to a double garage and a wrought-iron railing along the stairs to the front door. Jerry's house was dark green with black shutters and a cement planter full of flowers next to the mailbox. No other cars were in the driveway or parked in front.

Charlene must've been watching for the car because before I got my feet on the ground she had the front door open. She stood there, clasping her hands in front of her and waiting for us. She wore white pants and a blousy floral top that was long enough to cover her wide hips. Her hair was red but not a bright red. If it was natural once, it wasn't anymore. It had the faded quality of dye that has begun to wash out and show the white underneath.

As Jerry and I paused at the bottom of the stairs to negotiate who would go up first, she called down.

"I'm so sorry. If I'd known you were coming, I would've had a nice dinner planned."

"It's okay," I said, craning my neck to look up at her and trying not to fall down the narrow cement steps while holding enough food for a basketball team.

Losing Clementine   241

"If I'd known you were coming" was a nice way of putting what I'd done, which was to show up in the middle of their lives and demand to be seen.

Charlene was wearing coral-colored lipstick and blush and green eye shadow but not a lot of it. It was nicely applied, as if someone at the makeup counter at Macy's had helped. Her cheeks, like her bottom, were full, and as soon as I made it to the landing, she took the sacks from me.

"Oh, here, I'll take that. Come in. Come in. I'm sure you're tired. It's a long flight."

"Not that tired," I said.

"Oh, well, you're on California time. Can I get you something to drink? Iced tea?"

I followed her up the short flight of stairs inside that formed the split of the split-level. The carpet was such a light beige it looked white. Jerry stopped at the front door to take off his shoes. I took off mine when I saw him do it and left them by the sofa. Charlene was already barefoot. Her bright red toenails contrasted with her translucently fair skin. She walked into the kitchen, and I walked behind her down a clear plastic runner. I looked down the hall to the right. There was a runner there, too.

"Sure, iced tea is fine."

I'd thought she would introduce herself: "Hello, I'm your home-wrecking stepmother. Nice to meet you." Instead she set the bags on the counter and started pulling down plates. Only three. Silverware and napkins were already on the dining room table.

"Jerry, would you put the pie in the icebox, please? And get out the tea. I made a fresh jug this afternoon."

Jerry did as he was told, and I stood in the middle with nothing to do.

Charlene took serving dishes out and started opening Styrofoam containers. Halfway through dumping out potato salad that didn't look as if it had nearly enough mustard in it, she turned and touched her bosom.

"It's just so funny seeing you here in person," she said. "You're so much taller than you look in your photos."

Everyone was acting like it wasn't at all strange that I was there, like I was a minor surprise, a neighbor who had popped over for dinner. I didn't know whether to play along or jump up and down screaming.

"Photos?"

"Oh yes, we have a scrapbook of all your newspaper articles. Jerry, show her."

Jerry abandoned the iced tea jug and disappeared back into the living room. A dog barked outside. It was close by, but I couldn't tell if it was theirs or the neighbor's. It sounded small. I don't like dogs. I never have.

I walked up to the counter. There was sliced brisket and an entire pig worth of ribs. Along with the potato salad, there were macaroni and cheese, slaw, and baked beans floating in maple-colored gravy. Two whole containers were filled with nothing but barbecue sauce. Charlene got out the gravy boats.

"I feel like I know you from cutting out your articles and hearing about you and things, but of course I don't, so pardon me if I get overly familiar." She talked to the brisket as she transferred it to a platter and fanned it out in neat rows. "And I hope you like barbecue. We're famous for it here. Is this your first time in Kansas City?"

"Yes," I said. "I've never had to track down a fugitive parent before."

There. I said it. It was out there.

"Some folks prefer Texas style. It has a thinner, more vinegary sauce, but here we use molasses. It's thicker and sweeter. Just coats the back of a spoon."

She wiped her hands on a towel. They were shaking. At least she'd heard me.

Jerry came back in and set a black, leather-bound scrapbook on the kitchen table next to the salt and pepper shakers. I walked toward him, and he backed off, moving around me and heading for the safety of the iced tea.

I opened the book. There were a few clippings from my early days, not many. There were a few reviews in art sections, most of them not more than mentions. They were starting to age and turn yellow, and the glue that was holding them down was hard and brittle. I turned a page and a clipping came loose and slipped down into the valley of the binding. The clippings got more numerous within the last five years and stopped being newsprint and started being computer printouts from Web sites. Someone had highlighted my name in the photo captions. One of the last articles, which had run more than a year before, had a picture of me taken at my studio. Jenny was in the background. They'd highlighted her name, too.

I closed the book.

Jerry and Charlene were bringing platters of food to the table.

"You didn't have any trouble finding me," I said. "You were a lot harder to find."

"Well," Charlene said, "none of us is famous like you are."

"I'm surprised you didn't send away for my autograph," I said.

"Don't talk to my wife like that." It was the first thing Jerry had said since we'd come in the door. He didn't look at me when he said it, but he said it nonetheless. "Sit down and let's have a nice dinner."

Charlene went back to the counter for glasses of tea. Jerry sat down at the table and put a napkin in his lap. I sat, too. My only other option was throwing china, and I was saving that for when I really needed it. Jerry picked up the plate of meat and held it out for me to pick from.

"Excuse me," I said. "I need to use the restroom."

I didn't wait for directions. I went down the plastic runner past the family photos lining the hallway. Some of them were school pictures of a girl taken maybe twenty years ago judging by the haircut and the clothes. I stopped. I'd never thought about them having other children. She looked familiar. My stomach started to swirl again. The girl got older the farther down the hallway I went, and the farther I went the more familiar she got. And I thought it was because she was my sister, my half sister, and that she was familiar just the way Jerry had been at the end of the row of cubicles. I thought maybe my brain recognized kin and blood even when I'd never seen it before, but the girl went from grade school to junior high to high school, and then I knew. I reached up and took the last photo in the series off the wall.

When I turned, Jerry was standing there at the end of the hall watching me. The paper napkin was still tucked into the waistband of his pants.

"She didn't want you to know."

I looked from him back at the photo in my hands. It was Jenny. Jenny Pritchard, no relation.

6 Days

I woke up in a hotel room in the city. I'd taken a cab the night before, run right out of there because I didn't know what else to do. I'd wanted to score something like I used to in the old days, back in New York, when I was young and immortal and pickled in vodka and cocaine, but I hadn't scored in years. More than years. A decade. I'd grown up. I didn't know how anymore. I'd been medicating myself at the pharmacy with an insurance card, and I didn't even have that.

Fuck.

I was wrung out. I was the kind of tired that sleep wouldn't fix. I wanted to lie there in a puddle of betrayal and self-pity, but I hadn't eaten the night before. I was hungry. I sat up. I reserved the right to feel pitiful and betrayed, but I would do it with eggs.

There was a room service menu beside the bed. I opened it and dialed.

I turned on the news and let it drone while I waited for my food. When it came, my milk was still in its little cardboard carton, the same shape as Jerry's house. I looked at the expiration date. It would still be drinkable after I was dead. I didn't know how to feel about that. I didn't feel much. Somehow it seemed like there were more pressing issues.

There was an early hurricane forming in the mid-Atlantic. I watched the colored swirl on CNN and listened to the anchors trying to drum up end-of-the-world excitement. I picked up another piece of bacon. I wasn't hungry, but it was there. Bacon is one of those things you shouldn't waste.

There was a knock. I'd forgotten to put the DO NOT DISTURB sign on the knob.

Fuck again.

I got up and padded to the door without my pants. I wasn't in the mood for pants, and you didn't need pants to tell the housekeeper to go away.

On the other side of the door, Jerry was wearing his pants. Khakis with athletic shoes and a polo shirt tucked in. He looked me in the face, which I suppose was better than looking at my underwear.

"Oh. I can wait," he said, "until you're decent."

"I'm never going to be decent. How did you find me?"

"I called Jenny. She paid all your bills before, you know, online. So she looked up your credit card. There was a charge from this hotel on it."

Ratted out by the Internet.

"Jenny has known all this time?"

"Not always. Since she was in art school. Charlene told her."

I turned and walked back into the room, leaving the door open. He could follow me if he wanted. He did, but he hung back by the bathroom, not quite willing to commit.

"Why didn't she tell me?"

"I asked her not to."

Losing Clementine 247

Of course he did.

"Well, that just fucking explains everything, doesn't it?"

He didn't say anything. He looked as if he wished he had something to do with his hands, a hat to hold maybe.

I sat on the edge of the bed with the messed-up sheets and the dirty room service tray. I was so angry I didn't know what to do.

"So how did this work?" I asked. "Did she call you and tell you what I was doing? Thinking? Feeling?"

The humiliation of what Jenny had access to burned in my cheeks and brought tears to my eyes. The thing about being crazy is that you know you're crazy even when you can't do anything about it. You know how you look to other people, and the shame of it is almost worse than the thing itself.

"No." Jerry shook his head. "She only told us when you had shows and things, when there was an article about you in the paper. But it wasn't . . . She didn't tell us personal things, if that's what you're thinking. She didn't even tell us she wanted to work for you until she'd done it. We didn't ask . . . I told her she had to quit. That it wasn't right, and it was just going to hurt everybody."

I felt both furious and impotent, like a declawed cat.

"I hope you won't punish her," he said. "Jenny is such a good artist. It was just too much for her to have a big sister like you and not get to know you. She said it was a big opportunity. I know she's learned a lot from you."

"Yeah? Well, if I'd known she existed, she wouldn't have had to sneak around washing my brushes and folding my damn underwear."

"She wanted to do it. She loved working for you. She was devastated when you let her go."

God. I had fired my own sister.

"She wasn't yours to withhold." I was standing up, and I

couldn't remember when I'd done that. "It could've been different. What is wrong with you?"

I wanted to shake him, to shake something, to shake it and shake it until the stuffing came out and there was nothing left. I wanted to tear it up and scream.

"I didn't have any choice. I had to hide." He made his hands into little fists at his sides.

"Bullshit!"

I remembered after he'd left, when I realized he wasn't coming back, kicking my bedroom door. I kicked it and kicked it with my little kid-size shoe until the hollow core at the bottom splintered and my sister cried and yelled for me to stop and my mother came running and I kept kicking until I fell down. I was crying and crying, and I didn't want to be. I was angry, just as angry as I was right then all these years later.

"No. It was all my fault. I couldn't do it any other way."

"You're just selfish. You're a selfish, controlling coward!"

"You don't understand."

"How could I possibly understand? You ran off. You just ran off and left us all there like we didn't even matter, like we were old clothes you were done with, something for the Goodwill!"

He looked like he wanted to grab handfuls of his own hair.

"I couldn't take it anymore. You don't know what it was like. I thought you would be okay. She always wanted to be a good mom, but when—when Ramona died—I knew I couldn't ever contact you again. Not ever."

"What are you talking about?"

"I killed her! I killed Ramona and your mother." Tears spilled down his pale, wrinkled cheeks, running down past the rimless lenses of his glasses. "I left you girls there. It's all my fault she did what she did."

"I'm the one that found them! I saw the blood and the brains all over everything. And you were gone, and you never came back, not even then. I didn't even know if you knew, if you cared!"

He walked over to the side of the bed closest to the alarm clock and sank onto the mattress.

"I prayed for them every night."

"Oh good," I said. "That's just great. I'm sure that was real helpful. Did you ever think about doing anything for me? Did you ever think that I needed you? The kid that was still alive!"

"You had your aunt and uncle."

And then I did hit him. I ran over and shoved him hard in the chest. He fell backward onto his elbows. His bones were prominent under his skin and under my hands. It was like shoving a bird. He was weak, and that made me angrier. I was bigger and stronger and full of enough rage to fuel ten men. He put one arm up to block his face, and I kept coming. I slapped him and shoved him again and again until he was flat on his back, and his glasses had come off his face.

And then I backed off. It wasn't enough. It wasn't nearly enough, but the only thing that would be enough would be to wrap my hands around his throat and squeeze until he turned purple and stopped breathing, and then maybe that wouldn't be enough. This, I thought, this right here is how people end up stabbed two hundred times.

I took two steps back. This wasn't how I wanted to feel. He was supposed to make it okay. He was supposed to take all the bad feelings, the holes, and fix them, so I could die without that pain. And he didn't. He didn't at all. He talked about his pain. His feelings. He was at the center of his own story. I'd come all that way, so he could help me. And he couldn't.

I went into the bathroom. I made the water lukewarm and let it pool in my hands and rubbed it on my face, again and again.

When I stood up and dried myself with the rough white hand towel, I looked in the mirror. I had been crying. My face was red and blotchy. I looked old. I had lines around my eyes and lines running away from my nose toward my chin. I had purple bruises under my eyes. That's exactly how I felt, too. Old. Lined. Bruised.

When I came back out, Jerry was standing next to the window, looking out on the street below. The cable news was still playing on the television. A country I did not care about was having elections.

"You're still here," I said.

"Did you want me to go?"

"Do you have anything else to say?"

He shook his head.

"Then yeah," I said. "I want you to go."

And he did.

I spent the day at the city's art museum. It was bigger and nicer than I would've thought it would be. I ate lunch in its cafeteria, which was set up in an enclosed two-story courtyard with a center fountain. That was nicer than I thought it would be, too. I had carrot soup and a pressed sandwich with melted white cheese and salami. Then I went back to the counter for a cookie and a coffee. I took my time. I went through all the rooms, even the African basket weaving that everyone else skips, and I tried very, very hard not to think about anything.

5 Days

"Congratulations," the woman wearing a neckerchief with her company-branded chambray shirt told me. "Your flight today qualifies you for ten thousand bonus miles in our valued customer program."

"Swell," I said. "Can I get a window seat?"

"No, I'm afraid not."

The descent into L.A. seems to take longer than that into other cities. For ten minutes you're low over the tangle of freeways and cloverleaf interchanges. Houses and buildings look like Monopoly pieces, and the bright blue pops of backyard swimming pools are everywhere. Angelenos play Name-That-Freeway with themselves and each other on the way down. The 210? The 605? The 10? The 405. Definitely the 405.

When you take off from LAX, you soar over the open ocean, and when you land it's a slow creep over urban sprawl. I think that means something, but I don't know what.

When I got home, Richard was still there. He was sitting on the floor with his laptop on his legs playing *World of Warcraft*. Chuckles was lying on the floor next to him, looking brushed, fed, and smug. When your face is shoved in like a deflated football, smug is an easy look to pull off.

"How did it go?" Richard asked.

I sank down next to him and then into him, letting my knees curl up and my head find his chest. We stayed there on the floor, letting the light change around us and the cat get bored and wander off and the Thai food take-out containers appear and collect around us.

"I thought he would fix everything."

"Why did you think that?"

"Because he's my dad."

Richard leaned his head back against the wall and ran his hand over my forehead, brushing my bangs off my face. It felt warm and nice there with my head in his lap. "Parents aren't magicians. When yours stick around, you learn that. Sometimes they're even more fucked-up than you are."

"I was stupid," I said.

"No, you weren't. You just didn't get to learn that when everyone else did. You didn't have any examples."

"When does everyone else learn it?"

"College. Midtwenties at the latest."

"I dropped out of college."

"That's the other part of your problem."

He smiled down at me. He had lines around his eyes, too, and his breath smelled good, like soap and pad thai. His thigh was muscled under my head, and I couldn't help but notice how close his cock was.

"You have to go back to Sheila," I said.

His smile dropped.

"You do," I said. "You have to get over this guilt thing. It's yours. You get to walk around with it, and you don't get to give it to anyone else or use it against them. It's not Sheila's fault we had sex. Go back to her."

He didn't say anything, and I was out of things to say. So I just lay there and let him pet my forehead.

By nightfall he'd gone. Really gone. Back to her, I was pretty sure.

I got up off the floor. I felt bruised and stiff and had to fumble for a light switch. It was quiet. Chuckles had found some cranny to hide in, and nothing made any noise, not even the refrigerator, which was too new to hum the way the old-fashioned ones did. I was barefoot and the polished concrete was cold under my feet. The air was dry, and I was glad for it after the midwestern swamp.

I picked up the containers of leftovers and threw them out. I should've taken them out to the trash chute that emptied directly into the Dumpster, but I didn't. The next morning the whole place would smell of rotten fish sauce.

I turned on more light over my work space. Aside from the work in progress still propped on my easel, I had a dozen finished canvases from months ago leaning against the wall. I had intended to leave them to Jenny. She knew enough to be able to sell them. The money would be hers. Now I wasn't sure. She was no longer merely herself but an extension of my past and my father. She had split into two people. There was the Jenny I thought I knew before and the Jenny I knew after. I had gone for closure, to tie everything up with a neat bow, and I had come home with nothing but a new mess.

Maybe I would sell the paintings myself. I could have a studio sale, where buyers came to me. I wouldn't have to choose a gallery or split the proceeds with them. I could do that. I would make a good bit of money, and then I could decide what to do with it. I was still considering that when the phone rang.

I pulled off the piece of blue tape that was still stuck to it and picked it up.

I didn't know if I'd be wanted there. If I wasn't, I would leave, but Elaine had called me from Carla's house and asked me to come. To not go would've been a statement I wasn't willing to make.

I had known Carla for ten years. If our relationship was a child, it would be in the fifth grade, and I had still never been to her home. I couldn't recall a conversation that wasn't about the gallery, a show—a conversation that wasn't, at its core, about me. I thought about that as I drove, and when I pulled up to her house, the one I'd never so much as imagined her having, I felt ashamed of myself.

The driveway was full of cars, and I had to go a block down to find parking. Venice has always been the roughest of the beach communities. But in the past ten years or so, gentrification had taken hold. There are fancy gelato shops now and restaurants where it's possible to spend a hundred dollars on dinner. During the real estate boom, people bought houses and condos for far too much money on the litter-prone streets that zigzag around what's left of the duck-shit-choked canals that give the city its name. A city that isn't even a city anymore. Los Angeles proper swallowed it and its tax base right up. But Venice's history is like red paint on the walls: you can put coat after coat of beige on top, but it still shows through.

Cars were stacked up nose to ass under NO PARKING signs with hours and restrictions so complicated they required a graphing calculator and a phase chart of the moon to understand. The strip of street that remained clear was only wide enough for one car at a time to pass, despite the fact that the street was two-way.

I walked back to Carla's in the dark. The houses were mostly hidden from the road behind high wooden fences that blocked them from the riffraff on the street. Adult trees with feathery leaves and drooping, whiplike branches hung over the sides and littered their detritus on the sidewalk. Jacarandas left purple confetti everywhere, including on parked cars, so that everything looked like the day after Mardi Gras.

The gate that stretched across the driveway was open, and the last arrival to get in on the private parking was hanging well out past the sidewalk with its back bumper grazing the street's gutter. The house was a small bungalow of the kind L.A. built by the bushel in the 1920s. The blinds, if there were any, were open, and the lights inside were on. There was also the porch light, a series of blue bulbs inside a minimalist water-wall fountain in the front yard, and a row of small lanterns along the slate footpath, as though all of that could be enough to keep the dark out. The front door was ajar, and I could hear voices above the splash of water.

I stepped inside. Three-quarters of the faces were black. I didn't recognize any of them. The rest were white. I knew them all. Art people. I wondered, for the first time, what that was like for her.

"At home, she called herself 'Token.'" I turned to find a young man with skin the exact shade of Carla's standing next to me. "You know, after that cartoon character."

I didn't know it.

"Anyway, you get the idea," he said. "You're one of the gallery people?"

It was a question and not a question.

"Clementine Pritchard," I said offering my hand.

He took it. "Michael Jones, Carla's partner's son."

"I'm so sorry for your loss," I said.

"Thank you. Dad is planning the funeral. I'm sure he wishes he were here to greet you himself."

"Actually, I've never met your dad," I said. "But he must be impressive to have been with Carla. She was impressive."

"Thank you for saying that."

"If there's anything I can do."

I hated the words as they came out of my mouth, but I couldn't help saying them. He wasn't going to call on me, and I wouldn't be much use to him if he did.

"He's holding up well, considering. My sister is helping him, so I stayed here to . . ." He gestured at the assembled crowd.

"Keep order and play host" was what I guessed he meant.

People had brought food. I could see through the small living room into the dining area. The table was full of the sorts of things you're supposed to eat after someone dies. Cold cuts and pickles and potato casseroles. I wondered if people would eat salami in my honor.

"Please excuse me," he said.

Someone new had just walked through the door. Color code indicated she was family.

The house was warm all over. The walls were painted a deep terra-cotta and baskets hung over the leather sofa. If I'd paid more attention in my African and Asian art classes, I could've told you more, but I didn't and I couldn't. I wound my way through the crowd and passed several potted palms. The atmosphere was subdued, but no one was weeping. It had the feeling of a company party after a very bad earnings report.

I went past the table and the food. A middle-aged woman with graying hair was up to her elbows in dishwater at the sink, and someone else was standing in front of the open fridge looking for a place to put another casserole dish.

The sliding glass door that led out to the backyard was open, and more lights were on out there. They were attracting bugs.

Everyone outside was standing in segregated groups. Elaine was in one. She looked over when I stepped down the stairs. I nodded to her and she to me. She didn't motion me to join her, and I didn't walk over. Our reconciliation was, it seemed, a private affair.

In the end, I didn't find anyone to talk to at all. Carla's world was her family and the Taylor, and I wasn't part of either of those. I watched the mourners from the sidelines. She had gone suddenly. A heart attack. She had been too young and not even the right sex for such a death. It was shocking, the sort of passing that should shake you up, and yet there was a sense of normalcy. People died. We knew what to do. We brought casseroles and cold cuts and fought for parking and arranged for a family member to greet guests at the door. We had a script for this, and even though we would all agree to enter a collective mild depression over the whole event, we would still go to Starbucks in the morning.

Maybe that's why Carla's partner wasn't present. Maybe he wasn't making funeral arrangements at that very moment. It was late, after all. Maybe he was just too sad, too racked with grief and sobs, to stand in her tiled kitchen and direct guests to where they might find spare toilet paper rolls. I hoped so, for Carla's sake.

I started not to feel good. I felt the blackness creeping in through the bottoms of my shoes and worming its way like a parasite under my skin. I could feel it coming on the way you feel the flu catching up to you and breathing down your neck. If this feeling had a Hollywood score, it would be jungle drumbeats, the kind that tell the audience that doom is impending. I wasn't surprised. I accepted it. The only thing to do was to get home while I could still move under my own power.

I walked around the side of the house and let myself out.

4 Days

Chuckles jumped up on the bed. I could feel his weight on the edge, the dimple it made in the mattress. He meowed. I felt his whiskers graze my bare leg as he sniffed me, and then the release as he jumped down and the dimple sprang back.

I heard traffic outside the window.

I told myself I didn't have time for this. I had things to do. Time was running out. *Tick-tock-tick-tock.*

I pushed up. I put my feet on the cold floor and breathed. It was a struggle. It was like being deep underwater where the pressure starts to collapse your lungs. I walked to the bathroom with Chuckles trotting beside me and turned on the water in the tub. I took the bottle of tranquilizers down from the shelf and took it with me to the water, setting it on the bath's edge. I got in before it was full and let it fill up around me. First my hands were submerged, then my calves, leaving my thighs and knees poking up like a South Sea archipelago. I slipped lower and my thighs disappeared while my knees rose up like volcanoes coming out of the deep. I imagined them spurting lava, which I supposed would look a lot like hitting an artery. I let the water keep coming until it was almost at the edge of the tub. I had to stay very still to keep it from sloshing over. I looked at the bottle. It was beautiful in its simplicity. Clear glass with a white and blue label and a red seal on top. It was patriotic that way. The liquid inside was perfectly clear, too. It looked like water. Innocuous. Water, water everywhere.

I stayed there for a long time, even after the water cooled off and everything around me was the same ambient temperature. I thought about things in the vague way you can think about things when you're at the bottom of the ocean and the pressure is deflating your lungs like a beach ball. I thought about Jenny. I thought about Richard. I thought about Jerry and Ramona and how much trouble it was to breathe all the time.

3 Days

I had taken five baths in two days. It was all I could manage
to do. I sat in the tub watching the level of the water where it
hit my boobs rise and fall a tiny bit with each breath. I stayed
in there until my fingers shriveled and the water began to get
bits of fuzz and other things floating in it. Then I got up and
went back to bed. I no longer had a television, so I couldn't
even watch that. Sometimes I could hear the drone of the
neighbor's television. No actual words, but that was okay. I
listened to it anyway, the rise and fall of conversation, the
laugh track. I mostly slept. Sleep and soak. Sleep and soak.
That morning I called the food delivery boy. I thought about
making a joke—"No green bananas"—but I wasn't up to it.

I thought more about Jenny. I thought about Ramona. I
thought about my mother. I thought about Jerry, but only in
relation to the other three women, who were the ones who
mattered to me. I had achieved nothing of what I wanted when
I had gone to see him, and yet he felt like finished business.

I worried about Jenny. I had fantasies of what it would've

been like if I had known about her. I had nightmares about the things she might have said to Jerry and Charlene. I wondered why I had hired her in particular. Did I recognize something about her? Probably I did. She was talented, but so were a lot of the people I interviewed. What she was was organized, and I knew that I wasn't. She yinged to my yang.

She was also apparently a wily, sneaky, snakelike secret-keeper to my slobbering, open-book, black hole of emotional need, which is not a particularly fun thing to realize, not on either end.

I wondered what I should do. I didn't know. I felt as if my limbs had been sucked into the bed. I slept some more. When I woke up, it was dark. I thought maybe the black monster was distracted, his hand a little looser around my throat. The thought gave me enough courage to make myself a sandwich.

The food got to my stomach and awakened it from the starvation coma I'd put it in for the past two days. It was angry, and it would not be assuaged by one mere sandwich. I emptied the bag the grocery boy had brought, which had been left sitting on the counter minus a small carton of orange juice I'd managed to shove in the fridge before returning to bed.

Because I like to think of myself as generous, I'd ordered a couple of cans of wet food for Chuckles and a bag of catnip treats. I popped the top on the food, which brought Chuckles running out of the bathroom as if his fur were full of flaming ants. He catapulted his body up onto the counter and shoved his head into the can before I'd managed to remove the lid the whole way. We had a dispute about this. I argued that he would cut his face cramming it in there with that sharp edge still exposed. He argued that I was a miserable excuse for a human being and an owner and perhaps I might like to kiss his fluffy white ass. I won but only by virtue of height. I held the can up above my head to peel the lid free while Chuckles stood on his hind feet and tried to scale my chest. He got as far as one foot on my chin before I got it open and set it down for him. He gave a meow to complain about the tardy service and then shoved his face into it. As his face was wide and flat and the can small, there were a few minor physics problems to be worked out, but he overcame them with sheer determination and a lack of dignity.

I reacted similarly to a bag of Fritos and a banana Whoopie Pie, which I didn't know still existed. Aunt Trudy used to bring them back with her by the case when she traveled with Bob on his business trips. I would sneak them, which would lead to loud screeches of "Who stole my Whoopie?!" which is just as funny as it sounds. It was one of the few bright spots of my years with them. Maybe there had been more. I wished I could remember.

"Who stole my Whoopie?" I asked Chuckles.

He didn't get it, but then again he had ground-up tuna meal not suitable for human consumption in his fur. So, you know.

I took the bag of chips and another pie with me to my worktable along with Chuckles's catnip treats. He didn't show much interest in them until I opened the bag. He wasn't used to getting treats but seemed to have some sort of ingrained desire for them lodged in his lizard brain. No doubt it lived next to the neurons that demanded he chase and consume any bug that got into the studio, no matter how poisonous the insect or how painful the subsequent vomiting. I wasn't judging. My lizard brain did that with tequila.

I gave him a nip treat and went back to work on what I was calling *American Centaur*. The sketching was already done. It had the body of a cow—a castrated bull, really—and the torso and head of the Marlboro Man. I started mixing paint.

2 Days

By dawn, I'd finished the human bits. I filled in the shirt checks with small bits of red and blue I'd cut from my magazine collection. I'd redrawn the hands and face, so Marlboro Man was reaching up to tip his hat, and had painted in the skin. I didn't have what I wanted for the body of the bull, so I left it and concentrated on the background. I filled in a dilapidated barn that included a side covered in advertising I'd pulled from my vintage magazines. I liked it so much I looked for other places to put bits of discarded consumerism, then doubted myself and peeled them back off. I cut and pasted until my eyes blurred.

Chuckles, full of half the bag of treats, had long since passed the point at which he could be bribed for company and had found a corner to sleep it off. I put down my brushes and did the same.

There was a Barcalounger with the footrest flipped up in the courtyard. It looked like it had been rained on, which was only one of the indignities it had suffered. The building was two stories tall with a center island of grass onto which all the front doors faced.

"I didn't pay you better than this?" I asked when Jenny opened the door.

"It's rent-controlled."

She was wearing blue-and-white-striped pajama bottoms and a light blue tank top, the same blue as UCLA's colors. UCLA was just a few blocks away. I was wearing a blue tank top, too, but mine was navy and covered with cat hair. I'd forced Chuckles into an undesired fifteen-second cuddle session before I'd left the house. I'd also given him another can of wet food that smelled as if something had died under the baseboards. He'd bitten me on the hand. I appreciated the irony. He did not.

Jenny's arms were crossed over her chest. She wasn't wearing a bra and didn't need one. I didn't like to think I did, either, but now that I was comparing, maybe I did. Maybe time and gravity had taken their toll. Her feet were bare. The toenails had been painted black, but it was chipping. She curled them under when she caught me looking at them.

We stood there having ourselves what you call an awkward pause.

"How angry are you?" she finally asked when I'd outwaited her.

"Angry is just one of the many things I am," I said.

"You look like hell."

"Sweet of you to notice."

"I didn't mean that the way it sounded. I'm worried you don't look good. Did you have a bad night?"

"I worked all night. I didn't sleep much. Are you going to ask me to come in or should we continue this inquisition on the chair out here?"

'Homeless people sleep on that," she said and stepped aside.

I'd never been to Jenny's apartment before. She had been my assistant. She had become my caretaker, and if you had asked me, I would've said she was my friend. I wasn't sure now that that was ever really true. It had been, in retrospect, an upstairs/ downstairs relationship. I hadn't meant for that to be the case, and I felt some twinge of guilt that it was so. She knew almost everything there was to know about me, and I knew very little— and as it turned out even less than I thought—about her.

"Do you want something to drink?" she asked.

"I think I better," I said. "It's gonna be a long day."

"I'm supposed to meet some friends for lunch," she said.

"Cancel it."

There it went. Upstairs/downstairs. Or maybe now big sister/ little sister. Bully/victim.

In any case, she didn't object. "I have soda. Mexican Coke."

"The best kind."

Mexican Coke comes in a glass bottle so thick and solid it's fifty-fifty whether or not it will break if you drop it on the side-walk, which is only part of what makes it great. The rest is the real sugar that flavors it. No corn syrup. It's sweeter than Ameri-can Coke with no aftertaste. It goes great with the kind of salsa that leaves a capsaicin burn down the back of your throat.

The front door of Jenny's apartment opened directly into the living room, which was less than ten feet long. I sat on the sofa squeezed in there and looked around. There was no dining area, which was fine as she didn't seem to own a table. The kitchen was to the right and just big enough for a refrigerator, sink, and stove. There was hardly any counter space, and the stove wasn't full-size. I doubted she could've fit a cookie sheet inside it. Her microwave was equally miniature and balanced on a small bar that formed the room's boundary. No wonder she cooked at my place.

There was one door that led into the single bedroom, and somewhere in there must've been a bathroom. I imagined it was no bigger than the airplane toilet I'd used a few days before. There was art on the walls that I would've bet was hers, but from art school days, not recent. She could do better.

All in all, it was a few steps above Irish William's rented room but not many, and it made me wonder about what life was like for young people in this city. Maybe it was too hard and wasn't good for them. Then I felt old for thinking the words *young people*. My first apartment in New York hadn't had a single closet, and the water sometimes ran brown out of the taps.

Jenny took the only other seat, a small rocking chair. It was next to a television the size of her microwave, which was sitting atop a folding TV tray meant for eating frozen dinners. She pulled her feet up into the seat with her and was waiting for me to take the lead.

I watched her face. Jerry had looked like Ramona, but Jenny did not. She favored her mother's side, which was both a relief and a little sad. "So tell me," I said.

"What do you want to know?"

"Everything I don't."

She looked overwhelmed by the question. I could understand that. The amount of things about my own family—or at least a small part of it—that she knew and I didn't went back twenty years. Then again, the things I knew about her family—or at least a small part of it—went back twice that long.

"Mom told me when I went to art school."

"So I hear."

"I wanted to just call you up, but she told me about your mom and your sister. She said I couldn't, that you wouldn't want anything to do with me. I understood." She said that last part as though apologizing to me for bringing up my moral failing, my inability to forgive something I'd never had the opportunity to decide if I wanted to forgive or not. "But I was still, you know, curious. After graduation, I decided to come out to L.A. I went to the Taylor just to see your stuff in person. Carla was there. She was the one who told me you needed an assistant."

Of course she did.

"It was like fate," Jenny said.

"It was fate mixed with intention and manipulation."

Jenny found a loose string on the hem of her pants and twirled it around her finger. "Dad stopped speaking to me for six months."

Perhaps she was suggesting I punish her similarly, as though I were a parent saying to her child, "What do you think I should do about this?" And the child knows that whatever the punishment is, it will end, and she will be loved again as before. Clean slate.

It was my day for feeling old. That was for sure. I'd gone years without really thinking about our age difference, not really. Instead I'd thought about the difference in our experience. I had more connections, more shows, longer to hone my skills, to work through the parrot phase where every artist tries to paint like someone more famous. But what all of that really meant was that I was just a lot older.

So I told her about Ramona.

I told her because I knew more than she did.

I told her about the time I got sent to the principal's office for punching Kyle Streeter, who made fun of my sister for crying on the playground after our dad left.

I told her about the pet rabbit we had—God, did it smell bad—and the time Ramona tried to make it sleep in her bed with her, which only lasted as long as it took for our mother to come investigate the squealing.

I told her that Ramona's grades were always better than mine, that she was nicer than I was, so nice she shared her Halloween candy with me even though I almost never shared mine, unless you counted the kinds I didn't like, like Smarties, which taste like stomach medicine.

I told her all the little things I could remember, which weren't nearly enough. Thirty years was a long time for memories to fade, until what you had were the memories of memories. They weren't always reliable. It was like a game of telephone you played with yourself. But I told her what I could, because Ramona was Jenny's sister, too.

"And then she died," I said, which was enough.

"Would she have been an artist, too?"

"No. She would've been something much more important. She would've saved the world."

"Maybe she would've cured your cancer."

"She absolutely would have," I agreed.

I thought we might end there on that note. If I had written the script, we would have.

"What about your mom?" Jenny asked. "What was she like?"

"Overwhelmed," I said.

"Is it true that—"

"Yes."

I got up from the couch and set my empty Coke bottle on the floor next to a pile of DVDs.

"Where are you going?"

"Church," I said.

"Why?" It came blurting out of her, and she looked as if she wished the words were on a string she could pull back into her mouth. I often felt that way, and I needed a very long string.

"I heard they keep God there."

"It's a rumor."

"Smart mouth," I said, sounding like my mother. "You need to start painting again." I nodded at an orange abstract landscape above her head. "That's old."

She looked up at it as if its presence offended her.

"The Essex Gallery will still do that show," I said.

"They won't. I don't have anything for it. I already told them."

"Call them back. Use my name. They'll wait for a little while. Not too long. Get something for it."

"It's not that easy."

"It's not supposed to be easy."

I went toward the door. Hugging her would be the thing to do, make a nice memory for her, for me as long as it lasted. I could put a nice punctuation mark on it except that I couldn't. She'd still hidden from me, lied to me, all but lived in my space under a false identity. It was what it was, and it couldn't be undone.

There is a big cathedral downtown, newly built. It seats thousands, hosts dignitaries, features the finest of everything: modern art chandeliers; a sleek, minimalist baptismal font; even a tapestry all the teenagers think looks like Jesus giving John a blow job. There are landmark street signs pointing the way to the cathedral just like the Hollywood Bowl. There is valet parking on holidays because when God takes a rest he most certainly doesn't worry about parking. They hid all the stained glass in the crypts, and the whole damn place is fourteen shades of beige as though it were decorated by the people in charge of making office cubicles. It is a place not of personal prayer but of collective showing off, and that is not where I went.

The church I went to was surrounded by eight-foot chain-link fencing and stood on a corner lot next to a bodega. Across the street one way was a Mexican seafood restaurant specializing in whole fried fish. Across the street the other way were a hair salon and a lingerie shop specializing in crotchless underpants and nurses' uniforms.

The inside smelled like church. That smell hasn't changed and will never change as long as people pick up and go somewhere to pray. It was hospital disinfectant, old books, and incense. There was a community bulletin board at the entrance with reminders about drives for the food bank and Sunday school hours, which I didn't stop to read. There was even a carafe of coffee with a stack of Styrofoam cups sitting on a small, rickety table. I did not have any, but I did touch it just to see if it was hot. It wasn't.

I went through the interior doors to the nave, crossed myself, and sat. They had not hidden the stained glass in the basement here. Afternoon light filtered through the primary colors. The infant Jesus's face was painted onto a beige circle of glass, giving him a flat, cave-painting look. He lay naked in Mary's arms with a halo hovering above both their heads. His sex was hidden by a falling piece of fabric, and she had robes of red and blue. He grew up from window to window, gathering apostles, performing miracles, and hanging in permanent crucifixion, agony etched on his flattened face. There was a window for every season, every age, birth to death in pictures.

I wasn't alone. This small church next to the fishnet stocking emporium was one of the few perpetual adoration congregations left. It wouldn't last. The women who came to pray in shifts over the Blessed Sacrament would not live forever or even much longer. They seemed to get older with each passing moment. There was no one to replace them. Even a priest could not be had for the asking. The confessionals were closed.

I could have checked the schedule, which was posted outside. I did not do that. I had not been to confession since Aunt Trudy made both Bob and me go, back when I lived in the small bedroom and was carving my initials in the windowsill. How would you fit twenty-five years of lapse into one confession? It was like cleaning house. If you took care of it a little at a time, it was manageable, but neglect to take the trash out for a few decades and there was nothing to do but take a backhoe to the whole house and start over.

Still I sat.

A Hispanic man came in behind me dressed in long pants and a shirt with his name embroidered on the front. It looked like he did lawn work. He knelt and crossed himself and then took a seat on the opposite side of the aisle farther up. I wondered what personal crisis brought him here in the middle of the day in the middle of the week, but we were not in a bar and so I did not ask.

In my own way, I had already called for mercy, directing the wish at my own self rather than above. I had not prayed about it, and I was not praying then, not in the way I had been taught. I did not believe doing so would help. I did not believe anyone was listening, and I was not worried—at least not excessively so—that my soul would be punished for all eternity.

What I was doing sitting there on the wooden bench, polished and smoothed by decades of tormented behinds, was allowing for the possibility. I did not talk to God, because if Moses couldn't catch a break and be let into the Holy Land, I was sure as shit doomed. So the Virgin it was, the übermother and kisser of boo-boos, the forgiver of schoolyard fights and messy bedrooms.

I talked to her. I explained myself. In case she hadn't been keeping up, I gave her the rundown of my reasons for doing what I was doing. I explained the things I had tried and how they had failed. Therapy—all kinds, medication—all kinds, work, money, marriage, divorce, sex—all kinds, drugs, a strong affinity for Motown. I told her that I really thought this was for the best. I told her about my mother and how that had ended. I knew, I said, that she would understand how important it was that no such thing happen because of me. I explained how I had carefully made sure that no one needed me and that nothing would be messy or complicated in the aftermath. I told her I hoped I had covered my bases. And when I ran out of explanations, I just sat. I sat and waited for something to happen. That was it. That was all I had. I felt like a child sliding the permission slip across the dining room table for a signature.

"Are we good here?"

Nothing happened. No one signed. I hadn't really expected anyone to.

"All right then, maybe later. Glad we had this time together."

Sometime while I was sitting there taking care of my "just in case," the gardener had left. Maybe his problems weren't so complicated or maybe he just knew the value of brevity. I had spent longer sitting in the pew than I had intended. I walked out into the warm, late afternoon sunshine and headed through the chain-link gate to my car. I was hungry.

Usually this restaurant required reservations, but they had just opened for dinner, and most folks had not yet shown up for their tables. I was in luck. Or maybe Mary was looking out for me after all. The hostess sat me next to the window at a table dripping with white linens. I had more glasses and silverware at my disposal than any single person should need. Despite its being plenty sunny outside, a candle was lit for me. The wine list was long, dense, and beyond my ability to translate. I asked if there was a sommelier on duty. Of course there was.

He arrived at my table in dress pants and tie with his shirt-sleeves rolled up, which gave him the look of a man who was putting in a vigorous and demanding day. He introduced himself and shook my hand. How could he help, madam?

Losing Clementine   273

Red, I told him, easy to drink. Not too heavy, not too light. A cabernet sauvignon maybe.

"Did you have a price range in mind?" he asked very politely.

"Let's worry about that later."

"In that case," he said and pointed at the menu.

It was expensive but not the most expensive. I chose to believe this was a sign he wasn't merely padding the bill. I told him I'd take it, and he was back before I'd decided on hors d'oeuvres. He opened it at the table with one of those basic, Swiss Army–type corkscrews that I can never get to work right and poured a sip into the appropriate glass. I swirled, sniffed, tasted, and just barely controlled the urge to lick the drip off the side of the bottle.

"Yes," I told him. "Yes, that's it exactly."

And it was. It was the Goldilocks of red wine. Not too watered down, not so heavy it made your teeth feel they'd sprouted fur. Just right.

He smiled, nodded, and poured a proper glass.

There were almost half a dozen categories of hors d'oeuvres and choices in each. I ordered the French onion soup. The broth was deeply colored and almost sweet from the caramelization. I didn't eat it all. I didn't plan to eat all of anything tonight so as to have room for everything. My taste buds had fully emerged from their medication-induced coma, and I wanted to let them run. Next I asked for the terrine of foie gras. The liver was unctuous and cut perfectly by the layer of port jelly on top. I smeared it in decadent portions on top of my little toasts and protected it from the waiter, who offered to take the remaining bit away before my next course. What I didn't eat, minus the wine topping, Chuckles would have.

I nibbled on a salmon tart with lemon cream and drank more wine before the main course arrived. We were going slowly. I was going slowly. An hour had passed, perhaps a little more, and the sun had sunk past the tall downtown buildings that surrounded the restaurant. The streets made narrow urban valleys that darkened early. It was both sad and romantic. It was the way old Italian movies make you feel.

I had eaten a lot of food already, but I was starting to get lightheaded from the wine. It was a happy, cozy feeling, like pulling on a sweater. The bottle was almost half-gone, and the glass I was working on half-gone, too. I topped it off and ran my finger through the butter, which was French. It was so much better than American butter. It tasted like fresh cream, like real dairy. It tasted the way butter must've tasted before we began pasteurizing the life out of everything. Why shouldn't food be a little dangerous?

If the restaurant had been Japanese I would've asked for the puffer fish. As it was, I had duck confit, salt cured and cooked in its own fat, with cherries and a side of haricots verts. I nibbled at all of it, savored my bites, smelled everything before I took a taste. God, it was so good to be able to smell things again, to have all of my senses back. Sane, unmedicated people don't know how good they have it.

I ordered a cheese plate with a selection of three. I asked for the chef to choose his three favorite goat cheeses, presuming he had three favorites. Goat, with its tendency to be sweet and grassy, was my favorite animal to squeeze for sustenance. The tray came with bites of dried fruit, nuts, and, best of all, a small pot of orange marmalade. I loved the gentle bitterness of the rind in the sweet jam. I loved the color of it, the translucency that caught the light and reminded me of church windows and of Miles, who had told me a clementine was a type of orange, in case I didn't know already. I loved how it mixed with the softest of the cheeses.

The leftovers, too, although there was none of the jam, I would take to the cat. Dairy and duck and liver for him, and a case of feline diarrhea tomorrow for his new owners. I poured more wine. *C'est la vie.*

I was verging on the sort of full that makes you hate yourself, that's painful and gluttonous and stupid, but I told myself I was not there yet when the waiter, a beautiful woman with dark, thick hair and dimples, brought out dessert. The chocolate pudding was dark and, like an orange rind, a mixture of sweet and bitter. Fresh whipped cream swirled on top to be taken bit by bit with each bite of the custard, and sprinkled over it all were crystals of sea salt large enough to crackle between your teeth. I sat at my table for two that was a table for one while the world went full dark, and I ate that pudding slowly and methodically until it was all gone.

The restaurant had gone from empty to full while I had eaten. Not one table was unoccupied, and couples and trios stood waiting at the bar and clustered around the hostess stand. The din, when I stopped and listened to it, was loud enough to keep dining companions from being able to hear each other across a table. Voices rose above the clatter of silverware and glasses. Still, it was quiet in my own head. I felt deliberate and calm. It could've been the wine. It most certainly was a little bit the wine, but that wasn't all of it. Choosing death was different from death choosing you. I wasn't a fresh-caught fish flopping on the bottom of the boat, desperate for that last rush of water and oxygen through my gills.

I lingered over my last glass of wine. A quarter of the bottle remained, but I was done. I asked my waitress with the dimples to box up those things I wanted for the cat and slipped cash into the leather folder with the check. I included just enough to cover the bill then reached into my back pocket and took out the title to my car. I asked for a pen, and she brought it, leaving it on the table for me and then going on to her other duties. I signed the title and slipped it, the key, and the valet receipt into the leather folder, got up, gathered my to-go box, drank the last dregs of the glass, and went to call a cab.

1 Day

Meow.

I had emptied and washed Chuckles's food dish and packed it up in a paper grocery sack along with his half-empty bag of dry food, the leftover cans of wet, and his treats.

Meow.

The moving of his things was making him nervous. He'd rubbed his body around my ankles as I washed and packed, and when I sat down on the floor, he put his face very close to mine, almost to where his whiskers could touch my cheek, and sniffed, his pink smooshed nose twitching. "Explain yourself," he demanded.

I petted him. I'd already given him a good brushing, and his thick coat was shiny and soft. I petted him all over, running my hands down his whole body and the length of his fluffy tail. He rubbed his face against my hand, marking me with his scent. "Mine," he said. "Mine, mine."

"I am yours," I told him. "I promise. You're going to hate

me, but I swear it's for your own good. You're going to be so happy with your new people."

Huge tears rolled down my cheeks as hot as bathwater. They rolled down my neck and dripped off my chin.

Meow. Meow.

Chuckles put his two front paws on my leg.

Meow.

None of this made any sense to him. He didn't know what was happening or why. This whole month had been confusing for him. And things, as far as he could see, were going from bad to worse. That was the worst of it. He wouldn't understand why he was in a new house, where I had gone, and why I hadn't come back for him.

I picked him up and buried my face in his fur, and for once, he let me. I breathed him in, loose fur and all. He smelled like cat, like my cat, and when I pulled my face away, he reached out a paw and pushed it into my cheek. "Weirdo," he said.

I laughed, and it made him jump down. Then there was a knock on the door. Once again, someone had left the street entrance propped open. I rubbed my face dry with the back of my hand and went to look through the peephole.

It was them. I knew it would be.

I opened the door.

They looked like such nice people. That's why I'd picked them. They were in their early thirties. The wife worked part-time at a children's museum, and the husband was a city engineer. He wore a lot of golf shirts.

My face was red and blotchy, and the wife reached out and squeezed my wrist. "Oh, I know you're sad, but it's going to be okay."

It was the voice I imagined she used with small children who

Losing Clementine 279

had been separated from their teacher on field trips, and it made me sob all over again.

The husband didn't know what to do with his hands, and Chuckles was hanging out in the kitchen, unsure of this new development but not quite ready to hide.

"We'll have to put him in the carrier," I said. "He'll meow a lot on the way home. He doesn't like it, but don't worry. He's not like that all the time."

"It's okay," she said, patting my back and rubbing it in little circles. "We know."

She was a foot shorter than I was, and it seemed so silly to see her there taking care of me like I was in grade school, but my shoulders were shaking, and tears were splashing on the front of my T-shirt. My mouth was gummy. I had a hard rubber ball deep in my throat that made it hard to talk, but I kept pushing the words out because there were so many things they needed to know.

"He gets lonely, and he really likes the wet food so give it to him sometimes, okay? And the catnip, but not too much because he'll eat the whole thing if you let him. And his fur gets dirty and you have to brush him a lot or he'll get tangles. He likes to watch you in the shower sometimes, and he eats bugs. Sometimes they make him sick, so be careful. I wrote down the name of his vet. It's in the bag." I took a ragged, wet breath. "And just love him, okay? Love him very much, and tell him he's a really good cat because I don't want him to think he did anything wrong."

"We are going to love him so much," she said. "I promise."

The husband held Chuckles while I buried my face in his neck one more time, then helped me put him in his carrier. "I love you," I told Chuckles. "You're a very good kitty, okay? A really good boy."

Meow.

And then they hugged me, and Chuckles wailed, and I cried harder. And then they were gone. I looked down at the white fur all over my black T-shirt, and I left it there and wondered if I had made a horrible mistake.

I went to the worktable and pulled out the folded bits of leather I'd bought at a craft and sewing supply store on Pico Boulevard. I had light browns and medium browns and red browns and browns that were so dark they looked black. I laid the pieces out next to each other and moved them around and around looking for just the right composition, the whole process like a shell game on a New York City street. Where's the ball? Where's the ball? Where it stops, nobody knows.

I kept my hands busy, moving as fast as they could. My heart began to beat too hard and too fast, and I refused my mind permission to roam. This and only this, I told myself.

When I had it, I started to cut. Using patterns I'd traced from the painting onto thin, transparent paper, I made the same shapes out of the leather. The pieces that made the body of the centaur looked like a butcher's map of the cuts of meat. And when I'd done that, I took out my tackle box of tools. It was the same tackle box with my name written on the outside in Sharpie marker that I'd bought my freshman year of art school. I'd dropped out as a junior, but I kept the box. I'd been adding to it for twenty years.

I found the wooden-handled awl and a small hammer. Not worrying about the worktable underneath, I lined up the awl on the strip of cut leather and whacked it with the hammer. The pointed tip went through and lodged into the table. I wiggled it free and punched the next hole. I kept punching, keeping the holes equidistant from each other and lining them up with the holes on the neighboring scrap. I went all around the edges like I was tin-punching a pie safe. *Whack-whack-whack.*

The line I'd bought to stitch with was something between twine and yarn, dark red and far too thick to go through the eye of any needle I might have. I found the lighter in a drawer and held the end of the string in the flame. The fibers burned and melted, and the tip cooled quickly into a hard nub that I pushed through the holes with my fingers, whipstitching the quilted body together.

When the pieces were assembled, I took a pot of rubber cement off the shelf and tried to open it. The lid was glued shut, and for a moment, I panicked. What if I couldn't get it open? What if the glue was bad? I didn't have a car, and I had to finish this before Carla's funeral that night. My heart picked up speed again and my fingers got clumsy. I set the jar down on the table, pulled a screwdriver out of the toolbox, and whacked the edge of the jar with the heavy plastic handle.

The lid came loose. I unscrewed it and pulled it open. The attached brush was dripping with good wet cement that looked like burnt honey and smelled strong enough to strip chrome off a bumper. I took it to the canvas and started to paint it on, working fast so it wouldn't dry before I was ready. When the canvas was good and coated, I picked up my cowhide of many leathers and, starting at one end, gently pushed and pressed and smoothed it into place.

And then, just like that, I was done. I looked for something else to do, some detail to fix or to add. I stood there with the minutes ticking by loud in my ear. Nothing was ever done. There was always something, a change, an edit. It could be better. It could always be better. But right then, it was done. It was as done as any piece ever was. I could mix more paint, add more cutouts, but I would only make it worse.

I knew this time would come, this time of lasts. The last time I'd wake up. The last time I'd see Richard. The last time I'd use the bathroom or wash my hair. Some of the lasts I saw coming, and some I hadn't. But each time it was there. "This is the last time I'll do this. This is the last time I'll do that."

I reached out and ran my palm over the tips of my brushes sticking up out of the cup. They tickled my skin like pussy willows. Just one of a hundred little gestures to say good-bye to all the things there were to say good-bye to.

Then I had to turn away and take a shower.

I had arranged all my papers on the kitchen counter in neat stacks. I had already checked them twice, but I checked them again. Will. Yes. Deed to the studio. Yes. Banking information, investments, funeral plans, cemetery plot, copies of last month's bills. Yes, yes, yes. I had written out the names and numbers of people the police would need to notify: Richard, Jenny, the Taylor Gallery, Aunt Trudy and Bob, my lawyer, and my accountant. Jenny could tell Jerry and his wife if she wanted. I was sure she would, but I was leaving it up to her. His name was not on the list.

I had finished my suicide note days ago. Before I could think too much about it or read it again and decide it wasn't right at all, I folded it up, shoved it in a plain white envelope, and wrote Richard's name on the front. I laid it in front of the row of papers on the counter, next to my will. I had decided to leave Jenny half the paintings and Richard the other half. It was the fairest thing I could think of. Jenny got a little something of my investments, too, along with Aunt Trudy. I noted that I had given my car away and left copies of all my keys, in a straight line on top of the will, along with my passport. The cops already had my driver's license.

I felt better doing this. I felt organized and in control. My heart wasn't racing quite so much.

I went over the papers again, thought of something, and added a note to the end of the list: "Chuckles's adopters." I wrote down their names and phone number. Richard, I said, should check in with them to see how things were going. "Cat reverts to him should adoption fail."

That made me feel even better.

I took a breath, let it fill up my lungs. It was funny to think about your lungs inflating, how the oxygen got to your blood and then traveled around your whole body like a freeway system. I imagined I could feel it happening. My left hand felt more alive when the new oxygen made it there. Then my left leg got a little stronger. My spleen worked a little better. Each organ was happy to have the new supply. I thought about a little deliveryman leaving milk bottles at each stop. Here you go. Drink up. Then I thought about my brain, which wasn't a good citizen like my spleen but derelict and rundown with rot and holes. I imagined the deliveryman in his white uniform speeding up and throwing the bottles out the window. I didn't blame him. It was scary in that hood.

Speaking of milk, I opened the fridge. There wasn't that much there. I had already thrown out the blue chicken when it started to smell the way it looked. But there were a few other things. A knob of ginger, half an onion that had started to go squishy, part of a carton of eggs, some cheese slices. The cheese slices would probably be okay, but anything that might go bad, I tossed. I didn't want anyone to have to deal with rotting food after I was gone.

I remembered that after my mother died. I never went back, but Aunt Trudy did. She didn't go right away. There had been the funerals to deal with, and they'd hired someone to come tear out the carpet and the drywall and everything else that had blood and brain and bone stuck in it. It took a while for her to go back. She talked about having to throw away cereal and pickles. It felt wasteful. But who would want food that had belonged to dead people? She said that some of it had gone bad. The bacon had been green.

I wouldn't leave behind any green bacon. No, sir.

I cinched up the trash bag and hauled it out.

I checked my watch. I had to hurry. I needed to get my letter to the post office, so it could go out overnight delivery. I didn't want to be late to Carla's funeral. I sat down on the stool with a yellow legal pad Jenny had used to leave me notes.

To Whom It May Concern,

> *This letter is to report my suicide, which will have occurred*

I double-checked my cell phone and wrote in the next day's date.

> *in the early morning via chemical overdose. Mess should be minimal. I have turned up the air-conditioning to minimize decomposition. Nonetheless, please send the appropriate resources immediately. Documentation can be found on the kitchen counter. House key enclosed.*
>
> *Hope you are well.*

That was my little joke.

Sincerely,
Clementine Pritchard

I added my address, folded it up, and put it in an overnight envelope. I'd already addressed it to the local precinct.

I checked the time again. I really had to hurry. I gathered up my bag and the overnight letter and headed for the door.

Brrrring.

Brrrring.

I had my hand on the knob. Did that count as not home? I had to run—literally—to the post office. I had to catch a bus.

Brrring.

Shit.

I snatched up the receiver. "Talk fast," I said.

Jenny's voice sounded like she was two inches underwater, her words coming out in sodden bubbles. "I messed up really bad."

I should've hung up. I should've hung up right then, because nothing that could come after those words would be something I could handle. If she had simply locked her keys in her car I could have handled it. But, of course, she hadn't locked her keys in the car. I hadn't been that lucky since winning the door prize at a women's charity event in 1992.

Only half of what Jenny was saying made sense. There were gasps and non sequiturs before she could get it all out.

"How did this happen?"

I sounded like my mother. What difference did it make how? It only mattered that it had.

Jenny choked on her own spit and coughed, which set off another sob. "I don't know what to do."

I leaned over the kitchen sink, suddenly sick to my stomach. I had to stand over Carla's casket in an hour. I wanted to. I wanted to see how she did it. To watch how it all played out, a sort of fire drill for my own passing. Afterward we would all gather at our designated meeting spot outside the building, and our emergency response leader would take a head count and discuss how well we did. I didn't have room for anything else. I didn't have time. I had almost no time left at all.

"Stay there," I said.

I hung up the phone and opened the freezer just to feel the cold on my face for a moment. Then I marched out of the studio, slamming the door behind me. I was angry at Jenny for calling me, angry at her for needing me, and not at all in any sort of state of grace or forgiveness or any other bullshit that's supposed to happen as you walk into the light.

I knocked on Brandon's door, and he opened it. He wasn't wearing a shirt. I saw that with detachment. Beauty like that is the reason museums have to put DO NOT TOUCH signs next to statues, but I had nothing left with which to appreciate it.

"I'm sorry," I said, "but I need your car."

"You don't look so good."

"Bad day," I said.

"Are you going to be okay?"

"Last spring, you took those medications for a month. They worked, right?"

"The PEP? Oh God, honey, this on top of everything else?" He looked down at me as if I were a hopeless case good for nothing but pity.

"I'm asking for a friend."

"Sure you are."

"They worked?"

"I stayed negative," he said. "That's good enough for me." He handed me his car keys. "Drive fast. You only have seventy-two hours, and the longer you wait, the worse your chances."

I took the keys and started to turn away.

"Clementine?"

I looked back.

"They're going to make you feel like shit."

Losing Clementine   287

"I figured."

"I mean really, really bad," he said.

"Medications are like that."

"When you start them, come over. You're going to need someone to take care of you."

"I'll be okay," I assured him.

"No," he said, "you won't."

I turned up the air conditioner all the way and pointed the vents at my face and chest. My bangs fluttered in the artificial breeze, and goose bumps rose up on my arms. It still wasn't enough. My cheeks felt hot, and my nerves crackled. My brain pinged from emotion to emotion, unable to alight on any one and setting them all off at once.

"Damn it." I hit the steering wheel with the palm of my hand and pressed harder on the accelerator until Jenny's exit came into view. When I hit the off-ramp, I was going too fast and had to grind the sole of my shoe into the brake to keep from flying off past the guardrail and into the treetops. My heart fluttered. With the drop in speed, the engine switched to battery power and went silent. I hated that. I was used to the growl of internal combustion. It's how I knew something was happening.

I took my eyes off the road and scrolled through my phone to Jeremy's number. *Pick up, pick up, pick up,* I willed.

"Th-th-this is Jeremy."

I explained my situation, and he listened without interruption. And then he said, "What can I d-d-do?"

I asked for the name of a clinic, somewhere I could take her right then. He put the phone down, and by the time I reached my turn and had put my blinker on, he was back. I watched the traffic coming toward me, waiting for a hole big enough to make a left, while he read off the name and the intersection in the San

Fernando Valley where I could find it. I concentrated on the information, carefully committing it to memory rather than to the scrap of paper I didn't have.

"M-M-Mark says it's a good place. Th-th-they keep a doctor on call."

I told myself not to judge Mark for having the information I, after all, had asked for.

"Thank you," I said to Jeremy. "You're a lifesaver."

He didn't make the obvious joke.

"Anything for you," he said instead, and then he hung up.

This was my second time in two days driving to Jenny's neighborhood. I turned off the engine—not that anyone could tell the difference—and sat. A red sedan drove past me, parked two buildings down, and discharged a woman in a peach blouse with a gray work skirt down to her knees. The front was wrinkled as if she'd been sitting a lot that day. She parked in a red zone and ran inside on high heels that made her take too-small steps. She was back out quicker than even parking enforcement could move, holding on her hip a child too big to be carried that way. The girl's brown hair was curly and hanging in her face, and she clung to a construction paper art project her mother deposited in the backseat with her, then trotted back around to the driver's seat on her work pumps without knowing I was there.

I watched them without thinking, and when they were gone, I was alone with a steady stream of late afternoon traffic. I stared out the windshield at the space where the family had been. My stomach was clenching itself into too small a space. Jenny was inside waiting for me to come in and be something to her, and I wasn't even sure exactly what. Was I the big sister? The employer? The friend? I didn't know her well enough to be her friend, and I didn't know how to be an older sister anymore. I was the most useless person she could've called, and I couldn't think of another person on the whole planet, let alone within driving distance, to whom I could pass the buck.

Jenny answered the door so fast she must've been standing there watching through the peephole. Her cardigan, two sizes too big, was wrapped tightly around her with her arms following suit. It looked for all the world like she was trying to hold her organs inside her body. She stepped back to allow me room to come in, and when I did, she went limp against me. I thought she'd fallen and clutched at her too hard. She let go of her sweater and her insides and wrapped her arms around my waist, returning the too-tight hug I didn't mean to give. In my arms she felt insubstantial and hollow. It was like holding a wren and knowing one squeeze could crush it.

I didn't know how long to stand there. The door behind us was still open, and it made her dingy apartment feel vulnerable and exposed. Her head was pressed under my chin and her cheek against my sternum. Her hair smelled like lemon shampoo. Sounds from the street were blowing in. Somewhere close by a car door shut and then opened and shut again. One of the large black crows that plague the city, the ones as big as cats, cawed and flew toward us.

Jenny let go then, and so did I. She shut the door against the bird, and the room dimmed so much I had to wait for my pupils to adjust. She hadn't bothered to open the blinds, and the bright L.A. sunshine couldn't manage to do anything but shimmer feebly around the edges of the shades, which only made the room seem darker by comparison.

"Do you want something?"

It might have been funny, pleasantries under the circumstances. Her mother, the woman who had fed me brisket under equally trying circumstances, would've been proud.

"No," I said.

Jenny's arms went back around herself, and she held her intestines in place all the way to the couch. Wadded tissues were piled on the floor next to an empty bottle of Coke. She sat and pulled her feet up into the seat, forcing her body to occupy as little of the physical world as possible. I could've told her that didn't work. Mental anguish was not proportional to your footprint.

With the door closed, the apartment smelled of leftover takeout.

Her face was pink and blotchy, and the soft, puffy skin under her eyes looked bruised. "What'll happen if I have it?" she asked.

I took the spot next to her. It was a small couch, more of a loveseat. Sitting side by side our thighs were less than six inches apart. I didn't say anything. Whatever she was thinking, what I was thinking was worse. New York in the eighties was like living through an outbreak of the plague.

"You're thinking I could die," she said.

"No." Yes.

"I am."

"There are things you can do," I said.

She picked at her toenail. The black paint was still there and still chipping. "Maybe Ray's girlfriend was lying. She lies."

"How do you know?"

"How do I know what?"

"How do you know she lies?" I knew the answer was that Ray said so. It seemed Ray said a lot of things, and if I had known where this was all going to lead, I certainly wouldn't have let him walk out of my studio with that smug look still plastered on his face.

"Did it sound like she was lying?" I asked, glancing at the clock. We both needed to hurry.

Jenny shrugged inside her sweater cocoon. "She just asked if

Ray had told me he was positive. I asked her 'Positive for what?' "
She smiled with her mouth while the rest of her face stayed
where it was. She wiped at her cheeks. "I'm so stupid."

She reached down for her soda, picked it up a few inches, realized it was empty, and set it back down.

"You called Ray," I said.

"Four times. I left messages and sent a text each time."

"Since yesterday?"

"Yes."

I was guessing Ray didn't want to talk about it.

"He doesn't get good cell reception at his studio," Jenny said.

Or in his car or his apartment or the grocery store or the back
of the ex-girlfriend's Toyota, it would seem.

"The day before yesterday was the time without a condom?"
She nodded.

"The only time?"

"Yes."

"I need you to tell me the truth," I said. "The timing matters."

"I said it was."

I shifted my weight toward the edge of the couch. It was time
to go, time for movement and progress. Everything over the past
month was rolling downhill, gathering speed. I also didn't want
to keep sitting there in the dark smelling the congealed fat from
leftover Chinese food that was wafting out of the kitchen trash.

"We should go to the clinic," I said. I looked at my watch as
though I knew what time it closed.

"I haven't had a shower."

"That's really not important right now."

"I'm waiting for Ray to call me back."

"Why?"

She looked at me for the first time since opening the front
door. "What do you mean why?"

"Does it matter what he says? Are you going to take his word for it if he says no?"

"Why should I take her word for it? She hates me. She wants Ray back."

"I can't imagine why."

I could feel the shift and the weight of her angry fear as it settled on me and her relief in having found a target.

"You just don't like Ray."

"No, I don't."

She scrunched up her face. "I'm waiting until he calls."

"You don't have that kind of time," I said.

"He's going to call back."

"No," I said with absolute certainty. "He's not."

"You don't know that."

I stood up. I stood up and pulled myself to every millimeter of my six feet—more in shoes—and towered over her.

"Get up," I said.

"No." Her voice had the small quality of a child testing out her independence, unsure if it would work and unprepared for what would happen if it did.

I reached down and snatched her by the bicep, which was hardly bigger than her forearm. My hand was like the claw of the crow outside, and my fingers were no doubt making white marks that would turn pink when I let go. But I didn't let go. I picked her up—dragged her, really, to her feet—by her arm.

"Ow, you're hurting me," she said.

I wasn't. Not really.

Once on her feet, she stood on her own. I kept hold of her but not as hard.

"I won't go," she said. "I won't go to any clinic. Not without talking to Ray first."

"Where's your bag?" I asked.

Losing Clementine 293

"What?"

I scanned the floor looking for it.

"I said I'm not going." She tried to pull her arm from my grasp, but I held it so the ball of her shoulder was hitched up high and the angle was too awkward for her to get any leverage. "I don't want to. You can't make me!"

"Where's your bag?" I repeated.

I spotted it on the floor near the door and walked her toward it, my long legs making easier work of the distance than hers. She trotted the short distance to keep up, pulled along by the arm I still controlled. I scooped up her bag with my free hand.

"I said I won't do it."

"I heard you," I said, throwing her bag over my own shoulder and opening the door. I propelled her through, out onto her small stoop. I followed and shut the door behind us, leaving it unlocked. "We're going somewhere else."

"Where?"

"Ray's."

Her face flipped through three or four emotions looking for the right one before settling on resignation. The muscles in the arm I still held went slack, and I let her go. I walked toward the car, and she followed three steps behind me, neither of us saying anything else.

There was no traffic in the carpool lane. Brandon's hybrid was old enough to have the HOV OKAY sticker on the bumper, and I was using it, heading back toward the city on the 10. Everything about this was like having a dislocated shoulder shoved back into the socket: you never want it to happen, but if it does, you just want to get it over with as quickly as possible.

The ragged tops of palm trees were just visible over the sound-buffering walls that lined the freeway, and the only things to look at were brake lights and green highway signs. I veered left onto the 110, didn't stay long, and took the 4th Street exit headed west.

Ray lived in one of the neighborhoods surrounding MacArthur Park, which hadn't been a place of play since anyone could remember. The green urban square surrounded by botanicas and no-name storefronts selling cell phones was full to the gills with the homeless and hopeless sleeping off whatever they'd bought. Skeleton kids circled around, waiting for them to come to and buy from them all over again. There were always police around the edges of the park, but they, too, had given up hope. They were only trying to contain it. Do what you do inside the park, and try not to let it spill into the streets too often.

It did, of course.

Ray lived and worked in one of the houses that had been beautiful almost a century before but had been skidding and sliding downhill for more than half that time. The building had been subdivided into four apartments, two up and two down. The upper apartments were serviced by two self-made staircases nailed to either side of the house in violation of safety codes and good sense. The yellow paint outside was peeling, exposing bare wood to the salty Southern California air. What hadn't peeled off had aged and dirtied until it looked like the sort of stain that, were it on your upholstery, would make you throw the whole couch out.

I parked against the curb. The front yard had a chain-link fence around it. Inside, the lawn was too far gone to resuscitate and, in any case, had been a bad idea in a coastal desert.

"He has the apartments on the right," Jenny said.

"Both apartments?"

"He works upstairs and lives downstairs. The whole place is his, actually. He rents out the other side."

I added slumlord to his list of accomplishments.

"Nobody wanted to live in Venice, either," she said. "You could buy a house for less than fifty thousand dollars twenty years ago. Now they're worth more than a million."

I didn't have anything to say about Ray's real estate scheme.

We were sitting with the engine off, looking out. "What now?" she asked.

"We go in."

I opened my door.

"He might not be home," she called after me.

I shut the door on her voice, going around to the passenger side. When I got there, she'd opened it a little, just enough so that it wasn't latched. I pulled it open the rest of the way.

She stayed put. I waited. The silence between us made the ambient noise louder.

"I don't want to get out," she finally said to the windshield. "I didn't even want him to call me back."

"I know," I said.

"Like if I don't know, it's not real or something?" She turned her head just enough to catch me in her peripheral vision. Tears were leaking out of her eyes, a slow drip that matched her nose. She sniffed loud and wet and wiped at her eyes with the heel of her palm.

I wanted to offer her a tissue, but I didn't have one.

"Shit. Okay, let's go." Jenny got out so fast I had to take a step back to get out of her way. I shut the door after her and was going to press the LOCK button on the remote when she slipped her hand in mine and held on hard.

I didn't know how to respond to that. Holding hands with your sister was the sort of thing you were supposed to do in the dark under the covers after you'd sneaked downstairs to watch the *Twilight Zone* or when your mom was having one of her dark days and it scared you. Jenny was thirty years too late, and I couldn't remember if I'd ever held hands with Ramona. I didn't think I had. Maybe she'd wanted me to. Certainly at the end she'd have wanted me to.

"What's wrong?" Jenny asked.

"Nothing."

"There's his car." She pointed down the narrow, broken drive that separated Ray's house from a similarly rundown and subdivided house next door. At the far end of the drive, parked in front of a small detached garage, sat a black hybrid very much like the one I was driving. I didn't like even having that much in common with him.

Jenny wrapped her sweater around herself again with her one free hand. She looked cold, and it wasn't cold. Los Angeles was putting on its best show. Clear, blue, and warm.

I used my free hand to rattle the gate in the chain-link fence. It wasn't locked, but I rattled and waited anyway. Jenny cocked her head. I made a show of what I was doing. I had learned my lesson with the German shepherd outside of Fresno. When I was satisfied we weren't about to be mauled, I unlatched the gate and waited for Jenny to go through. Inside, I left it unlatched. I didn't know what was going to happen, but I didn't want to have our exit blocked.

We stood on the walk that led up to what had been the front door. Now it ended at a plain expanse of newer wall between the two lower entrances. Cars drove past, and I could hear a helicopter not too far away. Police probably.

"What time is it?"

I looked at my watch. "A little after five." The funeral would just be starting. Funerals usually started on time, I was pretty sure.

"He'll be upstairs. In his studio."

Upstairs meant up the narrow, too-steep steps that clung to the side of the house with a shaky grip. I went first, just in case the whole thing collapsed.

At the top, I stood directly in front of the peephole and knocked. Something inside moved. I wasn't, in retrospect, sure if I heard it move or if I sensed it move, but either way I knew something was in there and I knocked again.

Nothing happened.

"I know you're in there, Ray." Jenny was one step down from the landing, still holding on to herself, but her voice carried. "I know you got my messages."

I stepped back into the corner of the landing, making room for her to stand in front of the tiny one-way lens.

She let go of her sweater with one hand and rapped her knuckles against the door in the same place I had.

"Damn it, Ray." She was pushing back tears, and her voice was sodden. "It's Jenny. You know who it is. Open the door." She pressed her forehead against the wood.

I listened, watched for the shadow, kept an eye on the air currents. Nothing moved.

"Maybe if you leave." She said it quietly, and it took me a minute to realize she was talking to me. I was being kicked out, excused, and thanked for my service. I bit my tongue because it was the grown-up thing to do, though it was harder than it sounded. Hell of a time to learn a new skill.

I slipped behind her on the landing and went down the steps more slowly than I had to, stopping halfway down. I leaned my back against the side of the building and crossed my arms. I was looking out across the small driveway that separated Ray's tenement from the one next door. The concrete was cracked, but it was too dry even for weeds.

When I was settled, Jenny knocked again. She pressed the left side of her body to the door, her back to me, a human privacy screen. "Ray, come on. It's just me."

We both waited.

"Ray," she said again, "you can't leave me out here, please. Please. We were going to go down to San Diego next weekend, remember? We were—" Her voice broke, and I watched her back curve forward as her chest collapsed and her tiny bird body sagged inside the oversized sweater. Sobs came up and out of her, making her gasp between words. "We were going to take the train."

She rolled her head over her right shoulder and let it flop back, banging against the door. I winced and looked down at my shoes. They were black for Carla's funeral. I stared at them and listened to Jenny sob and beg. I didn't look up or go to her, because I had been there. I had begged, and I knew the humiliation of having to do it. Of standing on the wrong side of a car door in the middle of a parking lot with something bigger than a sheet of metal and glass between you and the lover inside and having to beg to be let in, beg because you didn't want to be left there in the middle of the night, in the middle of the day, in the middle of the cold or the rain, because you were afraid, because you were sorry, because you didn't want to be alone, and if he left surely no one would ever love you again. And standing there in public crying and asking for mercy was the surest sign that was true.

Only the truly broken and unlovable are paraded like that for everyone to see. And no one was more broken and unlovable than me. No one ever had to beg like I had to beg. I was sure of it. For years and years I had believed that like I had never believed anything else. And I knew how bad it was to have people see, so I looked at my shoes that were black for Carla's funeral and listened to Jenny sob at the top of the steps and pretended that I didn't.

"Ray. Ray, I don't have a lot of time. We can talk about this, but I need—I need for you to come out, okay? Okay, Ray?"

I remembered my mother begging my father. He must've threatened to leave a dozen times before he did. That was the thing. It never worked. How many men had I begged not to leave, and all of them, including Richard, eventually had, sometimes right there in the middle of the rain in the middle of the night in the middle of the parking lot, sometimes the next morning after not enough sleep and a blow job, sometimes days and months and even years later. We were Pritchard women. It seemed it was in our blood.

Jenny hauled back and kicked the base of the flimsy plywood door with the toe of her black-and-white Chuck. The door rattled in its loose-fitting frame. The sound made me jump.

"Open it. Open it and tell me it's not true. Tell me!" She kicked again. The wood rattled harder. "Ray!"

She was making enough noise to set the whole block on high alert, but no one came out to see. No one called the police. This wasn't the kind of neighborhood that did that sort of thing. People here had too many problems to take on someone else's.

"Open the door. Why won't you just open the door?!" She threw her body against the wood and sagged. "How could you do this to me? Who does this? Who?!"

The thin layer of muscle over my ribs contracted. My chest wanted to cave in on itself. That door would not open. Not for her. Not now and probably not ever.

"I could be sick. What if you made me sick? What if I have it?"

Jenny bent forward, and I took two steps up, expecting her to double over and scream or cry or vomit or whatever she was going to do, but instead she turned on her heel and looked down at me. "You make him. You make him open the door."

I reached up toward her. "Come on. Let's take you to the clinic."

"No one will want to be with me ever again," she said.

"That's not true. Come on."

She moved toward me. I'd gotten what I'd come for, even if she hadn't. I took her hand again and started down the steps, pulling her gently behind me.

"They're not closed yet, are they?" she asked.

I had no idea. I hoped not. "No," I said. "They're not closed yet."

She held tight to my hand all the way down the stairs, across the yard, and through the unlatched gate. She held on while I unlocked the passenger door and opened it for her. I shook her hand a little, ready for her to climb inside, but she wouldn't let loose. She took hold of my wrist with her other hand and held tight there, too. Her fingers were like cuffs, that thin and that strong.

"Don't leave me."

"What?"

"Don't leave me, okay? You can't."

"I'm not leaving. I'm going to take you to the clinic."

"But after."

"I'll take you back home," I told her.

She shook her head. "I don't want to be alone. Take me back to your house. Please."

No, no, no, no.

My freedom, my day, my release, my choice, my oblivion, my ending. No one relying on me. No one needing me. I'd given away my goddamn cat. All that was left in my apartment was a bed, some mustard that would never expire, and a clear, clean bottle of escape imported from Mexico.

I looked over her left shoulder, hoping a way out would materialize there. She shook my arm.

"You're going to take me with you, right? You're not going to leave me?"

Losing Clementine 301

I looked at her. She was ready to crumple. She was made of nothing more substantial than tissue paper. She could blow away in the wind right then or dissolve in the rain.

I felt responsibility throw a saddle over my back. It cinched around my stomach.

"You can't rely on me," I told her. "I'm the worst possible person to rely on."

"I know."

A car rolled by on the street, slowing as it passed us and then picking up speed again. It stopped at the end of the block with its blinker on, waited too long with no traffic coming, and then turned.

"You really don't." I tried to put enough weight into my words so that they could sink through the protective coating that was forming over her brain, keeping out all other pain. "Let's go," I said, putting my hand on her arm and pushing her toward the open door. She resisted, her lower body staying planted while my shove turned her top half. She looked like a swivel-waisted Barbie doll.

"I want to go home with you," she said. "I want to stay at your place tonight. Let me stay tonight."

My place. My place with my papers all laid out and my corpse in the bathtub by morning. I remembered I needed to turn the AC up.

"Will your mother come out here?" I asked.

"What?"

"To take care of you," I said. "I've heard the drugs they give you—I've heard you might need someone to check on you."

"I'm not going to call her. Why would I call her? I want to go home with you."

"I can't take care of you," I said.

"I know. I'm not asking you to."

"You are."

"I'm not."

I took hold of her chin with my free hand and tilted it up, forcing her to look into my face.

"I gave away Chuckles today. I gave away my cat. I am the sort of person who would give away her cat."

"We can get him back," she said, blowing past my point without a sideways glance.

"I can't take care of him anymore. I can't even take care of my cat."

"I know."

"You have to stop saying that."

"I know you stopped taking your medicines," she said, "and I know you don't have cancer."

I let go of her chin. I felt a flash of anger at her and shame over my lies, and I swallowed the part where I called her a sneak and a spy because I could do that much if not a lot else. She didn't need my shit on top of her own.

"I think you should start taking the pills again," she said.

Such a lovely, naive thought from a lovely, naive head that had not and would not turn on its owner like a sick animal.

"I am not going to get better," I said.

"You don't know that."

"I do know that."

Two doors down a woman walked out her front door. She had a teenage boy with her. She stopped to lock the door behind her while he continued on down the walk toward the street. His gate had an exaggerated lope, a self-conscious affectation meant to convey relaxed casualness. The woman caught up and then passed him, her steps quick and purposeful, making him drop the stroll to keep up. I heard the police helicopter make another pass, farther away than before. The normality was distracting.

"I want to go home with you," Jenny said, "and I think you need me to go with you, too."

"I don't."

"You're a bad liar. You should stop doing it so much."

"Jenny."

"You don't have to pay me," she said. "I'll be your assistant for free."

"This isn't about money."

"Would you take Ramona in?"

"You don't get to go there," I said. There are places in a person's past that are off-limits even to emotional pirates and plunderers.

"Why not? She was my sister, too, wasn't she?"

Jenny had let go of my hand, and I couldn't remember when exactly that had happened. Somewhere we'd moved from pleading conversation to argument, and she'd decided to fight with bare knuckles, which was more than unfair.

"It's not the same," I said.

"It is the same. It's exactly the same. I'm your sister, and you're mine, and she was, and we're all in this together, so let me go home with you."

I shut the car door and pressed the button on the key chain. A faint click came from inside as the plunger dropped into the lock.

I didn't want to have this argument. I didn't want to be here. Not on this street. Not in this city. Not on this plane of existence.

"Clementine."

I ignored her.

My plan was so good. So neat and clean. I had taken care of everything. No one needed me. No one was supposed to need me.

"Clementine."

She reached for the door handle and pulled up uselessly.

I had bought my own casket, for Christ's sake. I got points for that. The universe owed me. I did my part. I did more than anyone in my shoes could possibly have been expected to do.

"Clementine."

I had been responsible. Other people walked out in front of trains. I didn't do that.

"Clementine, open the damn door!" Jenny banged her fist on the passenger window. "You have to!"

I looked down at the car keys in my hand. I could just open my door. One click of the button. I didn't have to open hers. That was two clicks of the button. I could open mine and climb in and drive away with her screaming in the rearview mirror and things would almost be exactly the way they were three hours ago. Let her find her own way to the clinic. Let her find her own way home. Let her find her own way period.

"You'd do it for Ramona," she was yelling at me. "You'd do anything for her, and I've done a lot for you. I have. You know I have."

One click? Two clicks?

"We can take care of each other. We can."

I looked past her into the street.

"What are you going to do?" she demanded.

I really had no idea.

"I really have no idea."

"Decide tomorrow," she said.

"What?"

"You could do that. We could just get in the car for now, and you could decide tomorrow what you want to do. Or the day after," she added because why not buy a little time if you could?

"We can't go back to my place," I said.

Losing Clementine   305

"Mine then. Come home with me after the clinic. For tonight."

I tried to think of a logical, reasonable thing I could say to explain why I could not wait for tomorrow.

"Your apartment is a dump," I said.

"Yeah, my employer paid like shit. That means you should spring for the pizza."

"I didn't agree to this."

"Yes, you did, and it's only until tomorrow." She took a deep breath and started to cry again. It must've taken a lot for her to hold it in that long. She'd really been trying when no one could've expected her to. "Now take me to the doctor."

I clicked the button. Then I did it again.

Reading Group Questions for
Losing Clementine

At its heart, *Losing Clementine* explores the breaking and re-forming of relationships within the storm of mental illness. It's about families—the kind you're born with and the kind you make. It's about love and sex and marriage and food—and it's really about art and the creative process. *Losing Clementine* is about a lot of things. Here are some questions for discussion:

1. How do you feel about Clementine's decision to kill herself? Was she justified? Is there ever a justification?

2. Although Clementine is not a cook herself, food plays a prominent role in her life. Do you see any correlation in what she eats and her mental state at different points in the book?

3. Why do you think Clementine slept with Richard in Tijuana? Why do you think Richard slept with Clementine?

4. Was Clementine justified in defacing Elaine's work?

5. Did the gallery deserve any blame for the knockoffs of Clementine's work?

6. A major theme in the book is the effect serious mental illness has on the patient's loved ones. Clementine was one of those loved ones while her mother was ill and then is the patient during the book. How do you think being on both sides of the issue affected Clementine's behavior?

7. Do you believe Clementine acted responsibly in the way she planned her death?

8. How do you feel about Clementine's relationship with her therapist? Do you believe this relationship played a part in her decision to stop treatment?

9. How do you feel about Clementine's decision to tell her friends she has cancer? Was it a kindness or was it cowardly?

10. How important to the book is the city of Los Angeles? Could the story have been set anywhere, or did the city have an important role to play?

11. Richard wants to save Clementine and has wanted to throughout their relationship. How has this affected each of them?

12. Reflect on the art Clementine creates throughout the book— the perverted Americana scenes, the dying buffalo, the centaur figure. What symbolism do you see?

13. What do you think of Clementine's argument that art always belongs to the artist?

14. The three main art world professionals in the book are Clementine, Elaine Sacks, and Carla—all women. Do you think gender plays a role in how they interact with one another?

15. What do you think about Jenny's reliance on Clementine? Does it change in the course of the story?

16. Clementine's father feels culpable in the deaths of her mother and sister. Is he?

17. Clementine spends most of the book attempting to disentangle herself from her responsibilities. How successful is she?

18. What do you think happens after the book ends?

The Real-Life
Suicide Tourism Trip to Tijuana

by Ashley Ream

The first line of *Losing Clementine* was written in a coffee shop in Santa Monica, California, where I was briefly a regular. Followers of the Spiritualism movement would've called those first pages "automatic writing," a state in which the author is a sort of secretary taking dictation from an otherworldly source. Writers just call it "the muse" or, as I prefer, "flow." Whatever you call it, I hadn't sat down to write about Clementine, had never before made her acquaintance, and, in fact, was working on another novel entirely (which was going rather poorly). But the moment she barged onto the page, threw open the window, and started chucking crockery out onto the street below, I knew two things: Clementine was an artist and she was suicidal.

Several reputable newspapers, including the *New York Times*, have written articles about the suicide tourism phenomenon. Proponents of right-to-die laws are providing travel information to patients with painful and debilitating illnesses who are planning their own deaths. Although tightly controlled in the patients' home countries, a particular barbiturate used to euthanize animals can be had easily in Mexican border towns.

I wanted to find out just how easily, so I booked my own trip to Tijuana's medical dark side. Despite easy access to specific information elsewhere, I chose not to name the drug. I also chose to inaccurately describe the recommended method of taking it. Those looking for a how-to guide will not be well served by this book.

In 2010, the year of my trip, a number of Mexican border towns were experiencing more than their fair share of drug-related violence. In 2008, a war had broken out between rival factions of a drug cartel in Tijuana. There were 844 homicides in the city that year. By 2009, it was believed the factions had reached a truce, and the crime rate fell. However, in the first eleven days of 2010, four youths were shot, four people were decapitated, and at least ten more were killed in drive-by attacks. In addition, there had been five kidnappings—all in just more than a week, according to the *Los Angeles Times*. It was putting a serious dent in recreational travel south of the border.

By the fall, most of what would become *Losing Clementine* was written. A research trip couldn't be postponed any longer, and while no one thought it was a particularly good idea for me to go traipsing around alone inquiring about barbiturates, a line wasn't forming to accompany me, either. So I called Eric Stone.

Eric, another recovering journalist turned author, replied, "I know a good place for *carnitas* down there."

We loaded our bags into his aging Lexus and drove the 130 miles from Los Angeles to the Mexican border along Interstate 5. It's easier and faster to cross on foot, and the last mile of American soil is filled with nothing but long-term parking lots and Mexican car insurance purveyors. We abandoned the car, piled our bags on our backs, and walked the last quarter-mile.

There were no guards, no ID checks, no sniffer dogs—nothing but a large metal revolving gate and a parade of buskers and overpriced taxi drivers on the other side.

Although Tijuana is famous for its all-access *farmacias*, which are designed less like stores than walk-up windows, suicide tourists seek out the lesser-known veterinary supply shops located well away from the touristy main drag, Avenida Revolución, and other sightseeing destinations.

Obtaining turn-by-turn directions to one of the veterinary shops, along with the going price for a lethal dose of the barbiturate, had taken less than an hour. I'd printed them out and took them with me as Eric and I set out from the infamous Avenida on foot. Leaving behind the zebra-painted donkeys, strippers, and barkers, we made our way east until one dentist became a dozen, and we found ourselves surrounded by medical offices advertising orthodontic work for bargain-basement prices—all listed in American dollars. On the edge of the dental district was the veterinary supply store, just as my directions promised.

Despite the name, the store didn't give any indication of catering to anyone with a medical degree. It was small, narrow, and dark. The only light came through the front windows that were partially covered in long-ago faded posters, and it was as hot inside as it was outside. The only people there were a young woman who ran the place and a boy in her care. Both of them watched Eric and me, but neither spoke.

The front of the shop looked like a pet store that had recently experienced a holiday rush or maybe looting. More shelves, hooks, and displays were empty than were full, and there weren't more than one or two of each item available. What was there were links of chain wrapped around spools and available by the meter, dog collars of varying sizes, one doghouse, one birdcage, and some bags of food. Toward the back, one wall was lined with a waist-high glass case like in a jewelry store. Without lighting, the interior was hard to see, which didn't matter much as it was nearly empty. Behind the counter were shallow shelves with small glass vials and pill bottles that more closely resembled the *farmacias* we'd passed earlier. Some of the vials looked like the pictures of the barbiturate's packaging I'd come across while researching suicide trips—all of it easily available.

Authorities in the news stories had promised to crack down on the purchase of these drugs for human use, which are supposed to be available only to veterinarians by prescription. Shop owners denied knowledge of buyers' intent, insisting the drug was sold exclusively for use on animals. In any case, access didn't appear impaired. Nonetheless, I let the vials on the narrow shelves behind the glass case be. I didn't purchase any, and I didn't smuggle anything across the border, leaving that instead to Clementine.

With all the information I needed in hand, Eric and I left the store, the woman, and the boy, preferring instead to spend our American dollars on *carnitas*, music, and local wine. We spent two days wandering the streets, exploring the city's restaurants, clubs, and markets. The closest we came to seeing any of the drug war was listening to the *narco* ballads sung in the bars.

When it was time to return north, we piled our bags back on our backs and headed across on foot again. This time we stood in line behind hundreds of other travelers waiting to be admitted into the United States. Vendors took advantage of those in border purgatory, whether on foot or in cars. They offered fruit, candy, drinks, and kitschy souvenirs in case you hadn't had quite enough during your stay. Travelers filed through an air-conditioned building that resembled airport security. We formed lines, answered questions, showed our papers, and walked through metal detectors. My bags and Eric's were X-rayed but not searched, although they could have been. It wouldn't have been hard for Clementine to get her vial across the border, but it would not have been without risk.

Without exception, Eric and I were treated well by everyone we met. The drop in tourism was hurting those who depended on it, and everyone was anxious for us to return as soon as possible regardless of why we'd come. Eric did return, traveling throughout northwestern Mexico the following year to research his own book on trafficking.

The phenomenon of suicide tourism continues in Tijuana and elsewhere.

ASHLEY REAM got her first job at a newspaper when she was sixteen. After working in newsrooms across Missouri, Florida, and Texas, she gave up the deadlines to pursue fiction. She lives in Los Angeles, where she works in the nonprofit sector.

Ashley Ream